SARAHJAN

I Give You My Heart

Dear Gemma,
I hope you enjoy getting lost between these pages!
SarahJane xx

Hearts and Minds Publishing Limited

Hearts and Minds Publishing Limited
Aston House
Cornwall Avenue
London
N3 1LF

A paperback original 2018.

Cover design by More Visual Ltd.
Edited by Emma Mitchell, Creating Perfection Ltd.
Blurb written by Best Page Forward Ltd.
Typeset by Kerrypress Ltd.

A CIP catalogue record for this book is available from the British Library.

ISBN 9781999588519

This book is dedicated to my dearest old friend.
Life isn't the same without you; but between these pages I can still feel your heartbeat.

Part One

Chapter One

When the doctor told me I was dying a numbness washed over me. Nobody ever tells you that emptiness is the heaviest thing of all.

Brain tumour; inoperable; terminal.

I'm twenty-six years old.

I could smell a mustiness in the air, sitting underneath a chemical concoction that stripped my nostrils. It was a stark, bare room, in a neutral shade that had perhaps once been a brilliant white, aged now into an indescribable, dull colour. The room was remarkably non-descript, there was not a single human touch. I found that disconcerting. After all, this was a room that screamed with the memories of humanity it had borne witness to.

'Hello, Mrs Richards.' My doctor began. He was not the grey, wizened, old gentleman I'd expected to be caring for me. Rather, he was a vision of healthy middle age with a cheerful smile and an air of joviality that belied the news he imparted. His smile slithered off his face when he read my scans and he looked right into my eyes; his were a pale, cloudy grey. He moved words around his mouth, silently, testing how they tasted before releasing them into the air. His tense jawline gave the impression of him tasting something bitter as if a few drops of tart lemon juice had been dropped onto his tongue. His grey eyes gave him away most though – I saw flashes in them, flickers of sympathy, of sadness, of discomfort. Then the words rained down – heavy, sombre, and cruel. The doctor spoke them gently though, tenderly. They were too brutal to deserve such treatment.

He cleared his throat before he continued as though he could dislodge this reality from his body. Those cloudy, grey eyes of his, they held a lot that would scare a person, but to his credit those eyes never broke from mine as he spoke.

'I'm sorry to have to tell you but it is bad news. You have a mass, on your brain stem. Its location makes it impossible to remove surgically. It's advanced, I'm afraid, what we call grade four.' His voice was quiet yet steady and had a friendly timbre.

He paused, his gaze deepened, and his voice softened with sympathy. 'Now, there are things we can try to prolong life, minimise symptoms. We can discuss those now or you can take a day or two to absorb everything – it's entirely up to you.'

It was my husband who bravely confronted the elephant in the room, spear aloft albeit shaky.

'What exactly are you saying, doctor? What are we dealing with here?'

The doctor's eyes swept across to Alex's, which were bewildered and brimming with tears. His mouth tightened a fraction before he spoke, and that's the moment I finally understood.

'Alice has a Grade Four Brain Stem Glioma, which is a cancer - having developed to this stage it's a terminal cancer.'

It felt like the air was sucked from the room. My eyes locked with my mum's, fear and terror stretching hers wide. I looked across to my dad, whose hands gripped his chair arms so tightly his knuckles looked like they'd broken through his thinning skin. My husband let out a quiet moan; low, wounded, the sound of sorrow.

There was a silence stretching between us; separating us and uniting us. Eventually my dad broke it with a question.

'How long are we talking about, doc? How long do we have?' My dad's voice now cracked, broken.

'Nothing is certain, Mr Hadley, and it does depend on the course of action we take, but I'd estimate six to nine months.'

The windowless room, deep in the bowels of a huge, looming, maze of a hospital, was filled with shock. I was healthy looking, you see; young and vibrant, and I've been told that my laugh is deafening, my giggles ready, and my smile kilowatt. So, people didn't associate illness with me. I didn't even associate illness with myself and yet no one could feel its power more forcefully than I could feel its grip.

The news sat atop my mind for many minutes before I processed it. I've always been like that – deal with the practicalities of a situation first, feel later. So, as I sat with my family around me, the back of the chair lumpy and hard against my back, the rough felt chafing my skin in that sliver between my shirt ending and my jeans starting, I'd run many things through in my mind – my final words to those most special to me; my funeral service, complete with bright clothes, and an Abba finale; who would look after those I loved – before I shed my first tear. However, when those tears came, they nearly washed the entire hospital away in a disaster-level tsunami. They stung my eyes and spilled over my eyelids in a way that felt removed from me. I could feel their wetness spread through the thin fabric of my shirt as they dotted it with a darker pattern of anguish.

'Could we take a few days, as you suggested, please, doctor?' I asked quietly.

'Of course, Mrs Richards, you just let me know when you'd like to meet, and we'll make a plan. I really am so terribly sorry.'

He stood then, shook hands with us all, and we filed out silently.

I wasn't ready for this, I had so much left to do – so many ideas, and dreams, and moments. It wasn't my time … but I guess that's what they all say.

We were standing together on the fading tarmac outside the monstrous, grey, concrete hospital, huddled together. Mum pulled me into a hug so tight I couldn't breathe. I eased her back, and she clung onto Dad's hand hard enough to bruise. It seemed to snap him out of his distant trance.

'I don't understand, love,' Dad murmured. 'I thought these tests were just to rule various things out? Nothing drastic, you said.'

'That's what they told me too, Dad, maybe they were as surprised as anyone.'

'Just the odd headache you said, love, feeling a bit sick sometimes, a bit achy, that's right isn't it, I didn't get it wrong?' Dad asked, his brow furrowed, his mouth tight and his complexion paled.

'No, you're right, Dad, I guess this has caught us all out.'

'I'm so sorry, love.'

'Me too, Dad.'

Alex pulled me into him gently, strongly, and tucked my head underneath his chin in our favourite embrace. To see our silhouette, you'd never know where one of us ended and the other began. We had thought we'd be standing like that one day in a cottage by the seaside, grandchildren playing around our ankles. It just proves, you never know what's coming for you.

You are never prepared for a day like that day. The sun may well be shining, birds singing, children laughing. For someone, somewhere the best moment of their lives will have occurred. But you, very literally, don't know what to do with yourself. It doesn't seem right to deal with the dishwasher when you've just found something like that out, but there's nothing else to do, and the dishwasher still needs emptying. The world still spins, the sun still sets. Everything is happening exactly the same. And yet nothing will ever be the same again.

The leaving itself I could handle. I wasn't afraid of the endless night that lay in wait for me. I'm a soul-believer, you see and knew I'd be around to protect the people I loved and haunt those I was less fond of. I fancied myself a Jekyll and Hyde spirit – worthy of a sainthood or clown of a practical joker depending on who I was dealing with. Joker Ghost, I'll have some fun with that. I intended to leave little messages and signs for those who believed; it would be like a lifelong game of hide and go seek between us – they'd know I was always around somewhere, they just wouldn't be able to see me.

The doctor told me there'd be a slow descent into pain, exhaustion, and other nasty things ahead of me, and I abhorred the thought of that far more than the end itself. There would be no miracle here, just a slow slide into the abyss. So, I came up with my plan.

I would save or improve twenty-two lives. I'd donate every piece of healthy tissue and organ I could. Because of my corneas a blind man might see again; my liver might be the reason a woman gets to see her grandchild enter the world; a piece of my bone might allow someone to walk again who would have been wheeling round in a wheelchair for the rest of their lives.

The reason my plan would work is that despite my illness being deadly it's only one small part of me that doesn't work. The rest would have gone strong for seventy years. And in seventy years it's anticipated that they'll be able to remove my faulty part – with miniscule robots of all things, they just can't yet. I won't go into all the details – it brings me down getting into the scientific jargon, it makes it more real, and sinister. Suffice it to say, I have something inside me that's attacking and killing me. My own brain is a horror film.

Apart from what was perhaps a too lengthy affair with *Grey's Anatomy*, I had almost no medical knowledge. Don't get me wrong, I could slap a Mr Bump plaster over a little cut without having a meltdown, but I had none of the more technical knowledge I'd come to need in the months that followed. I would be dying, anyway, that was an iron-clad guarantee. So would the dozen potential recipients without the organs they so desperately needed. I wouldn't go out without a fight, and I would do my last good deed. I would not die in vain.

My biggest task was getting the people that loved me to understand – I know some people think we're crossing a line putting parts of one person into another person. Playing God, they call it. I hope, with time, they'll come to understand it's the only choice I could have made. I couldn't turn my back on my twenty-two.

Quality not quantity has always been my choice. I have friends who flit in and out of my life for a coffee here and there, but meaningful relationships are hard to come by in this fast world. The circle of my closest loved ones includes my parents, Alex, and Ryan.

It would have been impossible to have better parents. Yes, yes, I know, loads of people say that, but it really couldn't be truer for me. I know, and have known every single day of my life, that I'm totally and completely loved. My mum is my best friend too. We do girly shopping trips and spa days together, we talk about everything, and we're each other's shoulder to cry on. My dad is warm, and funny, and I know he'd do anything in his power to make me happy. Then we have Alex. You will hear no end of stories about Alex, but for now, suffice it to say, he is the love of my life and I'm the luckiest girl in the world that he chose to love me back. Last, but certainly not least, we have Ryan, my oldest and truest friend. He is the yin to my yang and the peanut butter to my jelly. We must have been made from the same star. My story wouldn't be complete without him. He isn't always there, but he's always there when it counts.

A haze descended on us all in the days following the diagnosis. Everybody fussed over me, and over each other, but we all still had our lives to lead. Alex and I lived close to Mum and Dad – I could never imagine myself living a life far from theirs. They brought fish and chips in on Friday, as was tradition, wrapped with newspaper and soaked in vinegar – just as they should be – and it was more welcome than ever after a week of rubbery chicken, and hard pasta. The smoke detectors in our kitchen went through more batteries than the Eiffel Tower light display. Alex and I never gave up, I hasten to add, our culinary talents had to be birthed eventually, though I'm not sure I ever wanted them to, since it was so much fun pulling disasters out of the oven and wafting the billowing smoke out of the open windows. There were more laughs the worse it turned out and I'd miss that far too much if we became the next Gordon Ramsey and Nigella Lawson. The supermarket's share price would crash too, since we had to be their biggest purchasers of ready meals, which we stock piled in the huge chest freezer to whip out once the smoke cleared. The ping of the microwave was the most comforting sound. It's funny that – it's rarely the perfect bits of life that make the golden memories and the tummy ache laughter. Besides, we'd always be sustained by Mum and Dad's Friday night delivery of those perfect fish and chips.

Alex and I spent a quiet weekend together at home. Our cottage was idyllically perfect and never failed to make me feel safe and secure when I was in it. It was filled with honey coloured oak, from the rickety floorboards that creaked and moaned as you moved across them, to the lopsided beams that hung majestically overhead and the low doorframes that elicited many a yelp and expletive from six-foot Alex when he forgot to duck for their five-foot seven demands. There was an old oak tree in the garden with a hanging rope swing that Alex had slaved over one weekend and was wide enough for us to sit on side by side.

I think the shock of the news had drained us both so we were very happy lying in both days, reading in bed for hours together – me with the latest Jane Costello novel and Alex with a crime fiction book. We made lunch together (sandwiches to be safe!) then cuddled up for movie marathons of our old favourites – Alex's go-to film was *School of Rock* and mine was *She's The Man*, so we started from there and over the course of the weekend worked through *The Blind Side*, *10 Things I Hate About You*, *The Eye In The Sky*, and the list goes on. Alex drove out for a takeaway both nights and we snuggled up in the duvet and each other for every possible moment. It was very unlike us to be so lazy, but we couldn't manage anything more. I think all we both wanted was to be curled up in each other's arms constantly, not even light separating us.

Alex had a high-flying journalism job in the city which meant an hour's train commute from our home in a beautiful old town outside London. My job in one of the town's florists involved fewer hours away from home than Alex's did, so I usually spent the couple of hours a day of me-time I had while I waited for Alex to crunch up the path, partaking in my customary bubble bath, chick-lit fest, and calling Ryan for long-winded catch-ups.

In the days after the doctor's appointment I also used Alex's commuting hours as prime thinking time. Although I'd never been somebody who wanted to save the world or had any kind of pressing notions of making a lasting mark, there is nothing like staring the night dead in the eye to make you evaluate what you will leave behind for when the sun rises again.

At this point, there were two things I was sure of. The first was I would find a way to donate all the organs and tissue I could –I would save or improve twenty-two lives. The second thing was that I would leave an instruction package for the lucky recipient of the most important part of me – the part I couldn't leave behind without certain provisions being made; after all it wasn't really mine to give. My heart, you see, it belonged to Alex.

Chapter Two

So, hello there my special new friend! Since you're reading this, you must have my heart! Can you do me a favour? Lay your hand right over it and feel it. Feel it beat underneath your hand for me. Ah, now that's something to savour! It worked!

Before we go any further I want to tell you what you're going to read. This is the key to my heart. A manual if you like. You see, what you're feeling beating right now, beneath your hand, is the part of me that loves. You might not believe that, but I do. And since it's spent twenty-six years being mine, I think what I believe counts for something at least, don't you? Let me tell you, that heart of ours, it's so good at what it does – it loves like you've never known love, until now I suppose. Now that love is inside you, you must be able to feel it, you must know its magnificence. If the strength of that amazing love feels overwhelming, please don't be afraid, that's what this manual is all about – showing you what to do with all that love. Let me explain …

I always told him that my heart beat for him; and I believed that with every fibre of my being. So, since it's still beating, you have to make him feel that love still. After all, what's love with nowhere to go? That heart of ours couldn't take that.

This package you've been given works in two ways. First and foremost, this is the story of my heart – I thought you'd want to hear it. Second, this is a request – to take action to help my love live on. I've organised things for you to start this just into the New Year. I'll cover a full year for you – all the things you need to do at every special occasion, season change, anything that could crop up that would be a defining moment in my love story. These things I've planned will deliver a piece of me, and my love, back to my husband. You see, I can't let those precious memories become tainted for him – I want those beautiful moments we shared to be the thing that pulls him through the grief, not what sucks him under. I need you to help him remember in the very best way and to hold his hand through to the other side. I need him to know that those special times will never die or be gone for as long as they live in our hearts. My heart will beat on so my love will still be alive, he needs to feel that. I pray it's not too much to ask, and that it's a price you're willing to pay.

So, let's start at the very beginning. I'll start where you'll start. And you'll start with coffee. That's the very first thing to do – have a cup of coffee with him. That's how we met. It's the oldest cliché in the book – we were both in a rush at the coffee shop counter. He spun round and spilled my caramel macchiato straight down my shirt. I lived for my morning coffee so this was a crime tantamount to murder – he'd literally killed my morning zest. That was until I looked up into his huge brown eyes and that old ticker you can feel beating, it skipped a beat. Ready for cliché number two? – I honestly knew in that moment that he was my One. That I would love him for as long as I lived. I was so right. And that brings us back round to you, and now. You have that piece of me and it's living. So, the love lives on. Meet him for a coffee – he'll know to expect your call. Don't meet him in a coffee shop though, that would be too much. Besides, I want you to show him that he's still loved – by me – not to fall head over heels in love with him yourself! Believe me, you'll be tempted. Unless you're a nun which would be disappointing – my heart wants adventure! Or unless you have a thing for the ladies, which I think would be unfair, since although I don't have an issue with it – live and let love I say – I don't think your new apparatus will help you out with the heart racing feeling for another lovely lady, if you know what I mean?

Sorry, back to the coffee. So, you need to do it in the kitchen at our cottage. Intimate enough – how could it be any other way – and yet not creepy, I hope. He likes it strong – pour that instant in. And he likes it with just a dash of milk, the smallest splash. And the milk must be skimmed. That's important.

Oh, and his name is Alex.

Chapter Three

I'm writing the instruction manual for my heart because I believe there are so many things we don't yet know. I believe our hearts hold our love. I've felt for myself the burning in my chest when I suffer hurt, and that hollow emptiness of loss in there. We literally feel those things in our hearts. Poets, writers, and lyricists for hundreds of years have believed it too – they call it 'heartache' and 'heartbreak' after all. I believe there is an endless amount that's yet to be discovered about the universe, including our fragile bodies. Scientists and doctors say the heart is just a pump, it's a bunch of cells that do a mechanical job, nothing more. But I can't help but wonder, when my heart has spent all day every day for years and years loving one person with all it has, the question is surely not, 'how could it remember?' but rather 'how could it ever forget?'

The days that followed my diagnosis were a bit of a fog. Time changed. It felt different. It felt precious and kind; and yet it felt sinister and violent. I felt things I didn't recognise. I was confused, and I was angry, and I was sad. Above all that though, I felt determined. The only thing I had left was this sense of purpose – the twenty-two lives. It gave me a focus, a job, and a lifeline. Boy, did I need a lifeline. Boy, did I need Ryan.

My best friend, Ryan, is my bouncer. He is the person I let see the very dustiest corners of my mixed-up soul. He is my person. The one who never judges, always forgives me, and who doesn't just tolerate my crazy but jumps right into it with gleeful abandon. We are so different, him and I, but that's what makes us perfect for each other. We challenge and inspire in equal measures, and that's a formula that gives fireworks in all their spectacular glory. It's important to say here, since I suspect you must be wondering, he is not Alex. I love Ryan, but not in that 'tummy-flip' way (which is just as well, given Ryan is gay). That's what Alex does – he makes my tummy feel like a pancake with all the trimmings – lashings of cream and piles of strawberries, drizzled with melted chocolate.

Ryan is very different from me in that he doesn't understand my fascination with feelings. He is Mr Logic to his very core, and he lands firmly in the realm of 'science knows everything'. He thinks it's hilariously funny that I believe in souls and that hearts are what love. He says I'm daft and asks me to provide one piece of evidence that souls exist. Obviously, I can't. But I just ask him to provide me with one piece of evidence that they don't. Alas, we meet a checkmate. So, he humours me, and I humour him, and we agree to disagree, and we have so much fun doing it.

Ryan wasn't there with my immediate family that day at the doctors' when we found out. It took me until the following week to make the phone call to ask him to visit for a coffee. I think it was because I knew telling Ryan would make it real. He was my person, and if my person didn't know it was real then why did I have to believe that it was. He was my one escape left; my one bit of unaffected, original, me.

I realised though that I needed Ryan. I needed him to be my custodian. It would be too painful for Alex to do. And I would never have wanted to request it of my parents – burying a child is an inconceivable agony, guiding the journey of one of their body parts would have been an unthinkable thing to ask of them. I knew Ryan would be the perfect guardian. No one knew me better. Alex knew me inside out, back to front, but Ryan knew every deep, dark secret I'd ever had. He would understand this.

Ryan is totally sassy, one hundred per cent classy, and terribly bad-assy, so he'd deliver for me. He had come through for me all my life. He had picked me up off the floor, dusted me off, and shoved me back into the ring more times than I can count. It's one thing to pick someone up and comfort them, it's another to get them back on the horse every time. Ryan did it every time.

I talked to Ryan about it at my house, on the sofa, curtains drawn, candles lit. He loved candles. I'd picked up a 'red velvet' one just for him that day. He loved the smells.

'Ryan, I have some bad news,' I said, my tone heavy.

'I wondered when you were going to bring up your eyebrows, Al. What has happened to them? Did two caterpillars go to sleep on your face and you just didn't notice? Hand me the tweezers and I'll get you sorted right out.' Ryan has always been good at lifting spirits. And to be fair, I'd left it a little long between shapings – those details tend to feel unimportant in situations like mine. Still, Ryan had a point.

'I'll go and fetch the tweezers,' I said with a resigned sigh. What? It couldn't hurt.

I laid a soft towel over one of the cushions and rested my head back on it on Ryan's lap. He began his mastery, plucking away. Despite the fact it stung a little each time it was very therapeutic and restful.

'Ryan, it turns out I have a mass in my brain.' I knew there was no point circling the issue any more, or he'd just joke us into full facials and pedicures and the news still wouldn't be imparted.

'What do you mean, a mass in your brain?' There was a pause. 'You don't mean a tumour, Al?' He'd stopped plucking now and his face loomed over mine, but backwards, making it look comical.

'Yes, a tumour. It's terminal. I'm going to die.'

'No, you're not, Al, you're absolutely not.' Ryan resumed plucking, a little too fiercely for my liking.

'I know it's a lot to take in, but I am. I have about six months left.' I paused. 'I need your help.' I knew he'd be curious.

'With what? Your burial outfit, flower arrangements at the funeral? I'll sort it all, don't you worry.' He spoke with a lot of raw pain in his voice, barely disguised by the sarcasm. 'You aren't going anywhere, Al, so stop talking such rubbish.'

'Ry—'

'Shhhh!'

'Ryan, I'm serious. I want to donate my organs – change twenty-two lives with my one loss. I will leave it up to fate to determine who gets all the parts of me, all except for one – my heart. It has to go to the right person because my heart's going to love Alex for the rest of its life. So, they must be perfect. I want you to decide. I want you to find them. Well, find her. You know me the best, and you know Alex. You know our love story. And, Ryan, you're amazing with people. You know their secrets with one glance, their fears with one sentence, their souls with one conversation. It can only be you. Please say "yes".'

'What do you mean, Als? What are you talking about? I'm not sure I get it.' Ryan looked puzzled and a little alarmed.

'Well, all my love is in my heart so whoever gets my heart, gets my love. Hence, it's vital it's not just handed out in a transplant lottery but rather that it finds a home inside the chest of just the right person. It needs to be someone who will want to feel all that; someone who'll fulfil the recipient's manual I'm going to write.'

'Oh, Lordy!' Ryan's perfectly shaped and sculpted brows nearly disappeared into his lustrous hairline.

'Anyway, it's going to take someone very special, don't you think, to help Alex – the most extraordinary person of all – except you of course – through this trauma? She needs to be someone who believes in magic; who is vibrant and embraces life with gleeful delight; someone whose life won't be damaged by doing this for me; someone who is patient, kind, and electric; someone who, more than anything, loves to love.' I finished with a smile.

'It sounds like you've thought about this a lot, Al. You're sure?'

'One hundred per cent.'

'It sounds a little morbid to me. What will I have to do? Interview these people in hospitals? It's a bit creepy for my tastes. Do I have to? Can't I just profile them online and you decide?'

'No! It all has to be you. I don't want to know anything about them. I want to go to the darkness with this fairy tale notion of the perfect, angelic lady. I know perfect doesn't exist, but I want it to, for Alex. Let me go with that last thought.'

'Typical you, Al, head in clouds, while I'm down here, dealing with fucking reality as always.'

'And I hate to drop all this on you, but there'll be a lot more to it than that. You see, they aren't so happy about releasing patient information to random strangers, so you'll have to be a little creepy, a lot crafty, and do some Sherlocking yourself. I was thinking maybe you could hang around the Cardiology waiting rooms and work from there.' Ryan didn't look convinced. I changed tactic. 'Just think of the outfits you could wear for the sleuthing – I wouldn't deny you a monocle if you thought it might help the cause,' I said with a sassy grin.

'Well, I've always thought I'd be quite the fetching gent in a monocle. Few people could pull that off, you know?'

'Yes, but you could pull it off. Please say yes?'

'Well, holy shit.' Ryan screwed up his eyes, pinched the bridge of his nose and puffed dramatically for a minute or two. He then looked right at me and said, with a weak smile, 'Okay, just for you, Al, but only if I get to pick your burial fashion statement. And the flowers. For real.'

'Fine. But no dresses, and no carnations.'

'Deal.'

I felt there was a huge hurdle ahead of me though in the matter of donating my heart – Alex. I had given him my heart all those years ago. My heart was only at home in his hands. So, how could I do this without consulting him, without getting his permission? We were partners. What was mine, was his. And how did I talk to him about it? I brought it up one evening when we were curled up on the sofa with warm mugs of thick hot chocolate nestled in our hands. We were hot-chocoholics. Our legs were tangled up in each other's, the way we always sat, with as many body parts touching as physically possible. Time had never taken the shine off our romance. We were always nauseatingly in love. Right to the very end – and maybe even beyond. Touchy-feely, lovey-dovey, perfection was what we had. My favourite blanket was laid across our middles.

Aaah, the blanket saga.

This was one of those couple-defining issues. The behind-closed-doors realities of sharing your life with another person. A person who may, unfortunately, turn out to have different blanket preferences to yourself. My favourite blanket was thick, woolly, and a gorgeous deep purple. It was huge, warm, and cosy – what could there possibly be not to like, I ask you? Well, Alex always said it was scratchy. Alex preferred his blue fleece blanket, but it was smaller and didn't quite wrap around us both in the same enveloping way mine did. It could only be described in one word – puny. It was thin, little, and not at all snuggly. We had always agreed on the compromise of alternating – one night the woolly purple, the next night the fleecy blue. These days it was the woolly purple every night. Alex insisted. And he'd tuck it in tightly around me before slipping under it himself and gathering me into his arms.

I was slurping my hot chocolate noisily; a whipped cream moustache gracing my upper lip, silky, smooth, and always kissed away by Alex. The cream moustache kiss was hot chocolate tradition. He leaned across and pressed his lips into the cream before deepening the contact. I must have tensed, because he pulled back a fraction, his eyes heavy with a question.

'What's wrong?' he asked softly.

'Can I talk to you about something?' There was hesitation and reluctance mixed in with the confidence in my voice. Alex must have sensed it was serious because he then settled back into the cushions, put his hot chocolate down, and rubbed circles on my knee with his thumb.

'Always.'

'I want to become a donor. Would you be okay with that?'

Alex was quiet for a moment before replying pensively, 'It's your body, Alice, whatever you want to do with it, I'll support you.' I gave him a weak, tight smile.

'What about my heart though?'

'Well, what about it?' He looked puzzled.

'Wouldn't it be strange, knowing it was so much a part of me and that it's beating in someone else, that I'd be there, in someone else?'

Alex was silent for a moment and the colour drained from his face.

'When you're gone, I'll be living a horror like no one's ever known, Allie. I think knowing you'd done what you wanted to would be the only comfort.'

'You'll be okay, though, won't you? Promise me you'll be okay?'

'How could I ever promise you that? How could I ever be okay? Nothing will ever be okay ever again.' Alex had tensed, and his eyes were thick with tears. He got up, paced to the door, and walked out into the ferocious night which was swirling with rain, and wind, and despair.

He always dealt with things in this way – physically working them out. He was a sight to see – brooding and sweating out his problems. Any ladies who happened to be around him whipped out their fanning implements in moments like these. Sometimes it was running, sometimes weights at the gym. Once it was even yoga. Hot-yoga. In one of those steaming rooms – his mum had convinced him to try it with her, which was ironically the cause of the brooding on that occasion – Alex, it turns out, is not bendy enough for a convincing downward dog. Alex doesn't like being bad at things. I did what I knew was the best thing I could in these circumstances. I put some towels in the dryer, so they would be warm for when he got home. I put some of his favourite posh shower gel on the shelf in the shower and I tidied away the detritus of the night. When he got home, I jumped into his arms and after a few moments spent wrapped up in the tightest hug, I peeled his clothes off and got him in the shower. When he'd finished, I brought him the towels and wrapped him up in them. I covered him in thick, fluffy, white towels from head to foot. He always joked at this point how much he loved being my polar bear. I led him to bed where we were cosy and warm, and one. I rubbed Alex's back until he drifted off to sleep. We wrote each other messages on our backs like that sometimes to get each other to sleep if we were restless. That night, like I did every time, I drew him a heart, and I wrote 'always'.

It was midday the following Monday. I'd taken the day off work. Amanda – my boss and the owner of that little slice of heaven – had been lovely and understanding. Even with my recent headaches and feeling generally grotty I hadn't taken a single unexpected day off in at least six months. Alex had managed to arrange to work from home in order to be able to come with me to the appointment.

Alex was heroic, generous, and utterly wonderful in every way but, like everybody (except, perhaps, for Ryan), he had his flaws. One was that he was a fiend when it came to his work. He was, what's the tactful way to put it? Ah, yes – passionate – when it came to his journalism. He believed strongly in the need for the public to be informed so once he got an idea, or a topic, he'd sink his teeth into it, and much like a pit-bull, his jaw would lock on until he got his story told. Confession time … it did niggle me occasionally, because he was single-minded, focussed, and, like many men, unable to multi-task; so after a fleeting hug and kiss when he came through the door he'd vanish into a bubble for the rest of the evening, as if nothing and nobody else existed – any plans would be forgotten and people fell away – he was the king of compartmentalisation, and I'm not saying that as a compliment.

So, I was justifiably concerned that my appointment would fade into oblivion in Alex's world that day, but he'd padded into the lounge half an hour before the appointment time and, with a grave look on his face, had asked, 'Are you ready to go?'

I nodded in reply and half an hour later we were sitting in front of a sombre Dr Hunter.

'How are you doing today, Mrs Richards?' Dr Hunter began.

'I could be better, I could be worse,' I replied with a smile. Dr Hunter nodded at both Alex and me.

'Today I would like to discuss the treatment options available to you. It's essential you take the time you need to make the right decision for you, Mrs Richards. As I mentioned last week, there are two options – focal radiation and chemotherapy. The aim of these would be to prolong life – slow the growth of the tumour, give us a little more time. I'm afraid though, that we're talking weeks, possibly months, not years.' He paused, presumably to let us absorb the gravity of the situation. 'If you decided you did want to try one of the treatment options, we'd need to begin very quickly in order for it to be most effective.'

I was taking a moment to process the information when Alex – protective as always – spoke.

'I've done a bit of research since our last visit, doctor, and those treatments are very tough on a patient aren't they, with nasty side-effects? What sort of toll would they take on Alice?' Alex questioned, leaning forward in his chair.

'You're right, Mr Richards, they can take a heavy toll. It is slightly different for everybody, but they are, in their own ways, destructive. However, in this case, many of the side-effects are symptoms Mrs Richards is already experiencing or is likely to experience due to the tumour – headaches, vomiting, weakness, exhaustion.'

'But, worse, doctor?' I confirmed.

'I would expect so, unfortunately.'

'And is there any chance at all that either the radiation or the chemotherapy could cure me?'

'No. The mass has developed to the stage that neither treatment option would shrink it, and removal is not possible.'

'I know I've already taken a few extra days, but I'm sorry I need a few more – I don't want to give up, but I also don't want to give myself up. We need to talk it through ...' I gestured to Alex, 'and I'd like to discuss it with my parents too. Could you give me one more week?'

'Of course. I understand fully. I do just want to go through one more thing with you today – it might be a component of your decision. Symptoms – what to expect. The brain stem connects the brain to the spinal cord. It is located just above the back of the neck and is the lowest part of the brain. The brain stem controls breathing, heart rate, and the nerves and muscles used to see, hear, walk, talk, and eat. So, any of these functions could be impacted by the tumour as it progresses.'

'Okay, so that's what I'm looking at, all of that could be at stake?'

'Yes, or very little of it. Every patient manifests differently. Plus, there are things we can try to control symptoms in these areas, medications, etc. We are on this journey together, Mrs Richards, I promise you that.'

I smiled at Dr Hunter, or was it more of a grimace? The conversation trundled on for a few more minutes before we said our goodbyes.

'Thank you, doctor, I'll see you in a week.'

'Indeed. See you soon, Mrs Richards, do take care.'

I got my first taste for doing good when I started donating blood years ago. We're not a dramatic family, but my mum has always been one of those perfect mums who coos over the smallest success. Actually, not even success, just effort. She'd be the one on the front row of the nativity play clapping her hands red, her camera blinding all the children the whole way through the play, making her little darling feel like the next Leonardo DiCaprio while donning the back half of a donkey suit. She was the best. So, you can imagine the fussing I got when I first suggested going to a blood drive. She gushed.

'You're saving lives, Allie-pops; I'm blessed to have the most good, kind person to call my daughter; you're an angel, darling.' Yeah, my mum is prone to wild exaggeration when it comes to me.

'Mum, you're being a bit dramatic, it's a simple, small act of good – I don't hate needles, I don't find it unbearably painful, thousands of people do this – it's not quite the miracle you're making out. I just know that I'd want people to donate in case you or Dad need it one day.'

'Answer me this then, Alice, will people who might have died, live, because of the blood you're donating?'

'Well, we can't know for sure, Mum, it might not be a life and death matter.'

'Yes or no, Alice?'

'Well, perhaps, yes, Mum, maybe I will save a life.' I smiled across at her ruefully.

'See, walking angel, I tell you,' Mum replied with a big grin.

So, I was sitting on that chair, at our regular blood drive, the piece of metal sticking out my arm, draining my life force away, mulling over whether to go custard cream or chocolate digestive at the free biscuit table afterwards – I know, no contest, right?! I was such a creative genius, I had The Fray's 'How to Save A Life' running through my head on repeat and I was feeling great.

My mum is the best, but she was wrong that day – I'm no walking angel. I'm just me. Flawed and fallible, but bright and cheerful too. There's been better, there's been worse. For now, there's still ordinary me.

Chapter Four

So, when you both have a coffee, just chat to him. Tell him who you are. Tell him how you feel now that you have my heart. Just talk to each other, please. I need you to know each other, down to the very deepest parts. I need you to connect so I know that this will work.

I need to say here, because I fear that perhaps I will come across badly at times – pushily and dominant and like it's all about me –I never want you to feel that I'm taking over, that I'm suggesting you're any less you now. I'm not suggesting that your love will be diminished in any way. I'm just asking you to let that corner of our heart that's left, after all your love is given, find its way home; find its way to Alex.

Alex likes to talk, so I expect once you both get over the strangeness of the situation you're in, you'll find him an engaging and enjoyable person to share a coffee with. He will chatter away about anything given the chance – from football to travel to politics to his career. I warn you now, his political views aren't everyone's cup of tea (I know, I spat that tea right out the first time I tasted it! I'm an English breakfast girl through and through and I couldn't stomach that fancy Darjeeling at all!). So, I would advise you to steer the conversation as far away from taxes and the Prime Minister as you can!

I know how nervous and uncertain I would be if I was in your shoes right now. I'm quite fearless usually – I love ziplines, parachutes, and tiny bumpy planes – but Alex always brought the dancing owls out to play in my tummy. Anyway, you will be great, I just know it. Even if you're a shy kind of girl Alex will carry you through, even with all the pain he'll be living with. He carries everyone through, always. It's like he just knows when people need something.

There was one time, on our second date, when he suddenly leapt up from the workbench we were sitting at and flew out the door across the road. I was flabbergasted. We were both covered in flour and were wearing goofy chef's hats and smocks, so he was quite a sight – he'd taken me to a tiny little restaurant, in the tiniest back alley of the whole city, to make pizzas. We were in a place the city had forgotten, cocooned in a world of fun and safety. The restaurant was small and packed with benches of other people, the smells were heavenly and enveloped us, fresh dough being made, and cooked, and all the fresh herbs filling our nostrils. There was funky music playing, lifting us along with every upbeat note. The most fantastic thing of all was the colour – the whole place was full of vibrancy, from the blue and red walls to the yellow benches, orange wooden floor, and the green sweeping murals. There was laughter everywhere. There were families, and first daters, and older couples whose wrinkles told stories of whole lifetimes shared; and there was more laughter than that little room knew what to do with. The laughter was contagious, the whole feeling of that wonderful corner of paradise was contagious. Alex knew how to choose a date venue.

Anyway, Alex must have been looking out of the window at the right time because, comical figure that he was, he rushed to a lady's side on the pavement across the road. She looked ordinary to me, late middle age probably, dressed practically but neatly, carrying a bag of shopping. She couldn't have fitted in more. No pair of eyes would have lingered over her for even a moment. Well, no pair apart from Alex's. I didn't know what to think, so I just sat stock still and watched. And what I saw was Alex chat to the lady for a moment, and then she crumpled a little, so he guided her by the elbow to a house's front doorstep and he sat down beside her on the cold slab of stone. She put her head in her hands then and I could see her shoulders wracking with the motion of sobs. Alex put his arm around those heaving shoulders and I could see his mouth move with the formation of words. She looked round to him and her mouth moved with a long reply. I could see the fight leave her body and her sorrow take over. I could see her lean all that sadness into Alex. I felt like I should be there, but at the same time I felt like a terrible unwelcome intruder just watching. I felt a lot of things, and I was just sitting, wrapped up in laughter, and this place of perfection, a pane of glass making it like a film screen. It was one of the most moving films I've ever seen.

After a time had passed, Alex stood and helped the lady up, guiding her by the elbow to her front door. They hugged tightly for a few moments, exchanged a few words, and moved away from each other. Alex walked back across the road and into the restaurant with his head bowed and his brow thoughtful. His face lit up when he saw me, and that look was a match to the fire he'd laid in my heart. Our heart burns like a wildfire for him now, don't be alarmed when you first feel it, I promise you it's the best feeling in the entire universe.

Alex sat down beside me, smiled, and apologised for his abrupt departure. I asked him if he knew that lady and he told me that he didn't. He told me that he saw her break, out there on the street, carrying her eggs, bread, and milk home from the supermarket. He told me that he saw it, and he believed nobody should be alone when they break. I asked him what he saw in her, how he knew, because she'd looked fine to me at first glance. He said when you've been broken yourself, you can never mistake it. He said it's in the way you hold yourself. Nobody else would notice but suddenly it's like your body can't hold you anymore. It's like you don't recognise the world anymore. It's like you've lost your balance and are falling. I couldn't see any of that, but he could, obviously. He told me her husband had left her that morning - her husband of forty years, whom she'd loved since she was sixteen, had told her he didn't love her anymore, he didn't want her anymore, he'd met somebody new who he wanted to love now. Alex told me it had just sunk in for her, in that moment on the pavement, that the only love she'd ever known had died. She'd given a whole life, everything she could give, and still she'd been left all alone. Alex said nobody should face a moment like that without a shoulder to cry on and arms to hold them. I knew then that I was making pizza with a hero.

That's the exact moment it happened – the moment my heart became his, I knew that I would love this kind, incredible, spectacular man for the rest of time.

So, you have nothing to worry about when you meet Alex for coffee – he will know what you need, he will know what to do to ease your pain, or discomfort, or nerves. And if you're at all broken, and I suspect that you must be with what you have been through just to have this manual in your hands, then I promise you, you're about to meet the best person you could ever hope for. Maybe, just maybe, you might walk away from that coffee a little fixed.

Alex is magical like that.

Chapter Five

The rest of the week passed in its normal rhythm. However, the next Sunday I woke up, surprised, to find Alex looming over me, the delightful aroma of a strong coffee wafting into my nostrils, and darkness.

'What time is it? What's going on?' I asked with a voice thick with sleep.

'It's time to get up, Allie, we're going on an epic adventure!' he proclaimed, wriggling with excitement.

'Seriously, Alex, the time?'

'Well, it's 5.00 a.m., aka adventure time – we have a long drive ahead. So, let's get moving.' He clapped his hands. 'I'll take the first shower, give you time to come around, drink up, then jump in the shower yourself. We need to hit the road for 5.30 a.m.' He was positively bubbling, eyes widened, smiling away. This was most alarming – Alex is not a morning person…at all.

'Grrr, Alex, what on earth!?' I exclaimed, pulling the covers up and over my head, burrowing down into their warm embrace.

'Oh no you don't, Allie, up and at 'em. Where's your adventurous spirit? You're going to love this!' He hurried off into the bathroom where he could be heard belting out, terribly out of tune, 'I Believe I Can Fly'.

I dragged myself up and reached desperately for my coffee which I lovingly cradled in my hands and sipped away at, hoping this whole debacle would look a lot rosier in five minutes when this dream-like substance had kicked in. Sundays are our lazy mornings – catnaps in each other's arms, croissants in bed, the full shebang, so I really hoped Alex knew what he was doing, sacrificing this precious sanctuary.

'Come on, Alex, I need some answers!' I called out in the direction of the bathroom. He emerged damp, with a towel round his waist – it was quite a sight, and my pulse got a fraction speedier.

'I promise it will be so much more fun as a surprise, I also promise you will love it. Can't you trust me?' Alex said, having made his way to the bed. He leaned in for a long kiss. I enjoyed it until I realised I must have morning breath, at which point I pulled back.

'I suppose surprises are your forte, you've never let me down. Fine, then, if I must.' I gave a mock sigh, followed by a smile, and headed for the bathroom.

Twenty minutes later I was fresh-faced from the shower, smelling deliciously of raspberries and vanilla thanks to the wonderful new body wash I'd just discovered, and trying to force my damp leg into one side of a pair of jeans. It was not going well.

Alex appeared through the bedroom door decked out in full sports attire as if about to embark on a gruelling triathlon.

'Sports gear is the order of the day, Allie. You've always looked breathtaking in these, they'd be perfect.' He threw a pair of running leggings my way. I just heaved a big sigh, wrestled myself into them, and stumbled to the car.

Alex had packed my pillow which I gratefully nestled into and dozed off against immediately, only to be woken a few minutes later by the barely stifled scoffing giggle from Alex. I squinted my eyes open and emerging down his driveway was Ryan, dressed in an ensemble that would warrant most mothers pressing their hands over their children's eyes.

'When I agreed to this, I did not envisage being up before the sun, Alex. You don't look as fresh as I do by missing out on beauty sleep you know!' Ryan exclaimed in an exasperated, high-pitched tone as he settled himself into the back seat of the car.

'Ry, what on earth are you wearing that for?' I asked, incredulous, once Ryan had strapped himself in.

'Your darling husband said sportswear, Als, so voila, here I am,' Ryan explained, gesturing down at his outfit.

I just slowly shook my head, a bemused grin on my face. Ryan truly is one of a kind.

'I see, but why is it so … tight?'

'Shape is so important, Als. All these baggy jogging bottoms and shorts you see men wearing, well, just no. There's no definition, no style – why would I ever conceive of walking around looking as if I have a nappy on underneath my clothes? So … uncouth, and entirely unacceptable for a gentleman. Do you not know me at all? Besides, you don't cloak a masterpiece, Als, if you've got it, flaunt it.'

I laughed. The leggings Ryan had on left nothing to the imagination, and I mean absolutely nothing, but they were decent. Technically everything was covered, and they were sportswear, as per Alex's brief. Ryan was always entirely, unashamedly himself. I was unbelievably proud of him, and inspired by that, so I couldn't say anything to dampen his spirits, especially given the herculean effort I knew he must have made just to relinquish his suit for the day.

'Absolutely, Ry, you do you!' I said to him cheekily, turning around to give him a huge grin. Ryan just shook his head at me in mock consternation before giving a good laugh back.

Ryan nodded off pretty quickly, lost beauty sleep to top up on, and Alex encouraged me to doze too.

'You'll need every bit of energy you can muster for what we've got in store.' He advised. The radio played quietly (horrifyingly, Alex is a Radio Four man) and we left the Home Counties and headed north, road signs overhead initially leading us towards Birmingham. Each time I came around enough to open my eyes for a second, I noticed the roads were clear and the scenery was typical of spring – bright, fresh, and promising. Green fields rolled by outside our windows, copses of trees lining the roads were carrying vulnerable new shoots and leaves. After nearly four hours had passed, the signs changed to complicated gobbledegook words alongside the English versions. Alex nudged me half awake and gestured to a welcome Starbucks which was indicated by Gwasanaethau/Services, heralding our arrival in Wales. We fuelled up on delicious lemon and poppy seed muffins and coffees, Ryan terrifying the Welsh baristas ordering his favourite double shot, soy, mocha latte while Alex and I shrunk up against the wall as he did so, trying to avoid the stares from the other customers who I'm sure didn't encounter many Ryans. We then piled back into the car, restored, and drove on until there were towering mountains around us, and we passed a sign for Snowdonia National Park. I was getting excited.

'Okay, Mister Adventure, what exactly are we doing here?' I asked Alex.

'Well, I'm just the chauffeur.' Alex replied, shooting a sideways glance my way. 'You and Ryan will be Miss and Master Adventure, with me waiting at the end, as acting cheerleader.'

'Oh, well, okay, why are you wearing the sports gear then?' I asked.

'Had to look the part, didn't I? I couldn't be missing out on all the fun,' Alex answered with a shrug.

'Having dragged me four hours each way crushed up in the back of this small car I hope you'll be breaking out cheer moves worthy of a role in the next *Take it to The Limit* movie, Alex. Hmmm, add that to the girls' night list, won't you, Al.' Ryan spoke in a way that brokered no argument.

Only Ryan could call a spacious mid-range, four-wheel drive small.

It hasn't always been an easy relationship between Alex and Ryan. They've each been such a huge presence in my life that jealousy creeps in between them from time to time. I think sometimes Alex struggles to get past the shiny surface to the depth and substance Ryan harbours beneath. That would be an easy thing to do – all the extravagance and hilarity can be distracting. Ryan makes it easy for people to misjudge him. It made it all the more special that Alex had organised this day for us all together.

Now, the strong caramel macchiato finally kicking in, realisation was dawning on me. Surrounded by majestic mountains in Wales, on a trip labelled an epic adventure by Alex, there was only one possible thing we could be doing today. I began bouncing on my seat with excitement. It just couldn't be, though. Alex has been ducking out of doing it for six whole years, each excuse getting more ridiculous and obscure than the last. Unless … that explained why Ryan was here – Alex wanted me to have the chance to do it finally, and with somebody I loved, but he was just too scared to manage to get up there himself. For all his style and girlishness, Ryan loves adventure and is stronger and more courageous than anyone I know. Alex, however, appears in the dictionary as the definition of a scaredy-cat (at least when it comes to high-adrenalin things). All of this meant one thing – we were here for me to fulfil a dream, to do the thing I'd been desperate for Alex to do with me for years – we were here to zipline.

At speeds of over 100mph and the longest zipline in Europe, it was heralded as the closest thing to flying a human could do – and I was sold! Lying in a harness setting out over a breathtaking quarry in the middle of Snowdonia National Park, that was me all over. I couldn't believe Alex had done this for me – this was something I'd longed to do, for a very long time.

As we pulled up in the carpark Alex turned around in his seat so that he could address Ryan and me.

'Rules of the day are,' Alex began seriously. That was very Alex – rules. 'No taking the mickey out of me. Allie, I wish with all my heart that I could do this with you, but it looks terrifying, and I would only have spoiled your fun having to hold my hand all the way through it.'

'That's not true – holding your hand is one of my favourite things in the whole world!'

I couldn't help but be distracted by the unmistakeable sound of Ryan fake vomiting. I looked around to see him doubled over in his seat, with bulging eyes, and his fingers down his throat. I rolled my eyes and gave him an affectionate shove before continuing.

'But I understand, Alex. I'm so grateful that you've brought me and organised it so I have a partner in crime up there.'

'I may be your superhero, Allie, but we both know that this superhero doesn't fly. Besides, your best friend is the bravest man I know. I'd be a fool not to call in the big guns when I can.' There was a pause, and then Alex continued, 'The next rule is no sad talk – this is a day away from all the bad, a chance for us to escape it and have a day of happiness, fun, and memories. Do we all agree?' Alex questioned. Ryan and I both nodded solemnly.

'Sounds good to me, boss, and don't worry, I'll take the best care of Als. I'm so excited!' Ryan exclaimed, knees bouncing with his enthusiasm.

Alex had booked us in in advance, so we were quickly whisked into a large room where clothes rails lined the walls, each one overflowing with identical red overalls in every conceivable size. There were two staff members standing next to these suits, emanating the paradoxically chilled yet energetic vibes that seem to define a 'dude'. They looked us up and down before rifling through the racks, selecting two of these fetching sets of overalls and passing them over to us.

'If you could just put these on over your clothes, then make your way over to Adrian in the corner who will get your harnesses fitted and you will be ready to fly!' He instructed enthusiastically, even giving us a keen thumbs up.

I looked over at Ryan, knowing he'd be preparing for war with his jumpsuit. He was holding the offending garment at arms-length, turning away from it, and stretching his head as far away from it as was physically possible, as if proximity alone would destroy his style-integrity. He looked like he should have had an act in the circus he was contorting himself into such an odd shape.

'Oh, God, no! You have to be joking!' Ryan exclaimed, horrified, with such heavy intonation the words took twice as long to say. I pinched my lips together to stifle a giggle, feeling great sympathy for the manly adventure dudes who were going to have to persuade Ryan to step into the suit. 'That is the most hideous thing I've ever seen.' Ryan was cranking the melodrama up further. His hands were flapping, his face a mask of despair.

'Sir, no suit, no flying.' One of the staff members calmly informed him. Ryan looked at him for a long moment before assuming his classic position of bridge of his nose pinched, eyes scrunched up.

'Give me a moment then, please,' Ryan said, gesturing the man away with a sagging hand. The staff member ambled off, a smile playing with his lips. I'll bet Ryan just made his day.

'Ryan, you have to, please. It's not so bad, it's just, in essence, a onesie.' I gently tried to persuade him.

'A humongous, bright red onesie, Als, which might as well be made of sandpaper it's that rough.' I just gave him one of my trademark huge, winning, kilowatt smiles. 'The things I do for you, Als, no one would believe me.' Ryan finally acquiesced, shaking his head emphatically.

As I turned away to put my own suit on I saw Ryan throw his arms to the sky, toss his head back and exclaim, 'Lord, why must thou test me so!?' with all the theatrics of a West End show performer. The thing is, he was serious.

They trundled us down to the start. We had a few practice runs to build our confidence, although Ryan's confidence needed no boosting, and he set off with a deafening, 'Whooooop,' every time. I loved every minute. It was so liberating; feeling weightless, gliding through the air, just myself and freedom.

'Now, it's the big one, guys.' The member of staff informed us. 'Have you decided on what order you're going in?'

Ryan stepped towards me at this point, grabbed both my hands in his and looking at me for confirmation as he spoke, asked,

'What do you want to do, Als? Do you mind?'

'No, so why don't you go first – you look as though you might throw yourself off this platform with the sling or without it if someone doesn't clip you on soon!' I laughed.

'Yes, please then!' Ryan was jumping us both up and down with excitement. 'Oooh, I'm having so much fun, Als. I think I might have to start calling your dream machine of a husband my superhero too after doing this for us.'

'Okay, sir, if you could step forward please.' Ryan did as he was instructed and got into position – head first, lying face down in the sling.

'I'll be waiting for you, gorgeous!' He gave me a huge grin as they counted down.

'You better be!' I called after him as he went. As he cut through the air, the spectacular blue of the water-filled quarry below, flanked by the slate-grey, stone walls of it, with the baby-blue sky overhead, marshmallow clouds dotting through it, it felt like we were in another dimension. Everything else had just melted away, it was just me, my extraordinary best friend, a whole lot of fun, and the love of my life waiting for me at the end.

They settled me into place next, and the first tingling of nerves set in. Then all I could think about was my spectacular husband waiting for me, and I couldn't get to him fast enough. I would enjoy the ride all right, but all I wanted was to be in his arms.

'Ready?' I was asked. I nodded. 'Three, two, one …'

Then, I was flying. My stomach dropped, my heart ducked and dived, my ears rumbled as the air roared past. It was incredible – up there, soaring, Alice Richards – a piece of the sky, I lived.

Alex came into view, standing on the platform, Ryan beside him. Then I was in Alex's arms, having the last bit of air squeezed out of me, as if being airborne hadn't done a good enough job of that. Alex buried his head in my neck.

I caught my breath enough to say, 'Thank you, thank you! I did it!' Then I grabbed Alex into a bear hug and spun us round and round.

'Yes, you did it, Allie, you did it all. You, are everything.'

He twirled me around and around, so that my feet were off the ground. Then he pulled Ryan in too, and we were all spinning together.

I carried on flying long after I was unclipped.

Chapter Six

I'm sure you will have got to know my beautiful best friend Ryan like you'd know a brother by now. That's your bonus gift – every girl's dream – a GBF! I know, I know, I've given you the jackpot – a hunky hero and a gay best friend. Life just doesn't get any better! Try to contain your excitement – you've just had heart surgery for crying out loud! To inherit Ryan is to inherit a soulmate. He will be faithful and true and there is nothing he won't do to protect the people he loves. I don't know how much he will have told you, but he chose you. He selected you as the closest thing to perfect he could find. So, he loves you. You will have a sheltered spot underneath his feathery wing for as long as you want it.

I've tasked him with the organisation of lots of your responsibilities. He knows everybody who is worth knowing, from maintenance men to CEO's. He's magnificent, and he's beloved by everyone he meets. So, he will get it all done. All the things that seem impossible, the silly things you're too embarrassed to ask for, Ryan will wave his magic wand and they will be sorted. He will also kick Alex into gear. Ryan was the one person Alex was scared of. All of Ryan's pink fluffy pens and perfect paisley shirts alarmed Alex. One stern word from Ryan and Alex will be putty in your hands. You will need that. For the bat house, and the train station, and maybe the Christmas lights. Sorry, I'm getting ahead of myself. So, don't be afraid to use Ryan's people genius. And please, love Ryan too. Just for you though, however you want. I'm not giving you Alex, quite the opposite, I'm just asking you to keep delivering me back to him. But I'm giving you Ryan. He is the greatest, most special gift you could ever receive. Underneath all that snazzy jazz he is a total teddy bear. He will be hurting so much. He lost his soulmate. His sister for all intents and purposes. And his best friend. He's so good at hiding his pain, he is so guarded and strong. But he will need the cracks in his soul kissing better. Slash some lip balm on and pucker up, please.

Chapter Seven

I phoned Ryan up from amid the abundance of bubbles I'd disappeared into during my daily bath ritual. The bathroom was bursting with the heavenly smell of strawberries, which put me in the serenest of moods. Isn't it fabulous the pamper-products you can buy nowadays? All I'd have needed were some cucumber slices, and I'd have had a spa in my very own bathroom. Self-care, you're a saviour – especially when you come to me in strawberry form!

'Hi, Ry, I'm not interrupting a hot date, am I?'

'Hello, gorgeous, no, sadly not, my only companions tonight are a bottle of prosecco and a mountain of work.'

'No Rupert Everett fest tonight?'

'Not tonight,' Ryan replied with a resounding sigh. 'I'm saving that delight for you and me on our next girls' night in – *My Best Friend's Wedding*, Als and I are coming for you!'

'Oooh, yes, you bet we are!' I flicked some bubbles into the air with an outstretched toe.

'Ry, there's something I have to ask you: will you come with me to the appointment with Doctor Hunter on

Monday? It'll be our chance to ask him all about donating, maybe get everything set up. I think it's best that Alex, Mum, and Dad don't hear about that side of things, and, well, I could really do with my favourite shoulder to cry on, there beside me.'

'Of course, I'll be there, Al, just name the time and the place, always.'

'I'll try not to smudge your suit if there's any tears.'

'Well, I should hope that goes without saying, even my most casual suit is Prada and we all know Prada doesn't grow on trees. Though, for you, Al, I'll splurge on a special dry clean – George knows how to take care of my babies. After all, what use is a shoulder to cry on if you can't, well, cry on it?' Ryan asked. I could just picture his exaggerated shrug.

'You could always wear something casual which doesn't need George to "take care of it" if a drop of water so much as lands on it. Something like, I don't know, a totally classy merino wool jumper?'

Ryan gave a mock gasp, and I knew he'd be covering his mouth with his smooth hand in an extravagant movement that was all stuck-out elbows.

'Oh, the horror, when will you understand that your fashion jokes just aren't funny. Besides, wool, on this skin? I think not. Have you seen me out of a suit since our school days?'

I couldn't hold back a mischievous grin that Ryan must have been able to hear in my voice.

'Since you asked, Ryan darling, I've seen you absolutely rock a certain onesie!' I remind him cheekily, to which he gave another gasp of mock outrage before bellows of laughter echoed down the phone line.

It was a crisp morning. There was a late frost glistening on the grass as Ryan and I drove to the hospital that next Monday morning. I felt sluggish though, and spaced out, as though I was merely a spectator watching all this play out on a television screen in front of me. Ryan parked us in the already crowded car park with the skills of Lewis Hamilton. Ryan is not only a vision of perfection, he is utterly faultless at almost everything he does. Having said that, I do think the secret to his success is that he avoids, with a vengeance, anything he's not one hundred per cent marvellous at. So, with him having manoeuvred his car into a space I would have totalled all three surrounding cars trying to reverse into, he grabbed my mitten-clad hand and pulled me to the sliding doors of the hospital building. I was grateful that the deep gulps of breath I took before we stepped inside filled my lungs with air so fresh they startled me into action.

Ryan looked round at me and asked, 'Ready, Als?'

'As I'll ever be.' I nodded.

We stepped through those doors and worked our way to the Oncology Department. There was a buzz in the hospital, the activity and bustle of cogs turning, a new day starting.

'Alice Richards to see Dr Hunter please.' I told the business-like receptionist, who was sitting behind her glass wall, rubbing up close to the pain but never quite touching it.

'Take a seat please, Mrs Richards, he'll be with you shortly.'

Ryan and I settled ourselves into two hardback chairs in the waiting area. This was as stark as everywhere else in the hospital: clean but worn; practical, never personal. We shrugged off our thick coats, unwound our snug scarves, and pinched off our mittens and laid them over our knees while we waited. We didn't speak – there wasn't anything to say. Ryan looked uncomfortable and out of place. His eyes darted about, showing his disconcertion. When he noticed me looking he smiled at me encouragingly, but it didn't even dimple his cheeks, never mind meet his eyes.

The hospital staff were always moving, brushing by and around us. They talked constantly between themselves in the hushed tones of insiders, among outsiders. Soon Dr Hunter emerged from his windowless office, or rather his head and torso did, as he peered round his door. His eyes swept the room and widened a fraction in welcome when they spotted me.

'Ah, Mrs Richards, do come in.' Dr Hunter offered. I stood up, looked at Ryan, and we walked in, sitting down on the lumpy, scratchy, but at least cushioned, chairs across from the desk.

'Dr Hunter, this is my best friend, Ryan.' Ryan immediately proffered a smooth, elegant hand which Dr Hunter gripped for thc briefest moment.

'Ryan Balfour,' Ryan said with a single nod at the doctor, his impeccable manners not hiding for even a moment behind the gravity of the meeting.

'So, Mrs Richards—' Dr Hunter began, but I cut in quickly.

'Please, call me Alice, if this isn't personal enough for first-names I don't know what is,' I said with a small smile.

'Okay, Alice, today we need to make a plan. Have you come to any decisions?'

I held Ryan's hand tightly in mine as I answered.

'I don't want to proceed with any treatment. I want to live every moment I can now and if there's no chance at all of a cure, I would rather take every moment of me that I have left. It's not that I'm giving up, quite the opposite, I'm fighting – for me.'

The doctor nodded at me.

'I understand, I don't exactly know how long you'll be looking at but with no treatment I would expect it to be in the three-month region. Obviously, we'll work together to manage your pain and symptoms as they present themselves. Do you have any questions for me?' he asked.

I looked deep into Ryan's eyes and he nodded at me and gave my hand a squeeze.

'Yes, I do. I want to donate my organs. I'm hoping that you can help me, advise me of what I need to do?'

'Well, in this case it might not be as straightforward as usual – cancer patients are usually exempt from donating due to the risk of the cancer having spread to other organs.' Dr Hunter looked at me with sympathy.

'Doctor, this is very important to me.' I implored. 'I could save lives. I've done my research – on average, twenty-two lives could be saved or improved by a single donor. You said that my cancer hasn't spread, all those organs, the tissue, it's all healthy, clean, cancer-free. Surely there must be a way to help, to un-exempt me?'

Dr Hunter looked deep into my eyes for a good while; I looked right back. We were all silent, patient.

'It's unusual, Alice, but I can see how much it means to you, and it's a wonderful thing to do. I'll work on it for you. Your specific type of cancer is so fast growing that, not to put too fine a point on the reality, you'll be gone before it spreads. I'll champion the cause, do my best I'm in!' He paused, and a smile tugged at the corners of his mouth. 'The twenty-two,' he said, nodding. 'It's quite something.'

'There's one more thing … I need my heart to go to someone specific.'

The doctor's brow furrowed into a frown.

'That's just not possible I'm afraid, Alice, deceased donations can't be directed – for ethical reasons – they have to go to the match who is in the greatest need.'

'I understand that's the law, but it's my body, my heart. This is … vital. There has to be a way.' I almost begged.

'I'm sorry, Alice, but there really isn't. It's legally bound up so tightly there are no loopholes or room for interpretation. It's impossible.'

Disappointment washed over me, I slumped back in my chair and put my head in my hands. Ryan shocked me with the intensity of his outrage as he spoke up.

'Well, that's plain insanity. How fucking ridiculous. It's Alice's body, she gets to fucking choose.'

The doctor's eyes widened at Ryan's profanities, but he chose to overlook them without comment when he replied.

'Yes – the choice is whether to be a donor or not. There is no scope for requests beyond that.'

Ryan was tense and agitated. It didn't feel right to me, though, something was scratching away at the back of my mind. Then it came to me.

'Dr Hunter, I know how ridiculous this will sound, trust me I hate to be this girl, but please, hear me out.' I paused, and the doctor gave a single nod. 'I've seen it – on *Grey's Anatomy* – a mother directs the liver donation of her deceased son.' I nod at him eagerly, which may have seemed odd given the topic of conversation. 'I expect Grey's Anatomy is the bane of your life, and that so many patients must think they have all the answers having watched Derek Sheppard hunched over an open brain, but it definitely happened – were they making it up?'

'You could well be right,' Doctor Hunter replied thoughtfully. 'Being in America it could be accurate – they do have a different system over there, and it's looser with its restrictions. I don't know for sure mind you, but it might be possible. However, I don't see how that helps us.'

Ryan's face had set into the determination I knew meant he couldn't be stopped – thirty carriage freight trains had less force than Ryan when he got like this.

'It helps us, doctor, because that's exactly what we'll do – we'll go to America, do it there. My gorgeous girl Alice, she's set me this one last task. Let me tell you, she deserves this, hell, this is not a fragment of what she deserves. If that's what it takes, rest assured, my good man, I will be making it happen.' Ryan spoke with a fervour and energy that seemed to take Dr Hunter aback.

'There will be a lot more to it than you think, I wouldn't want you to get your hopes up it will work out.'

'Noted, doctor, and thank you for your time.' Ryan stood up, swiftly followed by Dr Hunter who shook hands first with Ryan and then with me.

'Thank you for your time, Dr Hunter,' I said.

Ryan and I filed out of the office and linked arms as we left the building.

'Well, Ry, that's not ideal, is it. But, you've always wanted to go shopping in New York, maybe it's a blessing in disguise, hey?' I asked with a smile.

'I'm not sure I'd go that far but I like the way you think, Als, maybe you're right.'

I'd been told by Dr Hunter that I had three months left of useful life – three months as me. After that I would be declining – losing function, possibly losing memory, definitely losing independence. The monster inside me would take over gradually but completely. He would inhabit my head with more control and strength than my soul would my body. So, my plans were to enjoy those three months to the absolute fullest. I found time to be like they say in every cliché – like quicksand. I tried to grasp hold of it so tightly but the tighter I gripped the quicker it slipped through my fingers. I tried to plan all kinds of activities and adventures with Mum, Dad, Alex, and Ryan. However, it just seemed to cause more upset than benefit. Everybody had their responsibilities and lives. Try as they might, and they all tried so hard, they couldn't just stop completely. After all, when it was all over, they would still be here, they would still have the mortgage to pay and the house to clean. They spent every possible moment of time with me they could, but I was putting too much pressure on them. The best moments are the organic, everyday ones, like scratchy wool blankets and hot chocolate, not staged big debacles like artificial family photo shoots. So, I relaxed my grip on the time remaining and I let it follow its own course through the days.

That was okay though, because it turns out that dying takes a lot of paperwork, a lot of organising. I wrote a letter to every organ recipient I would be helping. I wouldn't have wanted a strange organ inside me, giving me life, without a little history of the life it had led.

There was so much to do. I wanted all the I's dotted and T's crossed for Alex and my family so they wouldn't have to worry about the small details, just about piecing their broken hearts back together.

I contacted funeral service providers, organised my insurance, changed all the details for Alex with bank accounts, bills etc – I wrote to every single person who we dealt with, so Alex never had to see my name on an envelope landing on the doormat or hear my name being spoken through a phone enquiry. I could only guess that those would be the most impossible moments to deal with in the early days – the ones where you're blindsided, unprepared, unguarded, and the pain invades out of nowhere. Those are the moments when your back slides down the hard door, envelope clutched, and creasing in your hands, the tears soaking your best work shirt, as you curl into a ball with the doormat spiking into your side and you stay there. You stay curled up there, in a ball on the doormat, cold, mute, still, empty, as the light fades through the frosted glass panel in the door and the blackness comforts you through the dark night, until somehow your phone alarm sounds and brings you back to face another day. Those are the real moments of grief, and they wound in ways that can never be healed. I wanted to spare Alex those moments of cruel reality. I wanted him to be able to cuddle our teddy on the soft sheets underneath the snuggly duvet and at least be held by warmth and cosiness while he cried the night away. If I could save him from the doormat and the cold hallway floor with a few phone calls, then there was no better way to spend my last days.

Alex didn't want to be, or maybe that should read couldn't be, involved in any of the conversations about the aftermath. I'd brought it up a few times, and it was a standard script that we couldn't break from. It went something like this:

'Alex, do you have anything you specifically want to include in the service? Or anything of mine you want to keep?'

'I can't talk about this now, Alice. I have to suffer through losing my entire life. I'm not wasting a moment of the time I have left to live it with you, working out little things for afterwards. Please, leave it.'

'But it's important, Alex. The one time you won't be able to deal with it is then. I want to make it as smooth as possible for you.'

'It will not be smooth, Alice. It could never, ever be smooth. Half of me will be ripped away. I don't even know if I will survive it. But rest assured your parents and I are more than capable of sorting out who gets your blue cardigan and who gets the green one. Okay?' Alex paused, and his tension fell away. 'Now, don't worry so much. Just love me with every beat of your heart, just love me with every last breath. Hot chocolate?'

I nodded. Hot chocolate solved everything. I resigned myself to making the best decisions I could and leaving the rest to Ryan to handle. I would leave some gaps in the service programme for Alex to play his favourite songs or say something if he wanted to.

I handed the funeral arrangements over to Ryan a few days later, with strict instructions to make it the party of a lifetime. Ryan studiously noted down my wishes with his fluffy pink pen in his big notebook with the inspirational quote on the front. If I was an organisational whizz, and I like to think that I was, then Ryan was an organisational genius, a mastermind. I think he was honoured to be entrusted with such an important task, though I don't know who else he could have imagined would be doing it. He was made for this. Being Mr Logic as he was, he didn't seem to have any issue talking about my death in black and white. He was the only one who ever made light of it or joked about things. It made him the easiest company. I loved my best friend days with Ryan.

'Ryan, there must be colour, okay, colour everywhere.'

'Mmm-hmmm, we'll go for muted shades, pastels maybe. Nothing garish.'

'No, Ryan, everything garish!' I laughed. 'Vibrant and lively.'

'It's a funeral, Al, not the fucking Rio Carnival. I'm keeping it classy, whatever you say.'

'Well, you're the boss.' I nodded at him. 'But cupcakes, yes, for after?'

'Fine, if that's what you want.' Ryan smiled.

'Bright cupcakes, orange, purple, red, yellow, all right?'

'Yes, of course, pastel cupcakes, sure thing.' Ryan chuckled. I couldn't resist joining in with the giggles. 'Seriously, Al, trust me, don't I have the best taste of anyone you've ever met in the whole of your life?' He was winding me up but that was exactly what the situation needed.

'Yes, Ryan, you do.'

'And don't I know everything I could ever need to know about you to make this perfect?'

'Yes, Ryan, you do.'

'So, stop fussing. Leave it to the master. You won't be disappointed. And if you are, I give you full permission to grind a pastel cupcake into my face as your first spirit act. Deal?'

'Deal.'

Chapter Eight

We go next to the surprise trip you're going to plan for our hero. Everybody loves a hero and not only was I lucky enough to love one but I'm passing the honour onto you through my heart. We all know every superhero needs their sidekick and ours may be feeling a little lost without his. I was never at the dizzying heights of Robin to Alex's Batman, but I held his hand through the turbulence of life and it can be a little lonely when your hand feels empty and cold where it once felt warm and safe. This is the first moment I think he'll know. You'll probably have to tell him about the manual at some point and I trust you'll know how and when the time will be right. I don't want him to think you and he are just puppets on strings and I'm the puppetmaster making you dance. I need him to feel the connection to me and believe it – that it's actually me with him, albeit from within you. This trip, if it all comes together just right, will be the moment he knows there's something more, that it has to be me, right there with you both.

Try to hold in your laughter when I outline the day you have ahead. Or else you might be spluttering coffee all over the manual and whatever pretty blouse you're wearing. And please try to embrace it, even if it's not your usual dream day out.

You will take Alex to the zoo. You'll need to select a day in the first two weeks of February, a day where it will be dry in the morning but with rain forecast for the afternoon. And you can't take a coat. When you collect him from our house and he slides into the passenger seat, say 'What a beautiful day for February!' He might not ask you why you don't have a coat since it would be too painful a repeat of us, but to fill in the blanks for you I was the fool who went to the zoo in February with no coat. I insisted you can't jinx a gift like sun in February by taking a coat. It's a commitment game. You commit to the weather gods. You have faith in them so they reward you. I lost my faith in the weather gods that day but a belief in Alex grew that I knew could never die. Never has a mistake been such total perfection.

I'm sorry you're ending up with all this reminiscing and I hope it doesn't feel like pressure to you, having to retrace the steps of our beautiful romance. I just think all these instructions need context. I need you to understand so you can get all the nuances and tiny details right.

That day at the zoo was only our third date. Alex had been desperate to plan this one, and we'd already agreed I would plan the next one. At this point I was just ecstatic there was definitely going to be a next one! We walked through the entrance gates and Alex whipped out the zoo map the enthusiastic, young, ticket-booth operator had thrust upon us. Alex carefully plotted us an itinerary. We had a conversation about favourite animals. I was the tigers and hippos to his brown bears and red pandas and they were all plotted on the map. Alex doesn't know it, I don't think, but I filched that map from his car when I got out back at my house that evening. I'm a sentimental type, and it went straight into my box of treasures. It is in the pack attached to the manual, so you can follow our exact route, see everything we saw, feel everything we felt. I hope you like bats.

You can follow the map together, hopefully one of my simpler directives, for this trip. Wander past the elephants and the hippos, the tigers, and the red pandas. I've always found that animals reflect to us all that we are and all that we are not. I hope you'll be able to relax and enjoy the morning. Maybe a bit of animal-driven-self-discovery will slip its way in.

About halfway round Alex's route, when you've just visited the rhinos, you'll glimpse the doors of the bat house a little ahead of you. At this exact point in time you need to morph from human to weather god, or at least cash in any chits you have with those who shake the rain stick. You need to make it rain. And I don't mean irritating drops of mizzle that you don't feel but sticks to your hair giving you a halo, I mean the heavy kind of rain. Clamouring rain. The kind that slices straight through your clothes and hits your skin. The sort of rain that has you soaked through in seconds. The type of rain that feels like so much more than just water falling from the sky.

Being realistic, I obviously don't expect you to be able to get that kind of timing perfection, but the point is you need to try to slow down, or speed up, on your route that morning to time it as closely as you can. The rain needs to start when you're somewhere in the approach to the bat house. I have to ask you a huge favour here. If you're scared of bats, please find a way through your fear. Don't forget you'll be standing beside a hero. A fixer. So, you will be in the best hands. And if that's not enough then you have my fearless heart to fill you with courage from within. I love bats. They are the fluttering guardians of the beautiful slice of time that is dusk. Neither an end nor a beginning; or rather both an end and a beginning.

Alex and I were marvelling at the rhinos that third date at the zoo. We were laughing together in the intimate, shared way of new lovers – still nervous, still aware of every millimetre of space between us, and yet wanting to share everything, falling in love with love. I knew Alex was special, that he was my One, I've told you that already. But rather than being a comfort, in those early days, it was petrifying. One mistake and I could lose the rest of my life. Having found him, I knew I needed Alex's love to survive this life. It turns out I was right.

The sun was weak but valiantly clinging onto its space between the clouds. Alex's elbow was brushing against mine, our bodies curving towards each other like the two halves of a heart. It felt like the whole universe was contained in those few centimetres of contact. I'd never given my elbows a second thought, yet in that moment I believed they would henceforth be my most revered body part. If they could feel that much, how could I ever dismiss them again. The day was perfect. And then, to interrupt that moment of pure perfection, it came fast and hard, the rain, the clamouring, soaked-in-seconds rain, came beating down.

More than anything it was the shock that made us move. One moment you're marvelling at the magical powers of elbows and the next you're being assailed by obese drops of water being fired at you by the sky. How life can execute tyre-screeching

U-turns. Alex grabbed me by the elbow and he ran towards the bat house, pulling me along with him. Alex has long legs, as you must have observed by now. I don't. So, his easy lope was an Olympic-effort sprint for me, but I made it. With the benefit of hindsight, I don't think Alex can have realised where he had led me; what creature fluttered among the rafters of that dry, safe haven. So, when it's your turn, he will be reluctant, because he'll know what flies ahead. You'll have to let the rain get heavy, then you'll have to look right into his chocolate-brown eyes, grab him gently but firmly by his elegant elbow and steer him through those bat house doors come hell or high water. However much he resists, know that it's important. I've a sneaking suspicion he will acquiesce easier than he may have once done. After all, he's faced far worse fears than what lies in that house now. He's lost more than the little bats could ever take from him. In fact, they can give him something back this time. When you've lost your everything, there is nothing more valuable than memories.

Once you're both inside those doors, the darkness will wrap around you. You will have to keep Alex moving and pull him through that plastic curtain into the warmth of the bat zone. That day when it was me attached to his hand he was trying so hard to play it cool, bravado was pulsing out of his stance, but fear was leaking out of his pores. I laced my fingers through his, and the way he squeezed them – so gently but also like I was his only lifeline – made me feel like I'd been a ship lost in the raging, angry storms of the ocean my whole life, and I'd finally drifted safely into a tranquil paradisiacal harbour.

When we wandered through that curtain the bats were everywhere. They were so used to humans they would fly right over the top of your head, so close you could feel the whoosh of breeze they left in their wake. I loved it. Alex did not. He flinched the moment he realised where we were. His head nearly disappeared into his shoulders and his eyes grew round and wild. The loveliest moment was when he pulled me tight against his side, his arm a shield of protection.

Alex gave me so many tiny hero moments.

He valiantly pressed on, giving the illusion of a cool, calm, collected twenty-something guy who enjoys a bat house as much as the next macho man. Nobody else could feel his trembling. The thing you don't realise until you've been inside a bat house is it's not just the sight of the circling winged beasts that can be overwhelming to those whom bats disconcert, it's also the sound. Bats chatter. I tried to out-chatter them for Alex, and you can do the same if you're so inclined. But it wasn't enough. There was a little part of the bat house that has a tunnel with displays in it. The bats love to fly through this. You can almost hear them laughing with glee at the frights they give people. Why deny the bats their own fun I guess the zoo keepers think? The bats must have been in hysterics when Alex and I walked through that tunnel. By now, it was less meander and more semi-jog. Alex wasn't interested in lingering with his newfound friends.

He had a hood on that day, and right as we were passing through that tunnel in our half-jog, a particularly friendly bat decided the hood looked like a comfy place for a rest. There are no words to describe how much Alex freaked out.

As I relay this tale, I wonder how you'll get him back in there. You'll have to use every possible method of persuasion.

Let's hope you're a hostage negotiator by trade, maybe then you stand a chance.

Alex was frenzied. Once I realised why, I turned Alex's hood out, dislodged the furry friend, and grabbed his shoulders to tell him it was okay. His wild eyes just stared into mine for a moment and time stood still. We became partners right then, I promise you.

We were forevermore Alex and me, me and Alex. A team, a pair, a package deal. Well, maybe not quite forevermore, I suppose.

He wound his fingers back through mine and we ran out. I was half-stumbling to keep up with his long-legged speed, but momentum kept me there. Outside, the rain was still pouring down, like pencils not droplets. Alex stood with his hands on his knees for a moment and then he looked up at me from beneath his floppy hair. This is where the story of that day really begins.

The rain was flying down, forcing its way into the fabric of our clothes like a SWAT team – suddenly and ruthlessly. We were soaked through in seconds – soggy underwear soaked. The water was dripping down our foreheads and our necks, our skin shining, lips glistening. The rain was so heavy all the other zoo-goers were seeking refuge in the various houses, and cafes. The air was filled with flying water, and the space around us had cleared of everybody else. It was just me and Alex, and a lot of dancing droplets. In that moment, the world began at Alex's head and ended at his toes, for me.

I'm not completely bonkers, I do accept it was a ridiculous situation to find any enjoyment in. However, we were grinning like the fools in love we were. We were beaming into each other's souls; my eyes were locked with his pools of chocolate brown. The rain had soaked through his eyelashes making them frame his eyes even more magnificently. I never underestimated mascara's mythical powers again after that day. Alex started laughing first; in fact, calling it a laugh does it no justice – it was a bellowing, doubled over with joy, howling laugh. Soon I was bent double next to him, and I finally knew why they called it 'crazy in love'. Being crazy never felt so undeniably, wonderfully perfect. The day turned from remarkable to magical with his next move.

Alex turned his head a fraction and lifted his shoulders into a bow. His laugh settled into a smile and his eyes sunk a little with shyness. The air between the pencils of rain became charged with enough energy to start a lightning field around us. Alex lifted his hand in front of me, and from his deep bow he asked, 'Dance with me?' I nodded, and he pulled me into him. His right hand found a home on my waist and I rested one hand on his shoulder and the other nestled within his left hand, in a stance just like in the movies. For the first few steps Alex just moved me in the silence. The quiet thrumming of the rain gave us a slight beat and took the edge off the empty space.

It became apparent very quickly that there was a hiccup in this scene of magic perfection – there were three left feet instead of the required two. I have never been a dancer. I've always been the girl who sits at the side of the dance floor. On the rare occasions I've been cajoled into releasing my inner dancing queen, there have been yelps, cries, black and blue toes, or split foreheads, and perhaps even a siren or two. Yet I never hesitated for a second to step into Alex's arms.

When he realised I lacked skills in the dancing department, the first thing he did was pull me right into him. So our bodies were flush against each other all the way up. I rested my cheek against his chest and felt his heart beating loudly against his ribcage. I let that be my rhythm to move to. I let that be the rhythm I moved to for the rest of my life.

We were pulling each other in so tightly it felt like we swapped the rain – that Alex pushed all the drops in his shirt into my shirt. We swapped our rain as we swapped our hearts. With Alex's heartbeat rhythm, I got a bit better at dancing. Good enough that I didn't worry about injuring Alex, or how far we were from the nearest A&E. It may not be pretty, I thought, but I could get us both through unharmed now. I let his thigh move my thigh, his foot move my foot. It was the most perfect, intimate form of connection I've ever known.

I felt a vibration in Alex's chest and moments later he was singing. His words were soft and gentle and slightly out of tune, but they were magnificent. They flowed around us, keeping us even more tightly bound. Alex sung like I've never known singing. He sang like reading alone in an empty library. He danced like the sunbeams dance with the raindrops to form a rainbow. He held me like the sky holds its bright diamond stars on a clear night. Everything about that day was so beautiful it hurt.

The melody was haunting, the lyrics flawless. The song filtered through the pores of my skin into my blood and my bones and my heart. It became a part of me. So, it's a part of you too. The song was Kodaline's 'The One' and it's one of the most beautiful songs in the world. If you've never heard it, give it a google and have a listen.

I expect Alex played it at my funeral. I hope he did.

Now, I don't really think organising that dance again is a good idea. I accept the evidence points to the contrary, but I do think I know where to draw the line. I think that dance would be too painful for Alex, and too false, and far too awkward for you. So, you can breathe a sigh of relief. You don't have to dance in the pouring rain. What I hope you can do though, is the bat house part, and then, if you can manage it, take a tiny Bluetooth speaker in your bag and as you set foot inside the bat house, play that song. Take hold of Alex's hand, squeeze it tightly, and wander through the house with the bats chattering and fluttering overhead, and let him remember that moment, relive our dancing in his mind. Maybe the bats will dance along for us.

Chapter Nine

I'd been back at work for a few weeks following the deluge of hospital visits, and it was wonderful to settle back into the rhythm of normal life, especially when I loved how I spent my days so much.

I have, what I consider, the best job in the world. I'm a florist – deputy to the owner, Amanda, of 'Sunshine and Roses'. She has been a wonderful teacher, and friend, to me. She works in the mornings, so I enjoy lots of learning time then, and when she's gone in the afternoons I have the place to myself, which is such fun. I feel like a child at playtime, not an adult slaving away. I don't have to go to work, I get to go to work.

Brace yourself for one of my gleeful ramblings! I think flowers are one of the things we are given as evidence there's something more, and I'm not specifying what that something might be, but I think flowers show that something cares. When you consider how beautiful even the simplest flowers are, and how amazing they smell, and how silky they feel, it's such a gift that we have them. Not only do I get to surround myself with these beauties all day, but I get to make other people happy too. What a win-win. I wish I'd videoed the wide smiles, the tears of happiness, and the shy looks of surprise people gave to my bouquets. I would so love to be able to settle back in my deep, squishy sofa, with my purple woolly blanket and a mug of hot chocolate, and play those videos back to unwind or to cheer me up when life got me down. It's safe to say I love what I do!

The florist's shop was in a beautiful old building, a rambling, grey-stone shop in the middle of a terraced row in the high street. It had a daffodil-yellow sign above the window that brightened you up inside, and the shop window was big and filled with a riot of colour. Amanda loved trinkets and wind-chimes, so these filled the window too, and our customers loved the little extra gifts they could find in our treasure trove of a shop. The loveliness of the shop front was nothing on the smell that assaulted you when you stepped through the door to the tinkling of the bell. It was a smell to rival home-baked cookies in the oven, or cinnamon-topped coffee, or the fancy bath bomb I loved to find in the bottom of my stocking on Christmas morning. It was a heavenly smell, and I always took the longest, deepest breath when I stepped into work in the morning.

'Sunshine and Roses' was in the old market town where Alex and I lived. The town had a higgledy-piggledy high street comprised of traditional buildings with architecture from across the ages set either side of a wonderful town square which hosted a market every Wednesday where local vendors, from cheese makers to egg farmers, brought their wares to sell. It was a town with a lot of character and a great sense of community. It was perfectly positioned for Alex too, being only an hour's train journey from London, meaning we got the best of both worlds – Alex got to have his dream job in the big city while we enjoyed a quieter pace of life together on his off time.

I'd been working for Amanda since I got my floristry qualification. It was my dream, and my goal, to open my own florist's shop when I was thirty, specialising in my flower language bouquets. There's a whole language of flowers, each flower has an individual meaning, and that was my favourite part of the job – floral matchmaking. Call me crazy if you must but it really works! I felt so sad to have to leave some stories I'd become an extra in, mid-telling – I'd become so involved with some of my customers' romances I felt excited to see how they ended. I suppose I'll have to let my imagination run wild with them now.

I might have fallen in love with floristry, but I was mature enough to realise college was only the first stepping stone and I needed to learn the realities of the job, gain skills beyond the theory, and become familiar with the business practicalities. So, Amanda had taken me under her wing and trained me up in the first step towards achieving my dream.

It was a sad thought to me that I'd never get to whip the cover off my own shop sign, that my dream would go unrealised. I'd imagined every last detail of my shop – the old-fashioned brass bell hanging over the door that rang out as people entered and left, the Aladdin's cave feeling of higgledy-piggledy shelves and bookcases crammed full of treasures and gifts in every free nook and cranny, fairy lights sparkling down on all the flowers. If I could find the right building I wanted to create a maze, an experience all of its own, with little rooms branching off, creating themed sections of the shop to allow customers to get to know the different types of flowers and how they could make them feel – from formal arrangements that shouted of success, to lively and vibrant overflowing arrangements that lifted spirits. There would be comfy armchairs, and a machine to make the frothiest cappuccinos, so that customers could settle into the soft seats with me, cupping delicious, rich coffees, while they told me their stories and learned about the flowers, so I had all the information to make their bouquet just right, every single time, for them.

Even though I would never get to see my ideas come to fruition it was of great consolation that I'd had the opportunity to follow my path this far and had been able to find work I was so passionate about and that made me so happy. There are different types of luck, and I know some people live to be eighty and never spend a happy day at work in their lives, so rest assured, this blessing has been counted.

I'd just finished a normal Tuesday at 'Sunshine and Roses'. The days were much the same there, happily flowing by to the same beat, and today had been no exception. We'd earned a few smiles for our bouquets, brought a little extra happiness into some peoples' lives, so it had been a good day. It was five-thirty in the afternoon, and I'd just stepped through the rustic oak door of the cottage and shrugged out of my coat when my phone rang. I couldn't help smiling to myself. Even after all this time, my phone rang at exactly five-thirty every single work day, and my heart still fluttered.

Alex may have had a work-mode to rival Mo Farah, but he never let it take priority over our special rituals. We usually finished work at similar times, unless Alex had a huge story or big deadline, but my journey home took five minutes as opposed to his commute. He used his journey time to work, but he always set the alarm on his phone for five-thirty (the time I arrived home) and called me as he was walking from his office to the train station.

'Hi, Allie,' Alex would say. 'You made it home okay?'

'Yes, thanks, I've just walked through the door.' At this point I always wondered what Alex imagined could have happened to me in the five-minute journey home, but I so loved that he cared enough to ask.

'How was your day? Scale of one to ten.' He would ask. I'd give him my answer, and if it was below a five he'd talk to me about it all the way home until he could scoop me up into a big hug as he walked through the door. Sub-fives were very rare at the florist's, though – it's a job of joy. So, usually I'd be giving him an over-five after which I would return the question.

'How was your day?' To which Alex would reply with his figure. Alex's number was far more volatile – he had some co-workers who sometimes made life difficult and, as his entire day was writing about the things that go wrong in the world, he took some of these happenings to heart. I'd do my best to chat his day through with him or tell him some of the tales from our customers – he loved to hear about happiness. We were at opposite ends of the spectrum in that way – he spent his days dealing with sadness, me with hope. Perhaps we balanced each other out – he kept my feet on the ground rather than swinging from chandeliers, and I brought some sunshine to the grey skies of his work world.

If Alex had a plus-five day, though, he'd simply say, 'I can't wait to see you, Allie.'

'You too, I love you.'

'I love you too, so much.'

It could've been scripted, such was its constancy. Alex had never missed a single call. It's the little things that really matter, because they're not so little after all.

Although Alex had a natural affinity for people who were struggling, he sought to distance himself from personal involvements. Therefore, I'd often wondered where Alex got his thoughtfulness and romanticism from, since he had this remarkable gift for those things when it came to me. Lately, I seemed to have developed the habit of asking the questions that popped into my mind, so once we'd got through the details on that day's call I asked him, 'Why are you so amazing when it comes to me, Alex? Where has it come from?'

'What do you mean, sorry?'

‘Well, you’re so thoughtful and caring sometimes I have to pinch myself that you’re real and you’re mine.’

‘Do you think so?’

‘I know so.’

‘Well, I expect it came from my dad. When I was, I don’t know, thirteen maybe, and just starting to think about relationships, I asked him – how do you get someone to love you for the rest of your life? It seemed like an impossible notion to me at the time. And Dad told me, “Son, you have to fall in love again every single day. The person you love has to be your number one priority, no matter what. Even the brightest sparks fizzle out if they run out of oxygen – it’s your job to be the oxygen.”’ Alex paused.

‘He was a bit of a guru, your dad. I wish I’d been able to know him.’

‘I wish you’d known him too,’ Alex replied, subdued. ‘I love you so much, Alice.’

‘I love you too, Alex, you are truly the best. Thanks for always being my hero.’

I was coping brilliantly with my diagnosis by throwing myself into work and driving forward with writing the manual. Ryan kept me laughing, and Alex kept me nurtured and whole. However, as I think was inevitable, anger, resentment, and frustrations started pushing their heads over the parapet every so often. Therefore, it was lucky I had a top-notch gym buddy. Her name is Serena, and she is bubbly, cheerful, and motivating. She is such a good gym buddy. She could be the poster-woman for the power of spinning classes – she looks like a Kate Moss and Venus Williams hybrid, while I look as svelte as one of the lemon and poppy seed muffins I'm so fond of. Serena drags me along to the gym one night a week – to a spinning class – and I whack my behind into the air and peddle as fast as my little legs will carry me. It works great because Alex works late on a Friday and, while I would love to add in a second film night with Ryan or a much longer read of my current novel while fending my way out of a cloud of bubbles in the bath, I've always liked to keep active and know that I'm helping my body to help me.

I'm grateful to Serena because when I first peered through the door at the gym it looked so intimidating. The music was blasting, brows were sweating, and I'd never been faced with a row of such peachy and toned behinds. I didn't know Serena, but she spotted me as she was walking into the main gym.

'Have you tried it?' She approached me with a big smile, and a nod to the door.

'Oh, gosh, no,' I said, shaking my head, furiously.

'Not your thing?' Serena asked, tilting her head to one side.

'I'd thought it might be, but looking in there, I don't think I would fare well. I mean, look at me,' I said, gesturing down at my, ahem, curves.

'Oh, stop right now. You're gorgeous,' Serena said, flapping her hand to dismiss my self-deprecation. 'I promise you – almost every single one of those ladies and men started off in exactly the same place you are now. It's so much fun, and we're a friendly bunch, well most of us.' Serena raised her eyebrows and grimaced, before smiling once more. 'I'm telling you, absolute truth, I was laid over the handlebars, wheezing like a steam train on my first session.'

I smiled warmly.

'Well, you've convinced me – maybe one day I'll brave it,' I said.

'What are you doing next Friday night?' Serena asked.

'Not much, why?' I asked, slow to connect the dots. Serena's face broke out into a huge grin.

'Perfect!' she exclaimed. 'Now you are. Now you're spinning with me on Friday evenings. I'm Serena, by the way.' She held out her hand to shake.

'I'm Alice, thank you, that would be great – I think!' I said, chuckling. 'But you'll have to be my A&E buddy too if I expire in there.'

'It's a deal, you're on!' Serena replied, laughing.

We've forged ahead together every week since, spinning until our buttocks are tender and our thighs are screaming. We often get a cup of coffee and have a chat beforehand. She's tried to convince me to attempt a Zumba class, but I peeked into one session and decided my presence would make it more dangerous than a lot of war zones.

I love those spin classes now. It turns out that those super-toned, lycra clad, peddling babes are a tribe, and they are now my tribe – my gang of sisters (and occasionally brothers). I've grown surprisingly comfortable with being face-to-cheek with a host of firm, pert behinds; and I rally along to the echoes of, 'Come on girls, you can do it!' Amid a sea of sports bras.

My spin class was a welcome release that Friday night. Serena's bright smile warmed me up better than one of Alex's hot chocolates would have, and the physical workout did exactly what it promised – it worked out a lot of my frustrations with my situation. For those forty-five minutes, I lost myself in the music, pumping my legs hard to 'I've Got the Magic in Me'. I might still have turned the same shade of red as the Coca Cola branding and sweated enough to fill a paddling pool every time but I held my own now. While my behind may not be peachy it's at least somewhat sculpted and no longer wobbling like a jelly with every peddle. The tension left me with every jump, and I forced my anger out with every climb. As the wheels span, and the funky beats boomed, I was cleansed. I felt like me again. Toned, honed, and ready for anything.

Chapter Ten

I feel like now is a good time to tell you, and I think you should know, it wasn't always this way for me. It sounds like it's all sunshine and roses with Alex, and as nauseating as it sounds, it really, truly was. But before Alex there was a lot of mess. And I mean a lot. There was a whole lot of mess to go alongside the happy childhood, doting parents, love of a lifetime. After all, everyone has a story they don't want to tell. And I have many. That new heart of yours, it has some scars. But, that's what helps to make a life, at least that's how it seems now I'm at the end of mine – the messes. The good times are amazing, but it's the messes that give you substance, and experience, and grit. And everybody needs those to get through this life. After all, as Atticus said, "I've never met a strong person with an easy past." Trust me, lovely, that heart of yours should be pretty strong with the past it's had. Although I hope you never need its strength, I'm glad you've got it.

Chapter Eleven

Ever since that initial time I spent at the hospital, during which I was known, and judged solely, by my diagnosis, I've been averse to telling people all the details of my tumour. It becomes all they see. Part of me thinks their eyes linger on the base of my head a little longer, as if somehow, they will actually see the mass, but I know that could be paranoia on my part. Perhaps it's because it's disconcerting for people and so they want some kind of visible evidence – that way they would see it if it was happening to them. Or, perhaps it's that they can't think of me as a human, as a soul, anymore, because it's too frightening that an invisible monster can ruin so many lives in one go, and nobody even knows it's there - terrifying. So, I tend to be casual about it. If they ask, I'll tell people I'm dying. Then, if they press, I'll tell them it's a brain tumour. I dodge any more questions. After all, that's all people need to know, I think. The rest is between me and my monster.

There are, of course, some exceptions to that rule, and those are my nearest and dearest. They know it all. Every gory detail. There was one person I classed as near and dear who I'd yet to tell. That person was Alex's mum.

Alex's mum is an interesting individual. She is paradoxically both an inspiration to me and at the same time an embodiment of what I've always wanted to avoid becoming. She is fierce, and feisty, and I love that about her, but that comes with a domineering and, at times slightly rude, edge that's unbecoming. She does whatever she wants, whenever she wants, which is how she came to be on a cruise of the Arctic while all of this has been happening. Alex and I see her about twice a year. She comes to stay and fills the house with the smells of her classic old perfume, fills our heads with her imparted wisdom, and fills our garden with delightful new plants. She comes in a whirlwind and leaves a big empty space when she leaves. She clearly loves Alex dearly but there is a huge amount of history between them I don't understand. I know Alex's dad died when he was fourteen and it changed them both deeply. Before his dad died his mum was a housewife. She was poster-perfect – cooked delicious meals; had homemade cakes and cookies waiting on the table next to a tall glass of cold milk for Alex when he got home from school; was on the board of governors at his school; ironed his dad's work shirts with crisp creases in all the right places – she was a domestic goddess. When Alex's dad died, she stopped all that the next day. Alex's grandparents moved in and took care of him for a while. His mum struggled, lost entirely in her grief. She came back to her life and Alex, but she was never the same again.

Although Alex doesn't talk much about his mum, I believe their relationship has been tumultuous ever since. When Stella visits, they appear to get along well, have fun together, and nobody could doubt they share a wealth of love. However, knowing Alex as well as I do, I'd say he keeps her at arm's length. He knows all too well how the blade of her abandonment feels so he won't let Stella close enough to stab him with it again.

I met Stella at my favourite local café. It had been the home of so many conversations in my adult life. Beneath the bunting and quote plaques I'd gossiped with Ryan, romanced Alex, and shared my day-to-day stories with Mum. It was the kind of café that imbued positivity. With a high ceiling and full height windows across the entire front, lined with white-painted lead latticing, the café was flooded with light, but retained its traditional character. It felt soft with its pastel coloured walls, furnishings, and crockery, but the shades were bright which gave warmth – sky-blues, chick-yellows, and candy-floss pinks. The plates and mugs were mismatched and patterned, the wooden topped tables with cream painted legs, and the walls were strewn with a hotchpotch of little mirrors, quote plaques, bunting, and paintings which came together as the perfect eclectic mix. There were tables and chairs mixed through with comfy sofas and armchairs, and there were a couple of little nooks that allowed privacy and quiet. A bookshelf was filled with paperback novels, magazines, and newspapers to help yourself to. The effect was a relaxed, cheerful meeting place with the best quality food and drinks. The coffees were sublime, and I never tasted a better millionaire's shortbread than the ones baked by May, the owner. It had a delightfully homely feel to it, with personal touches galore.

Stella arrived with every bit as much impact as she did everywhere she went. Dressed in an angry red shirt and a long black skirt; and holding her chin just a fraction higher than anyone else did, she made everyone around her feel as though the headmistress had just walked into their classroom. Eyes suddenly found the cups, or the tablecloth, or the quotes on the wall ever so interesting as they scrambled away from her gaze. The 'Stella effect' never wore off on me completely but I learnt to push it down to get the best from my relationship with her.

I stood up and greeted her with a warm hug and a big smile. Stella didn't smile often, but when she did she was so beautiful. She smiled back at me. I asked her the polite questions we all exchange while she settled in and we placed our order – a hot chocolate for me and a cappuccino for Stella. Once the drinks arrived Stella took charge of the conversation as she always did, and so it began.

'So, Alice, what news have you got for me today? I picked up a voicemail from Alex as soon as I stepped off the cruise – no signal out there you see – but I couldn't make head nor tail of it, what with all the crying. I phoned him straight away and he said that something terrible had happened, then all I got was a lot of sobbing. He couldn't bring himself to say it. So, I thought I'd come straight here and get it out of you.'

'Well, I'm afraid it's nothing good, Stella.'

'Go on then, tell me everything,' she said kindly.

'I have a tumour, Stella, on my brain stem. I'm on my way out. Quickly. I have about two months left now, the doctors think.' I let a pause hang in the air while Stella processed the information.

'There's nothing they can do? Surely there must be, in this day and age?'

'Sadly not. I have what's called a grade four brain stem glioma. Because it's on my brain stem they can't operate to remove it. Being grade four it's already very large, very advanced, and fast growing. I was offered radiotherapy but was advised that would only slow the growth and control symptoms and with my specific tumour it was unlikely to even do that. So, I decided the benefits, being so tiny, weren't worth the costs.'

'Alice, I'm so sorry.'

I nodded, tears in my eyes, and let silence sit between us for a few minutes. Stella looked stricken. She was wringing her hands and had gone very pale. I pushed the pause to one side and pressed on with what I had to ask her.

'It's obviously going to be very hard on Alex. My parents, and my best friend, Ryan, will support him in any and every way they can. He's their family too now. But there is no one like one's own mum. I know things aren't perfect between you two, but I would rest a lot easier knowing you'll be able to help him. Do you think you might be able to stay around here for a little while after I'm gone?'

Stella stared at me with wide eyes for a few moments too many. Then she jolted slightly, and she got up in a real hurry, her chair scraping loudly against the floor as she pushed it back.

'I'm sorry, please forgive me, but I just can't. I have to go. Goodbye, Alice.'

I was dumbstruck. I just sat stock still as I watched her flee the café, the tinkling of the bell signalling the end of her visit. It was all over before it sunk in. Then, I felt as though the floor had given way beneath me. I sat there for a while; and a few hot chocolates, a lot of anger, and plenty of thinking later, I got up and left with the lingering thought plaguing me that I couldn't work out whether the saddest part was that she could so badly let down the people who needed her, or that life had been so tough to her she could only survive it alone?

I was reeling for a while after seeing Stella. I welcomed my time working the next day – the flowers both lifted and soothed me. That was why I wanted to stay working for as long as possible – I loved what I did, and I saw no sense in empty days. However, I knew it was time to talk to Amanda about the situation and make plans for going forwards; and having had one such difficult conversation with Stella the day before, I wasn't relishing the heaviness of the impending one.

I approached Amanda about it during the quiet, late morning period between customers.

'Amanda, I have some news. I'm afraid I'm going to have to hand in my notice – I'm not well. I would like to keep working as long as I physically can, but I wanted you to know so that you had plenty of time to find someone else.'

Amanda seemed surprised and took a few moments to absorb my words before replying, 'Oh dear, Alice, I'm so sorry to hear that. There won't be anyone else like you. I'm happy to hold your position while you recover and hire someone temporarily to cover you while you're out. Unless you want to move on, anyway?'

'That's so kind, Amanda, and trust me when I say there's nothing I would love more, but I won't be recovering – it's a terminal brain tumour. I'll be moving on – I just don't know whether it's up or down I'm going.' I gave a little chuckle and a sad smile. These conversations were so heavy.

'Well, I promise you one thing, Alice, it's up you're going – there couldn't be someone more deserving of a spot up there than you.' Amanda had tears in her eyes that were threatening to spill onto her silk blouse. 'How long do you think it'll be?'

'A couple of months. I'd hope to be able to keep coming here for most of that time, even if I have to cut back to afternoons perhaps? I understand if it's better for you to get someone else in full-time sooner than that, but if you can bear me hanging around, I'd love to be able to pop in even just to lend a hand voluntarily?'

'Alice, you listen to me, you're the heart of this place and you will be welcome here forever. Besides, you can't let the customers down – they'll want their magic bouquets for as long as they can possibly get their hands on them! Those bouquets have changed this place, they've shown me a whole new depth to what we do, and you've touched so many lives with them. I don't know what I'll do without you. And the course of true love round here will run a lot less smoothly without your touch, I can tell you.'

'I don't know about that, Amanda, but thank you, it means a lot.' A blush was creeping onto my cheeks.

'Well I absolutely do! If you wouldn't mind, maybe you could teach me a little of what you do so I can carry on the magic in some small way. Ooh, maybe we could find an apprentice too, to undergo 'Alice Masterclasses' – it could be fun?'

'That sounds great, I'd love to do that.' It would be nice to know my work could live on and spending that extra time with Amanda sounded like a lovely way to spend some of my time at work.

'Just keep talking to me, do as much or as little as you can manage. I'm here for you in any and every way you need me, please know that.'

'Thanks, I've had the time of my life here, and I'm so grateful for that.'

She reached for me then and pulled me into a warm and tight hug. It lasted for a few minutes, and there were tearstains on her shirt when she pulled back.

It had undoubtedly been a tough day having that conversation with Amanda. On such days, when my troubles felt a bit heavy for my shoulders, there was one place I could go where I knew I would receive, if not a magic solution, at least someone to share the load and offer some comfort – Mum and Dad's house. Alex was my hero, but even that hero had a day job, as did Ryan, so I often spent my me-time hours while I waited for Alex's return in this way. Dad's shoulders are pretty broad, and very strong.

Mum has always dedicated herself to caring for Dad and me. She worked so hard to make sure everything was just right for us – one such example was the meals she prepared. She cooked us delicious dishes, but they were always eighty per cent vegetable, which, let's be honest, gets old. As a child, I'd been known to complain about the vegetable ratio, to which Mum would reply, 'It's my job to look after the both of you, and I want you around for a very long time. Vegetables is how I'll get my very long time.' A processed food item never entered our fridge, so while other children at school were eating cheese strings I looked on with envy while chewing on my extra mature Cathedral City.

Of course, she's always made exceptions to the healthy rules for herself if a decadent afternoon tea takes her fancy. As such, Dad cultivated a guilty pleasure that he brought me in on when I was a child – the golden arches. I loved going to work with Dad in the school holidays – Dad was a train driver. There was nothing like the rumble of the trains, winding through the countryside at high speeds. When I was a teenager he'd sneak me in with him, in the days when this was still possible, and it would feel like Dad and me against the world. I would eat a light breakfast – maybe a piece of fruit – and we'd cheerfully wave goodbye to Mum before he'd speed us into the McDonald's car park near the train station. Dad would be gleeful, and he'd say, 'Have anything you want, love.'

I would never hesitate.

'Double sausage and egg McMuffin meal please, with a hot chocolate.' I would order. Dad would smile a wide smile at me before ordering himself.

'Same for me please, but with a tea instead, if you'd be so kind.' He'd carefully count out the coins and I would proudly take our tray over to a booth by the window. We'd pick those stonking double sausage and egg McMuffins up with both hands and devour them eagerly, relishing every bite of deliciousness. We would chatter away between huge mouthfuls, and as Dad was not much of a chatterbox this was particularly special. His eyes would be lit up, and he'd tell me about the journey ahead of us that day, the number of carriages, all the details. McDonald's gave me my dad, entirely unrestricted.

We always had a ritual finish.

'There's nothing like it, hey, love?' Dad would ask, contentedly, subtly rubbing his belly.

'Nothing like it, Dad.' I would reply with a smile, rubbing my belly too, far less subtly, in the way that offspring do, mirroring the parent they adore.

Once exams started and revision meant school holidays were never my own, I stopped going to work with Dad on the trains, but we never stopped our sneaky trips to McDonald's, and Dad's love for it never waned. Neither did mine. It became his go-to move if I was down since our trips there never failed to cheer me up. Now he was retired, I would help him in the garden, and he'd save any acquisitions for the days I was there, so he could wander into the kitchen and proclaim, 'We can't get started without a bag of compost, love, why don't we head out now and beat the lunchtime rush.'

'Sounds like a plan, Dad.' I'd reply, and if Mum wasn't looking, Dad would give a cheeky little grin and wink at me. That wink was the code, the signal: the golden arches beckon.

We'd head off, and the whole cycle would repeat, exactly the same, except rather than chatting about train carriages and destinations it would be runner beans and tomatoes. I didn't mind at all, I still got my glorious Dad. We would always head to the garden centre too, without fail – he never went home without the item we'd come out for. There was a shed at the bottom of the garden full of these things, many of them we didn't need at all, he could start his own Garden World outlet if the fancy ever struck him.

'Can't have too much compost, love,' he'd say as he heaved the bag into the shed. I'd shake my head ruefully at him. I initially thought it was to maintain our cover, but that's not Dad at all. I asked him one day, why he always buys these things he doesn't need.

'Your mother might not know quite how we spend our time out, love, but she trusts that if I say I'm going out for a bag of compost then that's where I'm headed. Sneaking a sausage and egg McMuffin in on the way does no harm, but I'd be breaking her trust if I didn't keep my word and come back with that compost. I could never let her down like that.'

When I arrived at Mum and Dad's front door that day, I must have looked as forlorn as I felt because Dad immediately hollered, 'Alice is here, Anne, but I desperately need that thing for the garden, so I'll pop out now and get it, I'm dragging her along with me.'

'Okay, dear,' Mum called back. 'But, wait, not before I have a cuddle with my girl!' She finished as she appeared through the kitchen door. She bundled me up against her chest and held on tight, just the way I liked it. 'How are you doing?' she asked me.

'Tough day, Mum,' I said with a grimace.

'Make sure your dad takes care of you then.'

'He always does.'

'Usual time tomorrow?' Mum asked, even though we haven't changed the Friday night fish and chips time from 7.30 p.m. since the tradition started.

'Absolutely, Mum, thanks.'

'Well, enjoy yourself getting … what was it again?'

It turns out Dad's tomatoes simply wouldn't last another night without tomato food.

Chapter Twelve

Ah, here we arrive at the good old fourteenth of February. The marmite of all holidays. Those people who fill the checkouts with dozens of red roses, boxes of garish chocolates, and bright red cards are now your people. I kind of think it's ***our*** *day too, in a way. It's a day that celebrates hearts. And boy do we know about hearts and all they can do. So, even if you just can't bring yourself to pitch a tent in the campsite of romance, maybe you can catch a train to the station of celebrating hearts. Or, if you love the cheesy romance, of course that's great too!*

For the big celebrations of our epic love, Alex and I were always anniversary people but we always did a little something for St Valentine too. The first Valentine's Day, you have to remember, we were fresh from a dancing in the rain total soaking in the zoo. So, I came up with the genius idea of a themed umbrella – with bats flying about on the underside. I wanted Alex to have a reminder of that day, something that meant he could bring it back and relive the feeling time and again. It took some finding, I can tell you – an umbrella with flying bats on it isn't as popular as you might think. Where would we be without Chinese imports on eBay?

Alex had gone away for work on the day itself, chasing one of his hot stories, but he made sure we had a video call to open our presents together. As that bubbling Skype ringtone gave way to his smiling face my heart went wild.

We settled into the call, both a little shy, it being our first present exchange and celebration together. I 'gave' my present to Alex first, along with a soppy card, which I'll spare you the details of since I'm guessing you won't want to see your partially digested lunch again!

When he first opened the umbrella, I could see the confusion rise – top marks for Valentine's originality, bottom marks for romance it seemed. The moment it dawned on him why I'd given him an umbrella was the sweetest sight. A slight blush rose into his cheeks and he gave the loveliest little smile of delight. I'd been so nervous about it but when I realised how genuinely appreciative he was the excitement sort of bubbled over in me. I shocked Alex, I think, when I exclaimed, very suddenly and very loudly, 'You have to open it – go outside and open it!' Alex was clearly bemused, but he did as I asked.

He said, 'Fine, but you're coming too.' He whisked up his iPad and carried it, and the umbrella of course, out onto his balcony. The view was spectacular. Lights were dotted everywhere, the city spread out below him. It was a backdrop to rival any romantic film set. He set the iPad down on a table and opened the umbrella. When he first looked up at it he literally jumped back a few feet, shrieked in fear, and let the umbrella clatter to the ground. I was doubled over in laughter from my bed hundreds of miles away. Alex floundered around and then he staggered about on that balcony clutching his chest claiming I was early on in our relationship with my first attempted murder. Then he stared straight into the camera and whispered, 'It's absolutely perfect, Alice.' My heart melted a little. Alex quickly recovered, and it was the source of endless banter and laughs for the rest of time. Alex loved that umbrella. He never left home without it. He always did a little jig if it started raining and he always said with glee, 'The bats are coming out to play.'

Once we'd both recovered from the umbrella hilarity Alex went back inside and I opened my present. Alex had gone for very simple, but incredibly romantic. I peeled off the red tissue paper covered in hearts, glitter drifting from the paper onto my duvet, and there sat a very simple CD case. There was a homemade slip of paper in the cover, decorated with a photo of the two of us I didn't even know Alex had taken, and three little drawings along the top edge. One was a cup of coffee. The next one was a slice of pizza. The final one was a bat. Underneath the photo was the title 'The Story of Us'. I need to explain that Alex was no Picasso. This was actually a fairly ugly CD cover, but never has ugly been so beautiful. We had swapped roles completely. I was now grinning delightedly with a little blush gracing my cheeks. Alex was the excited face on the screen exclaiming that I should turn it over, turn it over! On the back was another homemade insert, this time completely plain. It had one line on it:

Kodaline, 'The One'

I welled up. Alex got a little flustered. I think maybe he thought I was disappointed he hadn't filled it with songs. He tried to explain, and for a man who spends all day in the company of words, he got awfully tangled up. I managed to pick out that he'd add every song that meant something to us to it along our journey together. I'd realised that, but it was wonderful to hear it from him, with all his stutters, and pauses, and, well, love. It was the most magical gift he could possibly have given me. That CD ended up being the soundtrack to years of blissful happiness. The soundtrack to the greatest love story ever lived.

Your role on this marmite of holidays is to start from the beginning. Go onto eBay, find yourself the wackiest novelty umbrella that you can, wrap it up in cheesy paper covered in glitter, and give it to Alex. Also, please find a tiny cuddly toy bat, and give him that, from me. Then between us, we've got the memory bases covered.

Chapter Thirteen

When it began, my idea, that day in the doctors' office, it was a noble theory, but that was all. The grisly reality was a little different. When I was younger, I was a cut and dried, black and white kind of person. Right was right, wrong was wrong, and there was no middle ground. I was, without doubt, too judgemental back then.

Some people labelled what I was doing as sinful – trying to play God. Yet, what I was doing had been labelled as heroic by other people. The philosopher in me finds it hard to fathom how both of those realities can exist within the same reality. That wise philosopher, all this life on from that young, judgemental girl, feels that there has to be hundreds of shades of grey to cover the space between the black and the white.

I spent a lot of time considering the options and making plans with Ryan. He sashayed into the cottage one evening, kissed me smack on the lips, and settled into the sofa, fluffy pink pen poised and ready.

‘Houston, we have a problem,’ he began. ‘This America idea, there are a lot of hiccups … I’m not sure we’re going to be able to do it.’

‘We have to do it – there’s no other way. My heart must go to the right person. If we do it here my heart will go to just anyone. The other twenty-one, they’ll be the people in the greatest need, whoever they might be; but can’t you see, Ryan, my heart, it has to be my choice.’ I slumped against the arm of the sofa.

‘Don’t even get me started, Als, I’ll fight to the death for your right to do this, really I will, but these are big issues. I might be good, but I’m not sure I’m that good.’

‘You are that good!’ I protested. ‘But, what kind of issues?

‘For starters, there’s the medical bills – for you, and for her. How can we ever afford them? Then there’s convincing her to travel to America for something that can be done here – why would she agree to that?’

My face must have crumpled, for Ryan glanced at me, and then his beautiful face set with his trademark determination.

‘You know what, Al, we can do this,’ he said, nodding vigorously. He pinched the bridge of his nose, brow crinkled, thinking away. ‘Brainstorm, brainstorm!’ Then he clicked his fingers, a lot of times, and exclaimed. ‘Pro bono! I’ll just have to take on my biggest charm challenge to date. I’ve got savings, no fabulous fella to spend them on, and I’d already worked out that I could cover everyone’s flights and hopefully your medical bills. I’ll just have to explain to the hospital. I'll have to work my magnificent magic – find a hospital that will cover her costs; do it for free. If I spin it well enough how could they not, right? This is a sensational story – a PR coup for them. Imagine the following they could get from this. Not only will the hospital be keeping love alive, they'll be saving, or improving twenty-one American lives. I really think it will work, Als! I'll make it work.'

Ryan's eyes were dancing with excitement. It was infectious.

'Well, we both know if anyone can pull it off it's you, spectacular superhero.' I paused. 'I hadn't thought about that though. That if you can do it, the other twenty-one will be American.' I considered this for a moment. 'One life is one life. Twenty-one lives are twenty-one lives.'

I thought about Ryan's other points before continuing. 'I think she'll go, why wouldn't she in reality – if all her costs are paid, she's well enough to travel, and she knows it could save her life. The hospital could tell her it was a directed donation, but not give any details, you can do your bit after. She'll do it, another chance at life, wouldn't anyone?'

'Okay, I'll get to work, gorgeous girl. Now where's the chocolate? Tell me you got my favourite white truffles for tonight, not that cheap and nasty stuff like last time?'

I brandished the gold box with a flourish. Though only Ryan could class a bag of luxury milk chocolate buttons as cheap and nasty. It was especially frustrating, but typical, given he polished off five-sixths of it.

'Phew, Als!' Ryan swept his hand across his flawless brow theatrically. 'Please God, let it be *My Best Friend's Wedding* tonight.'

I pointed to the DVD box sitting on the coffee table. Ryan leapt up and put it in before settling down underneath the blanket and putting his arm around me. I snuggled into his side and as the terribly annoying opening song came on I whispered to him, 'I love you, Ry.'

I didn't think it was loud enough for him to hear but he whispered back, 'I love you too, Als, more than you could ever know.'

A tear slid town his cheek.

I knew we had to make the journey to America. I had to get my heart to the right person. For Alex. The government here wouldn't let me do that, but the good old US of A would make the allowances – I'd done my research. They would let me direct my donation. I wanted to fly at the last possible moment though, so I could spend all my remaining life at home. I thought it was in the best possible hands with Ryan, so I let it be put aside in favour of the things that would take a lot of my time – the manual, the organising, the precious family moments. It turned out that was a good decision, because it soon became apparent that the three months of me was more like six weeks.

I felt the monster for the first time six weeks after the doctor's appointment. I awoke with a burning need to vomit, which I promptly did all over the rug beside my bed. It was one of the first things Alex and I had bought together for the house – 'his' and 'hers' bedside rugs. It was such a happy, hopeful, couple-y day. When we got home we laid those rugs down beside the bed with goofy grins all over our faces. Then we scrambled into the bed beside each other and cuddled all night long.

Now, that 'hers' rug was covered in a pool of disgusting sick. It stank, like all sick does, and it looked vile. I'd crumpled to my knees with the wave of nausea that accompanied the vomiting and usually slow-to-wake Alex was up in a flash. He took one look over at what had happened and flew round to my side. He knelt slightly behind me and grasped my arms underneath the elbows. His touch felt like home. He tried to ease me up. I resisted.

'Alex, please, just go, I'll sort this out.'

'Of course that's not happening, Alice. You rest in the lounge and leave all this to me.'

I tried to bat him away; he stayed strong.

'Please, I don't want you to see me like this, or to have to deal with this stuff.'

'I signed up for this stuff too. I think I can handle a little sick. It's a tiny price to pay for these years with you. Let me get you settled and then I'll come back.'

I reluctantly let Alex help me up, and he guided me down the stairs of our cottage to the lounge, where he wrapped me up in the purple woolly blanket. I hated that Alex had to do this, and if I had any choice at all I would never have let him, but to tell you the complete truth, I could hardly stand, let alone sort out the mess.

'Shout if you need anything, Allie, promise me?'

I held my pinky finger out to Alex, which had always been a thing of ours, and he smiled his gorgeous smile at me as he looped his pinky through mine. The promise had been sealed.

I heard him rattling around in the kitchen, assembling the things he'd need. This wasn't his usual territory, domestics, so he popped his head around the lounge door a few times to ask questions about what to use. Every question stripped a small piece of my dignity away. He came back down a few minutes later carrying the rug. The stench of vomit came down the stairs accompanying the rug and filled the air around it.

'I'll put it outside for an airing, okay?' Alex called out as he took it through the back door onto the patio. I didn't reply.

He came back into the lounge and sat beside me a few minutes later.

'Phew, all cleaned up and sorted. I'll try to pick up a carpet cleaner later to get the job finished top-notch. How are you? You still look peaky. What can I get you, some toast, some water? What do you fancy?'

'I'll finish the rug, Alex, thank you, you've done more than enough. And I'll get some toast later, that does sound nice.' I spoke kindly, to please him. 'But don't worry about me at all, you need to hurry to make it to work on time.'

'Don't be silly, I'm taking today off. We'll cuddle up with some films, some hot chocolate if you feel better later, I'll even throw in a full day with your purple woolly best friend and bench the wonderful fleecy blanket. It'll be great fun.'

'Alex, you can't. I'm so grateful, but we should save the paper's kindness for more important days. Who knows how many of these we have yet to come. I feel better already. I'll take it easy, I promise.' His eyebrows unknotted a fraction from their deep frown, and the corners of his mouth turned up in the hint of a smile, as he gave my hand a squeeze. 'Besides, I'll call Mum and get her to come around and spend some time with me – we both know how much she's been nagging me for a girls' day. Okay?'

'Well, it's not what I want, but if it's what you want then I'll do it, you know that. You're sure it's what you want?'

I nodded.

'It's the right thing. I'm so sorry, about all this,' I said, my voice breaking a bit. He scooped me up into a gentle hug.

'Don't ever say that, Allie, ever. Being your husband is the greatest honour on this planet, even if it comes with a little puke.'

I smiled weakly, before replying, 'Now, shower off the sick smell, and get yourself out the door. Tell the world a great story today. And tell it in the sky-blue shirt with the navy tie.'

Alex laughed.

'Okay, boss, will do. With the dove grey suit, I'm presuming?'

'Of course, could there be any other? When I'm gone, I do worry that you'll turn up one day in a hot pink shirt with a purple suit, you know.' The playful smile dropped off Alex's face like a stone released off the roof of a skyscraper.

'Too soon, Allie, and it'll always be too soon.' A pause hung between us.

'Okay, sorry, I love you so much, have an amazing day.'

I didn't call my mum for a girls' day. I sat in silence on that sofa for hours thinking about the unmitigated disaster it would be if this was the start of me becoming symptomatic.

When I felt strong enough I scrubbed that bedside rug for the whole afternoon, until my hands were red raw and chapped. I could never get the smell out fully, so it became the first symbol of what was to come – there was only a 'his' bedside rug going forwards, no 'hers', and that empty space beside my bed goaded me every day.

Chapter Fourteen

If you think I've embarrassed you before with what I've asked you do, lovely, then you need to buckle up for a serious shock for this one. If it helps at all, then I advise you to include Ryan in this adventure, in fact you may not be able to keep him away even if you wanted to once he knows it's in the works. He is the man to organise this with you anyway – he knows exactly who to contact and he's like a puppetmaster with the strings he can pull for this task.

This re-creation is the day I introduced Alex to Ryan. Alex and I had been together for about three months, we knew it was serious, and Ryan was desperate to meet Alex. I was petrified – Alex and Ryan were very different beasts, yet them getting along was absolutely vital to my future happiness. So, this one was important. I'd told Alex we needed to come up with an adventure to include Ryan in and Alex surprised us both with this epic night.

I have to confess it could have gone terribly wrong – I feel like Alex completely stereotyped Ryan, and Ryan could have reacted very badly to that. The saving grace was that Alex had clearly tattooed on his forehead the expression 'go big or go home' and had gone full steam ahead with maximum effort. He got it so right that Ryan didn't just throw himself into it, he chop dropped himself into it like Dwayne Johnson in his WWE days (ooh, just think how much Ryan would love to hear that comparison!).

The day started with just Alex and I, the planned adventure with Ryan due to commence in the evening. Alex pulled up to my parents' house in his beaten up classic Mini and scooted us off to Oxford for the afternoon. I was expecting a romantic picnic in the park like we had done before, so I was shocked when we pulled to a stop outside a fancy dress shop front as Alex gestured to the door.

'What are we doing here?' I spluttered.

'Preparation.' Alex informed me matter-of-factly.

'Oh dear … what have you done?' I gasped, horrified – I was always up for fun, but the variety that involved costumes had never been my choice.

'There's no need for that face, it'll be great,' Alex said, chuckling.

We went inside, and Alex was greeted warmly by the shop proprietor. It was then I realised this was no casual visit, this was, in fact, a set-up. This lady – Katie – was a vision of eclectic tastes – from her flowing gypsy skirt to her rock-band emblazoned tour T-shirt, she was bold in her style. I loved it. She pushed garments into our hands and ushered us towards two changing rooms hidden in the back of the shop – thank goodness they were hidden, for my outfit looked like it could overshadow any Las Vegas showgirl's for sequins and sparkles.

'You're doing this, Allie!' Alex called out cheerfully over the top of the dividing wall, as I unfurled the costume and exclaimed no way! I slumped down for a minute on the three-legged wooden stool in the corner before I heard Alex emerge from his cubicle and the striking introduction to Abba's 'Voulez-Vouz' blared out of a little stereo Alex had put on a chair outside my cubicle. As he started to sing I peeked out from around the curtain to see what on earth was happening. What a sight greeted me – there was Alex, dressed from head to toe in a sequin emblazoned, skin-tight, turquoise and orange jump suit, complete with orange gaga boots, and a deep V in the chest of the outfit, looking like a character from a drag Magic Mike. It doesn't end there, there was hip-dipping, shimmying, and all sorts of moves to complete the performance, including a prop microphone that Alex was practically making out with.

When he paused, short of breath to ask, 'Why aren't you dressed, come on, Dancing Queen!' I melted.

The fun was contagious. I pulled that dastardly jumpsuit of mine on, as Katie pushed some baby-blue gaga boots of my own under my curtain, and I jumped out of the dressing room, right into Alex's arms. He spun me out, and Katie handed me a microphone and we worked our way through 'The Winner Takes It All' and 'Does Your Mother Know' before collapsing in a heap on two nearby chairs. It was lucky those gaga boots were so chunky because Alex had some badly trampled toes and a few accidental elbows to the ribs mixed in with my moves. It was so much fun, though.

'Is this what we're doing later?' I asked.

'Sort of,' he replied. 'Now, what do you think of this for Ryan?'

Katie came forwards, brandishing a garment bag which she slowly unzipped to reveal the most dazzling jump suit I've ever seen. It wasn't just sequinned, it was a diamante masterpiece, in silver and gold, and with a metallic silver feathered boa draped round the neck of the hanger. The gaga boots had towering platforms, and I could almost see my reflection in the gold surface.

'Didn't want to outshine the star,' Alex said. 'Will he go for it?'

I didn't know what to say – Ryan was flamboyant and decidedly camp but being a spectacle had never been Ryan's thing – he was more poise and polish than dressing up and drag queens. But he loved a good time and a lot of fun, and if it involved Abba, Alex might just manage to persuade him.

'There's only one way to find out.' I replied.

We set off back to Mum and Dad's, barely managing to squeeze all our paraphernalia into the back of that tiny Mini. I called Ryan to warn him – I could tell he might be highly offended if Alex just arrived dressed in his gear, thrusting this monstrosity at Ryan.

True to his wonderful spirit, Ryan just said, 'Don't worry, Als, it sounds like an absolute blast! See you later.'

So, your part of stage one needs to be outfit procurement. Ryan still has his dazzling number and so does Alex, and I can't imagine any snags or issues for them with wearing the same ones. You just need to find a startlingly-sequinned eighties jumpsuit of your own, complete with gaga boots, and a big smile. The phone number for Katie's shop is in the file attached to the manual and I know she'd love to help. Take Ryan along for the giggles – it's far too good an opportunity for hilarity to miss.

Stage two is the night itself. The organisation of this is where Ryan will shine. Alex insisted that he pick me up in the Mini, all dressed and ready to boogie. I fluffed my hair right up, and, unusually for me, put on some make-up so I looked the full eighties dancing queen. I nearly fell off Mum and Dad's porch step when I glimpsed Alex through the car window, with eyeliner wings that could have made Amy Winehouse jealous. I was a little alarmed by how much he'd embraced his inner diva.

His plan was to turn up to Ryan's house with twenty minutes to spare to give him time to warm up to the idea and then get ready to go. As soon as we rang the doorbell, Ryan whooshed the door open with a 'Wooop-whoooo, the party has arrived! I don't know whether you're a hero or a monster for doing this to us, Alex, but you certainly look like a dancing king! Are you happy to share that position for the night, give our gorgeous dancing queen double trouble?' Ryan asked happily.

'I wouldn't have it any other way,' Alex replied gallantly.

I shoved the fully concealed jumpsuit and boots at Ryan and told him we'd wait for him in the car while he got into his outfit. Alex and I chatted for the ten minutes it took for Ryan to emerge and when he strutted down his driveway I wound the window down and let out a piercing wolf-whistle.

'How does he do it? He's made these ridiculous outfits look like the latest couture. I feel like a Philistine now, seeing how he's pulled it off.' Alex asked, incredulous. I scooted through

into the back of the Mini, scrunching myself up so I fitted, since Ryan would never have managed to with his long legs – it was enough of a squeeze when he folded himself into the front seat.

Alex drove us back into Oxford and as we walked along the streets we attracted a lot of attention from the evening crowds. It was a positive impact we seemed to have and making people smile fuelled us up and into the mood for fun. Alex led us to the doors of a theatre, which had billboards up announcing 'Abba Mania' – one of the UK's finest Abba tribute acts, and Ryan and I nudged each other and let out little squeals of excitement. We have done underwear karaoke to Abba classics more times than I can count, booty wiggling and bumping hips with each other to 'SOS' – this was our night, and we were so ready to get stuck in.

'Does he know what he's let himself in for?' Ryan whispered to me as Alex handed the tickets to the doorman. I just shrugged. 'I hope he loves a good performance, because he's got Abba's two biggest fans as his dates for the night.'

I thought back to the fancy dress shop and couldn't help but reply, 'Oh, I think he'll be all right.' Ryan just wiggled his eyebrows at me very dramatically and then Ryan and Alex grabbed one of my hands each and we dashed inside.

As soon as we'd got settled in our seats in the stalls, the opening chords of 'Take A Chance on Me' belted out, the curtains parted, and there they were on the stage, dressed every bit as funkily as we were. The audience was split about half and half into those who'd gone for the dancing diva apparel and those who'd kept themselves firmly restrained into everyday clothes. It looked like those tame audience members already had some regrets that they hadn't got more into the Abba spirit. For the next two hours, tune after outstanding tune rained down from the speakers – they may have been a tribute act but they all had more energy, enthusiasm, and talent than you could ask for. Our make-up must have run, the fabric under our arms a shade darker than the rest of the jumpsuits, and our hair flatter than an American highway with all the dancing and singing we were doing – we'd got started with 'Take A Chance on Me' and never as much as faltered. We were a trio having the time off our lives, in a theatre full of more fun than I've ever known in one space.

As things were winding down, Alex managed to communicate over the raucous 'Waterloo', 'I just have to go to the men's – I'll be right back.' Ryan and I just nodded, not wanting to miss a note of this lively belter that was one of our favourites.

As the final notes tailed off, one of the Abba Mania singers announced, 'Last one of the night, ladies and gentlemen.'

It was my all-time favourite and Ryan grabbed my hands and jumped up and down with me. 'Super Trouper' the perfect cocktail of meaningful, heartfelt, and vibrant. Ah, what a way to finish. Then, about halfway through, a figure emerged from the side of the stage, and went to stand beside one of the lead singers. The figure was wearing a turquoise and orange sequinned jumpsuit, orange gaga boots, and eyeliner wings that would have made Amy Winehouse jealous. My heart nearly beat right out of my chest.

The other singers went silent as Alex took it away for the last chorus, loud, clear, and looking straight into my eyes, pointing right at me.

'I love you, Allie,' he whispered into the microphone at the exact moment a bright beam of light landed on me as a cheer erupted through the theatre. As it turned off again Ryan swept me into a tight hug.

'He's a keeper, Als!' he shouted above the noise.

'He really is, hey,' I replied with tears in my eyes.

The next morning, Alex added 'Super Trouper' to 'The Story of Us' CD.

So, over to you and Ryan. Ryan now knows one of the members of Abba Mania – don't ask how, he's just a wizard I think! He's all set to organise another performance at that theatre in Oxford for whenever you give the go-ahead. Ryan will sort out all the logistics, so all you need to do is arrive at the cottage with Ryan with twenty minutes to spare, all dressed up in your dazzling numbers, and ask Alex to meet you in the car in ten minutes in his wonder suit. Boogie yourself exhausted all through the performance, slip away as 'Waterloo' comes on, and, you guessed it, walk out onto that stage and get ready to belt out that 'Super Trouper' chorus. There's one vital detail, you absolutely can't leave out, and that is, keep your left hand held right over our heart all through your magnificent performance, so that Alex knows it's me pouring out.

Get up on that stage and sing our heart out!

Chapter Fifteen

It became finalised that I was responsible for finding and then training my replacement, to specialise, as I did, in the language of flower bouquets, since they were so popular now. I thought this would be a fun and rewarding exercise. So, the search began.

It turns out that recruitment is no picnic. People are so fake, and who can blame them when the process is what it is. It's hard for employers not to make judgements about applicants who show the full spectrum of their personalities, but then when candidates avoid this personal judgement by saying standardised things that sound appealing, it's impossible to see the individual through the mask. I had some very interesting interviews, but I found my perfect match in the end. Her name is Susie, she is twenty-three, and quite remarkable with flowers, she has this vision for them, and flair, that quite frankly make me as green as the Grinch with envy. She is five-foot-five, with straight brown hair, hazel eyes, and medium-weight. She has a list of B and C grade exam results and she has an everyday history.

She loves flowers, though, and boy can she create flower-magic when her fingers touch the stems. I met her, and I knew with every fibre of my being – even the tumour knew – that Susie would become an epic florist. Visually, her arrangements were far lovelier than mine and if we added in the language the flowers whispered, Susie could create floral masterpieces – I just knew it.

Although the finite nature of the remaining days sat more heavily on my chest with every passing moment, life continued much as it always had done. Susie proved to be a fast learner and a complete joy to work with, and though she'd been told I would be leaving in a few months, Amanda had agreed not to tell her why, which was a mighty relief to me – it was already proving suffocating how much Amanda was fussing, and the vehemence of my protesting to such fuss was far more tiring than any of my daily tasks themselves. So, Susie and I had fun with the flowers, and with her sunny smile and warm heart I was confident I would be leaving my special customers in the safest, and loveliest, hands possible.

I decided to fill Susie in on all the histories for the regular special bouquet customers, while at the same time, leaving a little of the magic of their stories left untold for her to discover herself as time passed. It was a Friday, which meant Rob would pay us a visit that afternoon.

'So, I expect you'll meet Rob today.' I told Susie, as we were refilling the displays after the lunch rush. 'He's in his thirties, married to Nadine, they have one child – Charlie – he's very cute. He's been in once or twice with his dad and he loves daffodils, so I always let him have one just for himself when we have them in. Reading between the lines, Nadine and Rob are hoping there might be another little one along soon. They've been married maybe five years and every single week Rob calls me up on a Wednesday with the message for the week and I make him up a small language bouquet with that message for Nadine. He comes in every Friday to collect it and gives it to her when she gets in from work.'

'That sounds so sweet, but what sort of message is it if it's every single week? I understand how flowers can give messages for big occasions – first time saying I love you, first date, weddings, funerals etc, but what messages can flowers deliver week in, week out?'

'One week, Rob wanted a message of apology and sheepishness, because he'd been due to collect Charlie from playgroup and had forgotten. He told me Nadine had been really cross with him because the playgroup leader had made a big fuss about it, but when he gave her the flowers, and she looked up what they meant in the little card we included, she laughed, and they've joked about it ever since – because she realised he understood her feelings and was genuinely sorry.'

'Okay, yes, I see what you mean. That is romantic. What other ones has he asked for?'

'Sometimes, it's as simple as "I love you forever", sometimes, it's "keep the faith", it's been anything and everything, and it can be very challenging; some of the messages aren't the easiest to match to the flowers. I've had to do some deep digging to find the right match for Rob's orders more than any other. It can be the flower combinations too that put the exact right slant on things. The tough challenges have made me grow into the best that I can be.'

'You can't stop now that you've just got going – give me some more of Rob's messages, Alice, please.'

'I can't ruin it anymore. Let it unfold before you week by week, it'll be much more special for you that way. It's such a wonderful feeling, being part of a real-life love story.'

Susie gave a huge grin.

'It really is.' Susie looked cheekily across at me. 'Not even just one more?'

'Not even one! Discovering it for yourself is what will make you great, Susie, and I see greatness in you.'

Susie blushed beetroot red to the roots of her hair.

'You really do? That's the nicest thing anyone has ever said to me, Alice. Are you sure you mean it?'

'I'm one hundred per cent sure. You have such a flair with flowers, and I see how you handle them – with tenderness and respect. That's so special. It's just the people to crack now and that will come quickly. Then I'll have the Pablo Picasso of floristry as my protegee. I'll be the proudest mentor around.' I gave her a confidence boosting smile as she busied herself with the stems. 'Now, this week Rob wants the message to be "congratulations, good health and new beginnings" take it away solo for me, let the magic happen for Rob and Nadine. You can do it.'

Susie nodded nervously and began studiously flipping through the pages of the notes I'd compiled for her which detailed every flower we could get in and its meaning.

One of the toughest parts of my remaining days in 'Sunshine and Roses' was telling the customers I was leaving. The customers I'd formed relationships with took the news hard, and it let sadness creep into the otherwise cheerful and happy building. Rob was one of the customers who didn't yet know, and I knew today was the day to tell him – it had proved in past cases the smoothest way to Segway into the topic was to introduce Susie as my replacement.

True to form, Rob appeared at the glass in the door at 4.30 p.m. that afternoon – he always came in on his way home from work, which was an early finish on a Friday. The bell tinkled as he pushed the door open, and he gave his heavy construction boots a thorough wipe on the doormat as he stepped across the threshold.

'Hi, Alice. How are you today?'

'Hello, Rob, I'm doing okay, how are you? I can only guess the answer is good based on the message to Nadine this week? Is there something for me to get excited about?'

Rob blushed slightly and nodded with a little smile lifting the corners of his mouth.

'Actually, there is, we aren't supposed to tell anyone yet, but I'm sure you already know, since you know more about our relationship than even we do! Nadine is expecting.'

I smiled a huge smile and scooted round the counter to wrap Rob up in a tight hug. It was a very personal business and I could never help myself from riding every high and low with my customers as they faced them. Susie let out a little squeal of joy and clapped her hands together happily. Rob made eye contact with her and smiled ruefully.

'Wow, that's so exciting, Rob, I'll keep my fingers and toes crossed for a smooth pregnancy for Nadine. Huge congratulations. I have to admit I have been harbouring a lingering hope since your call on Wednesday – a congratulations, good health, and new beginnings brief left me with a good clue.'

'Shall I call you Sherlock going forwards, Alice?' Rob asked with an eye-roll directed at Susie.

'Perhaps you should you know, Rob, I could get quite used to that!' I gestured towards Susie, who held her hand out in front of her in readiness. 'Rob, this is Susie by the way. She'll be taking over from me in a month or two.'

'What do you mean, taking over, gone, and got yourself a promotion have you, Alice?' Rob asked me with a supportive grin.

'No, Rob, not this time, I'm leaving actually.' I shrugged.

'What a shame, Alice, how will I keep my marriage strong without you? Where are you going if you don't mind me asking?' Rob seemed genuinely disappointed underneath his light and jokey tone.

'Well, you'll do absolutely great without me, Rob, that's why I'm getting superstar Susie all prepped and ready. A fresh take on things might just liven things up anyway. Now, let's get you home to your beautiful family – here's your bouquet.' I handed Rob the bunch of flowers and seemed to skip safely past the dangerous territory of future plans. Susie seemed to take the hint as she wandered with Rob to the door, keeping him chatting with questions about Charlie and Nadine – subjects he'd happily talk about all day. I stepped up to the counter, placed my hands on it as I braced my arms and breathed a very shaky breath out. It got harder every time I had to tell it, it got harder every day.

'Well, if all the customers are as lovely as him I'll be the happiest employee in all of England.' Susie beamed, once Rob was safely on his way home to Nadine and we had the shop to ourselves again.

'You will be delirious all the time then, since we don't have a single grumpus or bad apple.' I smiled back at her.

'I really love it here, Alice,' Susie said and then paused for a moment before continuing. 'Thank you so much for taking the chance on me, and for spending so much time teaching me your wonderful ways. I'll never be able to do what you can do, but I'll never let you down, I promise.' The words tripped from Susie in a rough and tumble somersault of hurry. I forced a smile at her, and I think she understood that it was all just too much for me, and maybe it had turned into a little more than she'd expected herself, because before I could muster a reply she'd spun on her tail and gone to tend to her most precious of charges in their buckets and bunches.

Chapter Sixteen

This next one may come at you a bit out of left field. Sorry, but I can't let Alex miss out on a whole lifetime of these. He's missed enough before. Alex had a loving but rather staid upbringing. I've had to drag him into the headspace of celebrating all the little things, taking every single chance to be happy. So, we come to Pancake Day. I've always thought of this as the opportunity to inject fun into everyday life handed to you on a plate – haha, I love being punny. Alex will remember me as a pun-lover, but more of that later. Anyway, on the first time we celebrated Pancake Day together, when I told Alex to get home early because we had a big night of flipping ahead of us, he seemed disbelieving.

'We can have pancakes any day – I don't get it.' Was the response I got. Let's just say his mind was changed after that first pancake night.

This one is a bit out of order – we'd been together over a year by our first Pancake Day as Alex was away overnight with work for the first one. But Pancake Days are so, so important that it has to be included!

I'd prepared all the possible ingredients, and they were all laid out on the counter – so you'll need to do the same. It's just the usual pancake list – they have to be made from scratch, obviously – plus Nutella, bananas, whipping cream, strawberries, raspberries, blueberries, sprinkles, vanilla ice cream, maple syrup, lemons, icing sugar, and whatever your favourite topping is if it's not on that list.

When Alex got home from work I gave him a big old kiss as always – you should leave that out – and I told him he was on a ten-minute countdown to get changed. He hurried away, taking it all seriously, but mumping about how silly it seemed. He is the sweetest man because he humoured me all the way. I would ask him sometimes why he went along with my crazy ideas when he so obviously didn't find them as fun as I did, and he'd always say, 'You happy is me happy.' So, he came down, his brow slightly furrowed as he surveyed the huge mountain of supplies and I stood behind him, hooked his apron over his head, tied it behind his back, and gave him a huge cuddle and a thank you.

We each had our own beloved aprons. They were our second skins when cooking. They unleashed our alter-egos. We had so much fun together in the kitchen. Hopeless, disastrous fun. So, you'll need to get your own special apron for Pancake Day and other culinary moments.

When you arrive at the door make sure your apron is already on, and once you've laid all the ingredients out on the side ready, make sure you ask him to put his apron on. Wait until he's done that and then maybe you could lay mine over the back of a chair to keep me there in spirit as well as heart.

Once we'd reluctantly pulled away from that cuddle the frenzy began. We whisked, and we mixed, and then we began the flipping. There was a lot of cleaning up to do, since he took a while to master the true flip. He's a man so it was then onto the double flip of course. Don't let him try the triple flip, I'm telling you, huge mistake. You'll have to be firm. Though that was one of the most fun moments of them all – him hoisting me onto his shoulders to scrape the triple-flipped pancake off the ceiling. So, yes, be firm when it comes to his triple flip ambitions! We had one of the best nights of our life that first Pancake Day. He flicked the mixture at me, and then kissed it off my nose and my cheeks. We had flip-offs and who could make the most creative topping contests. Some were so disgusting they were delicious. We just laughed all night long. We ate so much we were round enough to roll into the bedroom after the lengthy clean-up we did side by side. We were always side by side.

It's strange for me to think about you and all that you could be – an astronaut or a shelf stacker. Uptight or a wild hippy. You could even be mean and aloof and have just ignored this whole thing, I suppose. Whoever you are, I hope you're creative, or if you're not, you can entice a creative streak out for Alex tonight. You see, you need to get the pancake mix right, and you need to just throw yourself into the flipping. Ask Alex to show you how, even if you're a chef of dizzying flipping ability, because then he'll probably remember how I wrapped my arms round him from behind (even though I'm so much smaller and they only reached his forearms) and taught him the right wrist action and how to duck and dive to catch the pancake. There was an electricity between us in that moment, and the stars shone out of our smiles. I'd like him to remember that moment.

Then comes the creative part – the toppings. Once you've made a good batch, cover the mixture, turn off the hob, and prepare yourself for some topping mastery. I would recommend starting with something simple, to ease yourself in and appreciate the wonder of Pancake Day – maybe a strawberries and cream, or a Nutella and banana, depending on your tastes. But then, oh wow, nothing is too daring, no combination too wacky. The more unbelievable the better! Be creative, and wild, and you both have to try every single effort, that's the most important rule. One mouthful minimum swallowed down, I'm A Celebrity Bush Tucker Trial style – you'll be surprised by which ones become your favourites, I promise you.

I'll never forget that night, or the ones that followed which got even more extravagant and fun with every passing year. I don't think Alex will either, so every Pancake Day, help him remember. Make him a triple stack, chocolate, raspberries, strawberries, and ice cream extravaganza from me.

Being in February I know this will have come early for you. And I know it's a silly kind of fun. So, please just try your best. Just let loose, enjoy, and be free. Put on an Abba or a Mika album, we always did our crazy, fun things to them. Now I look back, maybe that's why our cooking always went so badly wrong, all that dancing. Mika's 'Big Girls You Are Beautiful' never failed to bring out some colourful moves. We did them all, the cheesier the better. Once, and yes this is for real, we danced the 'Macarena' while cooking a Sunday roast chicken. It explains a lot. So, that's the most sure-fire way to get the

Pancake Day party started. That's how it should be – a two-man party! Two people and maybe a ghost. Don't think of me as looking over your shoulder though, I'll just be enjoying the view, and maybe skipping the CD player to 'Big Girls You Are Beautiful' if the mood seems a little flat. Don't be embarrassed to dance like a madwoman either – Alex dances about as well as he triple flips pancakes, but that makes it all the more amazing. I think it will break any last shards of ice between you. Maybe this time it will even be Alex who initiates you into the glorious abandon of some crazy fun, rather than me dragging a reluctant Alex into it. I'd like that. If he could have learnt how to embrace the ordinary fun, the little blessings, I would know he'd be all right. So, if he's forgotten, this is how you can remind him. This is how you can make him be all right, for me, from me.

Chapter Seventeen

Time continued its steady march and before I knew it, and certainly before I was ready, I was staring down the barrel of the one month to go mark. There were so many things I was certain of in the last weeks. I was certain that I was doing the right thing. I was certain that I was scared, terrified in fact, by what lay ahead for those I loved. However, I was filled with uncertainty too. I'd learnt over my twenty-six years, and well before my diagnosis, that life doesn't come with an instruction guide. There is no clear-cut way to handle things, and schools certainly don't teach you the stuff that really matters. What use is algebra to someone finding it hard to get out of bed because their heart is so badly broken?

I was uncertain about many things but nothing more so than how to deal with a certain person. There was an individual in my life who I didn't know what to do for, or whether I should, in fact, do anything. She was one of my oldest friends. We had fallen out a few years ago. But she'd been my friend for far longer than she hadn't. We'd lost touch completely, but if she was dying I'd want to know. I would want to apologise, maybe not for anything specific I'd done, but perhaps for not finding it easier to forgive and patch things up. It seems so small – what we choose to make so big – at the end.

I decided the right thing to do was to call her, so I did, but the line had been disconnected. I drove to her house, but new owners lived there now. I could only conclude she'd gotten herself lost and didn't want to be found. I wrote a letter to her, for Mum to keep, in case she ever got in touch. It was compassion I found among the lack of time.

As well as being a soul-believer and true love enthusiast I complete the fanciful hat-trick with being a star-gazer. I love to sit, surrounded by silence (or the soft chatter of my knight in shining armour), admiring those bright beauties looking back at me from light-years away. Not only are those stars breathtakingly stunning, but I love the way they make me feel – they balance me, and, despite living in the distant skies, they ground me. The small stuff fades away when I'm in their magical presence, all the niggles and irritants of everyday life fade into inconsequentiality to make way for pondering the big things – the meaning of life, my purpose, the power of love, why we get out of bed in the morning. I love the Alice that has that perspective so much more than the one who gets grumpy about the milk being left out after breakfast.

I love being there in that spot in the field behind our cottage, laid out on a blanket, the inky night cloaked around me, my eyes twinkling with the reflection of the stars. Just like I know Alex needs to be polar-beared and cuddled once he's physically worked frustrations out, Alex knows that I need to be dragged, purple woolly blanket in tow, to that field, on a clear night when I'm getting wound up. He will lie beside me, often sharing the silence, my head resting in the crook of his elbow, my body tucked in tightly beside him, until he feels the tension ebb away, and pure-Alice makes a welcome return.

It was the evening before my last day at work, and I was rather down when Alex walked through the door. A cloak of melancholy had settled around my shoulders, but I got up, padded over to him, and he folded me into his arms for our customary hug. When he pulled back he took one look at my face, and, noticing the droop in my shoulders, asked, 'What's wrong, Allie? I'm so sorry the signal was so bad on our way-home call.'

'Nothing much, it's just been one of those down days – you know the ones, when everything just hits you all at once, like an avalanche you never saw coming. You just can't help but feel overwhelmed by it all.' I shrugged. 'Or maybe it's just girl stuff – hormones – taking over my emotions in that annoying way they're prone to,' I said, trying to make a slight joke out of a heavy situation.

'Come on then, talk to me about it,' Alex said, pulling me through the lounge door and settling in next to me in the squishy sofa.

'Well, I think it's just the feeling of the ending – tomorrow being my last day at 'Sunshine and Roses' makes it all feel quite final. Susie's settled in great, and she's so wonderful I know she'll do a good job but even that's bittersweet – I'm happy knowing the customers will have her, but it won't … be me. Plus, I couldn't get in touch with my old friend, to try to sort things out – I'm going to have to leave it unfinished. I don't like that feeling.'

'It's completely understandable to feel that way. It's definitely not girl stuff this time. It was always going to be a very tough few days, you'd have to be a mannequin not to feel down about those things.' Alex suddenly jumped to his feet and picked up my purple woolly blanket from where it was folded over the arm of the sofa. 'I'm not having my girl feeling down. You hang on here for five minutes, I'll get us a picnic tea together, and we'll head to the meadow and do some star-gazing,' Alex said with a hopeful grin.

'Alex, it's not even dark yet.' I pointed out, brightening up a bit.

'But it will be, in an hour. Time for us to get settled in before the show starts.' Alex, it seemed, wasn't taking no for an answer, for with that he bent down to place a gentle kiss on my forehead before turning on his heels and trotting off to the kitchen to gather supplies. A few minutes later I heard him thunder up the stairs as he called out, 'I'll just get changed, we'll leave in two!'

As Alex hurtled back down the stairs and through the door, dressed now in dark, well-worn jeans, and a thick woolly jumper, I marvelled at his enthusiasm and zest, even in the face of such difficult times. Yes, the mask slipped, and the raw pain came through at times, but to remain lit up, in all this darkness, was the greatest gift he could have given me.

He grabbed my hand and entwined his fingers through mine as he pulled me up. He dropped the contact, only for a second, to shuck the rucksack containing our picnic and supplies onto his back and lock up behind us and then we were off, hand in hand, wandering down the lane to the footpath.

As we walked, dusk was just settling in, the way one climbs into bed at the end of an exhausting day – with a peaceful joy at the familiar comfort. We clambered over the stile and found our favourite spot beneath an old oak tree in the hedgerow. This tree felt wise and protective, its huge width oozing strength and life. We always felt safe under its shelter.

Alex let go of my hand and unpacked his rucksack. First, the picnic rug came out, soft to the touch and traditionally tartan. Second, he produced four candles in glass jars which he used to anchor the rug at the four corners. Matches hissed to life and the candles glowed. Third came the feast – Alex had thrown in all sorts from the fridge which came together to make a delicious array – we had sausage rolls, a fresh French stick to break up and fill with sharp mature cheddar and rich honeyed ham, we had Alex's favourite Kettle Chips and a jar of fancy olives; Alex had brought plastic glasses and fizzy elderflower to drink, and two mini raspberry panna cotta pots for pudding, not to mention the essential Marvellous Creations chocolate. We both sat down, cross-legged, knees touching, and worked our way through every last mouthful as the night slowly found its way to us.

When we'd finished eating, and the black sky lay above us like the softest velvet, holding twinkling diamonds in its caress, Alex blew out the candles to give us the full effect, and we lay down next to each other. I lifted one of my legs to lay over Alex's just the way he liked it, and he pulled me in close to his side with his arm around me. He reached for the purple woolly blanket and tucked it in around us both. We gazed.

We needed no words, in fact they would have felt out of place there – too small and slight against the vastness.

I didn't know I'd fallen asleep until I squinted my eyes open to find myself in Alex's arms, my cheek against his chest, him wandering back through the meadow. The purple woolly blanket was tucked tightly around me, and he held me gently but safely. I could have walked back but I didn't want to miss this precious moment, so I shut my eyes and enjoyed every second of this closeness. Despite me being no waif, Alex took his time and he allayed my fears that he'd drop me as he climbed the stile by summitting it as elegantly as the hunky lead male ballerina lifts his female partner in Swan Lake. He even perched himself down on the plank of the stile for a moment on the other side, and, keeping me held tightly in his arms, my bottom now resting on his lap, he rested one cheek on the top of my head for a few minutes before getting up and plodding slowly home. He must have wanted to prolong the moment too.

I squinted my eyes open enough to see the beautiful diamond sky over head and I let the rhythm of Alex's chest rising and falling beneath my cheek form a lullaby.

Somehow Alex managed to unlock the door and he made it up the stairs without puffing in the slightest. Then he set me down gently on the bed before easing my shoes and jeans off. He tucked me in under the duvet, disappeared into the bathroom for a minute to brush his teeth, and then settled in behind me. His chin rested on my shoulder, our breath mingled, and his breathing fell into time with my own. I read about a scientific study which proved that lovers' hearts really do beat in sync when they're together. I believe that has to be true, for its not just mine and Alex's hearts that fuse together, it's every breath, every touch, every part of us becoming one.

Chapter Eighteen

Prepare for adventure! I'm a storm lover, a storm addict, and a cautious storm chaser. My mum is responsible for this. When I was a little girl she never got nervous about storms, rather she got excited. She'd lift me up onto her hip and dance, or, when I was older, pull me up and dance me round holding my hands. My mum always told me, on every single stormy night, that the storm was the angels having a party in heaven. She told me they loved to have fun, and to celebrate, and we should join in with them. Mum said the thunder was the angels' music and the bolts of lightning were their disco lights. She'd say this was the most amazing kind of party there ever was and we'd be so silly if we didn't party along with the angels. So, we did, we always partied with the angels. If Dad was at home, Mum would grab him, chuntering and shaking his head as he started, and twirl him round and round, laughing away. They'd pull me in after a couple of minutes, so the three of us were swinging round to the thunder. Mum was always beautiful, but never more so than in the white light of the lightning and the flickering candles' glow. Dad always let himself get into the swing of it so that by the end he'd have his head thrown right back with laughter bellowing from him. We had so much fun, and that's why I so dearly love storms.

The first storm I shared with Alex was a special one – it was forecast to be a big extravaganza of a storm: swirling winds, booming claps of thunder, flashing bolts of lightning, lashing rain, and fizzing romance. The angels must have had some incredible news, for they were set to celebrate hard. The full stormy works were on their way and my excitement started mounting as soon as the weather man's jovial grin turned to a serious glare at me through the television screen as he warned of the impending situation. I turned to Alex, who was furiously typing away on his laptop, with glee and my deranged leery grin proved enough to make him pause in his work and enquire what on earth was happening. So, I didn't just go full crazy on him the night it happened like something out of a horror film, no, he had days of notice.

I made sure we were well prepared with candles, a torch, supplies, etc. My mum had been wild in her abandon when the storms rolled in but my dad was Mr Practical, so I knew the drill regarding turning the electrics off – in case you don't know, you have to turn all the sockets off so any surges after a power cut don't damage the devices – so do that first when you arrive please, in case Alex is distracted by, well, you know, and forgets. Thank you!

The night it arrived it was every bit as fuming as predicted. It was so brilliant it felt like the storm had grabbed hold of the cottage and was shaking it – the windows were rattling, wind was hissing round the corners, it was tremendous!

I bounded from window to window trying to spot the lightning. There didn't seem to be any yet, but that didn't dampen my spirits. I had my eyes glued to my watch, counting the seconds between the thunder claps out loud. Alex tried to soothe me to begin with. He tried to entice me to settle down with concessions such as agreeing to watch my favourite programme instead of the sports news he currently had on. I spun round to the screen and switched the TV right off – what was he thinking?! He tried to start conversations to distract me. I think that eventually he realised it was futile, and I heard him mutter under his breath, 'If you can't beat them, join them.' Before whipping his laptop out of his bag and switching it on. I told him he didn't need that to join in, but he insisted that if we were doing this, we were doing it right – no amateur storm followers would be found associated with Alex, apparently. So, he located the storm updates, the current centre, and he created an excel spreadsheet to track its' timings and location – men, hey! I wasn't complaining though, seeing his cute smile and the way his eyes lit up with every thunder clap was infectious and delightful. Alex got more and more involved in the storm surveillance until I looked like a laid-back, casual, disinterested pleb next to the world's most avid storm fan. He even insisted that we turn off all the lights so that we'd get the maximum lightning effect when it finally arrived, so that we were flailing around in the darkness with only Alex's laptop screen (turned down to minimum brightness to prolong battery I hasten to add) to provide us with any light.

Soon enough, the lightning was with us, and when it crackled down it lit up the whole room in its beautiful white glow. I had to admit Alex was onto something – it felt so dramatic and magnificent. Amid Alex's cries of, 'Listen, it's here, we're right in the middle of it!' he came at me out of nowhere and before I could blink, I found myself slung over his shoulder and being run out of the back door. I was yelping but Alex just laughed from deep in his belly and said, 'Oh, come on, Alice, where's your sense of adventure? This is amazing!' He spun round and round with me in the middle of our sodden lawn, both of us soaked through, clothes clinging, in all the right places for Alex – who somehow managed to look like a Greek Adonis despite his days at a desk – and all the wrong places for me – who resembled a muffin made with a raising agent on steroids. He flopped us to the ground after he was dizzy and grasped my slippery hand in his as we lay side by side. Yes, it was absolutely ridiculous – I could feel the wet mud seeping into my clothes, and I tried to get up, but Alex held my hand tightly and said, 'A few more minutes, please?' The way his eyes shone, and his voice held a lethal combination of pleading and excitement, left me with absolutely no choice but to lay back and embrace the disgustingness of the mud and the wet.

The rain was lashing down on us, pelting our skin with its vicious strength. The thunder was clapping around us, and lightning broke the sky apart every so often. It was absolutely, unequivocally, hair-raisingly magnificent.

Alex turned to look at me, flinching as the rain assaulted the side of his face, and he said, 'Isn't this just glorious, Alice, you were so right. This is living, hey? This is the very best of this wild and amazing world, this wild and amazing life.'

I nodded, and he turned away, and I lay there thinking he was right, but that the very best of this wild and amazing life was not the storm but this incredible man lying next to me.

Now that I look back I feel even luckier than I already did that I had those kinds of moments. I lived my life, so fully and completely, that I had it far more special than most people do. I truly embraced this life for all it can be.

Before you ask, yes, we both caught colds from it, it was real life of course and real life is so far from perfect, I don't have to tell you that. But, yes, I wouldn't have swapped that stormy night with Alex for the world.

Now, instructions for this one are tricky, since I know some people are so afraid of storms it would be impossible to even fake it 'til you make it and pretend to be having fun. I think I'll just have to hope with all our heart that you're at least non-phobic and you can plaster a smile on your face with authenticity and leap about happily. Maybe we can mask any fearful jumps and shakes as leaps of glee and trembles of excitement. Anyway, the things to take with you will be lovely scented candles – Alex likes the fruity types more than the floral ones. You will need plenty – you've got to make the whole lounge glow, plus enough to make the kitchen and corridor safe in case you want a hot chocolate – which I highly recommend as the perfect storm beverage! You'll also need a torch, some playing cards, and lots of enthusiasm. When a storm is forecast, and the bigger the better, arrange to spend the evening with Alex. Since we're an electronics-free household in storms, Alex can get pretty fed-up (he's the TV and laptop type far more than a cosy up with a book man) so he may make other plans if you don't get in there quickly. Go to the cottage nice and early and set up the candles with him. He has this extra-long lighter (it's for gas rings really but don't tell him that!) that he loves to light anything and everything with. So, put the candles where you want them (he doesn't have an eye for these things) and ask him to light them. Then he'll be in a good mood before the first thunder clap even booms out with his typical boy with his lighter-toy attitude. Maybe then brew up some hot chocolates and snuggle in to wait for the party to commence! The playing cards are to give you both some entertainment – Alex and I would always play when storms struck, or in bed on Sunday mornings, or whenever the fancy took us. I was always game (ha ha, there I go again, sorry!) for snap which Alex barely tolerated, so you have to throw a round or two of that in there for me as well as letting Alex talk you into the more grown up games he prefers. He has a few special creations of his own which I'm sure he'll teach you. Just remember he has a ruthless carding streak and can be fiercely competitive so if you are too, it will be a long and bloody battle of an evening. Try to dampen it down, or if you have to, maybe even let him win if you turn out to be a card shark by profession, because a stroppy, sore-loser Alex won't be the man to spend the storm with, I can assure you.

When the storm hits full swing, make sure you persuade Alex to open his spreadsheet and get tracking! He'll have enough battery life on his laptop to not breach the sockets-off safety code. He will get very intense during this period, so you might have to step up and provide refreshments. He's very partial to Kettle Chips as a helpful hint! When he tells you it's reaching the cottage, close his laptop, ignore any protestations, and lead him out through the back door into the middle of the lawn. Take him by the arm and dance with him. If it feels natural put his hand over our heart and let him feel me beat. Get totally, gloriously, soaked through, and then head back inside to another round of thick hot chocolate and fluffy towels. Your work there will nearly be done. You'll have the time of your life, even if you don't realise that while it's happening!

The final thing to do, when you're still dancing in the lashing rain, the swirling wind, the booming thunder, and the sparkling lightning is this: I've told Alex the story my mum told me about storms. So, tell him this is his chance to dance with me once more, to party with his angel.

Chapter Nineteen

Alex had been given compassionate leave by the newspaper for my final three weeks and so that was when I left 'Sunshine and Roses'. I wanted to spend the final few weeks having afternoon teas with my mum, gardening with my dad, girly film nights with Ryan, and picnics and hot chocolates with Alex, and then flying to the USA.

Amanda must have told Susie why I was leaving them, even though I'd been so sure she'd keep her word, because the last day was a freight train of emotion running away down the tracks. There was a banner across the door when I arrived, beautiful in sky-blue and daffodil-yellow proclaiming 'We Love You, Alice'. Inside there was a mini flower party with more flowers in the shop than I'd ever seen, and mini cupcakes on the counter top. As soon as I stepped through the doors Amanda smothered me in a long, tight, warm hug, tears rolling down her cheeks. I'd told her the week before I wouldn't come back in after that day – I didn't know how my health would be and I didn't want to make promises I couldn't keep, or let such an inspirational person in my life have a last memory of me as anything but the vibrant goon with a smile that takes over her whole face and a laugh that overwhelms a whole room – she'd put up with it for all these years, I had to go out as myself, not as a vessel for the monster.

I was so touched by the effort Amanda had gone to, and Susie too. When Susie arrived, it was clear from the tears in her wide eyes and the tight hug all of her own that she'd been involved all along. Little did I know, this was only a small part of their master plan.

It began with Rob. This was a Wednesday, bear in mind, so he wasn't due to come in. He was supposed to be piling bricks up on a construction site somewhere, fulfilling his bricklaying duties. Instead, he found his way through our doors, bell tinkling to announce his arrival. In his strong, broad arms was a beautiful bunch of flowers. The flowers in the bunch were cyclamen, which means goodbye, and cattail, which is a very rare flower that means peace. Rob handed me the flowers. Trailing behind him were Nadine, and Charlie. In Charlie's hand was a single daffodil. Bright, sunny, and beautiful it had a glow all of its own. Charlie was standing before me, and, with a shy smile on his innocent face, he stretched out his tiny hand and passed that ray of sunshine to me.

'I'm heartbroken, Alice. Amanda phoned us on Monday, and she explained everything. She suggested this – that we chose two messages to give to you and that's what we wanted to say – goodbye, and that we pray you'll find peace – no one could deserve it more.' Rob spoke these words with a softness that was unexpected from this strength of a man. Still, from the greatest strength often comes the greatest softness.

Nadine followed on, with tears in her eyes and her hand clasping Charlie's tightly.

'We'll never forget what you've done for us, your flowers have truly touched our lives. Every week they bring a happiness, and a romance, which has brought us together in a way we never expected. Thank you for everything, it's meant the world to us.'

Amanda handed them each a cupcake, which Nadine and Rob thanked her for and held on to. Charlie had been silent and clearly affected by the sombre mood but not so much that he couldn't tuck straight into his cupcake, smearing icing messily on his chubby cheeks.

'You are all so special, I've loved every moment of being a tiny part of your story – it's a really wonderful one. I'll be pulling in any favours I can up there to make sure it stays as happy as it possibly can be.'

We all smiled at that and Susie took the lead in seeing them out when it became clear I was struggling. As Rob turned around to catch my eye through the window I gave him a gentle wave, tears streaming down my face, tears streaming down his.

They all came – every single one of my special customers. They all got the time off work or rearranged their schedules to make it in to the shop that Wednesday morning to say goodbye to me. I understand now why some people prefer to leave unannounced, with no ceremony, or actual goodbyes – it's such a painful process. I cried until my eyes were stinging with dryness, and yet there were still more tears to flow. Seriously, I got so dehydrated that day I must have been millilitres off IV drip requirements.

Mavis came, and she brought Bob too, which was a wonderful surprise since I'd never met him in the flesh before. Mavis and Bob are in their eighties, and Bob used to be the head gardener at the stately home outside of town for his fifty-year career. He used to bring Mavis a bunch of his favourite flowers home from the garden every week and he'd cook them a meal that night and tell her the stories of his week, and of his flowers. Now, Bob is in a care home, and he has Alzheimer's, so he doesn't remember everything. Mavis loved the flowers he brought home so much that she made a log of the flowers that Bob loved the most and the times of year he brought them home. Now, every week she orders a bunch according to the log, so not a message bunch, and she takes them to the care home, where she cooks him his favourite meal – steak pie and mash with proper thick, old-fashioned gravy – and they eat the steak pie and mash sitting at a table for two in his room with a red tablecloth and candles, and those flowers in the middle. Mavis says he doesn't have many lucid moments now, but he never fails to chatter the night away with old stories of his garden, and his flowers, and the nights they shared when he sees the bunch in front of him each week.

Mavis chose azalea for gratitude and gladiolus for remembrance. She left me with the final words, 'You've helped to give me life left with him – I would've lost Bob a long time ago if it wasn't for you, Alice. From the bottom of my heart, thank you. A hundred times, thank you.'

Next up was the burbling sound of Skype coming from the depths of the counter – where the laptop was stored on the shelves underneath it. Susie rushed to get it open and up and running in time, creating a real flap, and a stir as she did so, so I knew it must be important, but I had no idea just how much. Susie shared a look of excitement with Amanda and opened the screen towards me with a flourish. On that screen was a man wearing combat uniform – the sandy patches of camouflage gear. His hair was short in a buzz cut and the background was dark and dingy.

'Alice, hi, you're every bit as lovely as I imagined. I'm so glad I got to see you, but I haven't got long. Susie, would you do the honours?'

Susie handed me a small bouquet. I looked at her with my jaw on the floor.

'You can't be … Rory?' I asked the screen, shocked.

'I sure am – the one and only. The man, the myth, the legend,' Rory replied, cheeky and boyish and full of innocent charm. 'Sorry this can't be longer, but there's a line of lads twenty deep waiting to get a go on this thing. I just had to be part of this as best I could, and I had to say thank you. Thank you so much, Alice. It's helped keep me going out here, knowing that Michelle has been taken care of in this one small way. I know that your flowers, with my messages, have been a lifeline to her, as has your friendship. Take care up there, maybe I'll see you again one day, in the gardens up above.'

Suddenly his face froze on the screen before the bright blue of the Skype background re-emerged. Rory was one of my most favourite cases in the romance stakes. He was a soldier deployed in Iraq, with a new bride here in our village. He'd been gone a year and had set up a list with me before he went with messages he wanted to send his wife every fortnight. The messages were beautiful and heartfelt and so moving, and although the bouquets were simple, they were gorgeous. He'd asked me to deliver them in person, and to check in on Michelle with every delivery because she didn't have any friends or family here – it was his hometown, not hers. She'd become a wonderful friend, an inspiration, and a strength and I'd loved being the messenger in their challenging love affair. Rory had given me white heather for protection and yellow roses for friendship.

My next visitor was Beanie, who contrasted with her name in every way. Beanie was the only customer who intimidated me, though I'm certain she never intended that. She intimidated me because she was feminine perfection – she was tall and had a tiny waist with boobs that filled any blouse just that ideal amount. I'm as straight as they come, but she made my mouth water just a fraction. She looked elegant and flawless at all times and carried an air of control around with her as consistently as she did her designer handbags. Beanie bought flowers for her new girlfriend, Clara. They'd been dating for a few months and during that time Beanie had been in to see me for a bouquet before every single date.

'A lot about me is unconventional, Alice,' she told me the first time she came to the florist shop. 'But, I will most certainly convene fully in this one beautiful tradition. There could be no one more deserving or worthy of the most gorgeous flowers than my date, Clara.'

They seemed to have a blossoming relationship and were happy and becoming serious. Beanie departed after a tender hug and left me with a bunch of flowers containing camellia for admiration, and pine for hope.

Although not my closest customer, I'd enjoyed my time with Beanie, and I always felt like I'd been standing in the sunshine during her visits.

There were many more, perhaps twenty-five to thirty of my regular customers. There were enough tears shed that the floor was sparklingly clean, and all the cupcakes were thoroughly enjoyed. It was a send-off to remember and one filled with so much heartfelt emotion I felt so lucky to have shared in this wonderful adventure of life. The most painful and difficult goodbye of them all was at the end of the party with Amanda. Susie left me with a hug, a good luck, and a thank you and disappeared off into the flower fridge to leave

Amanda and I in privacy. I was grateful she hadn't made a spectacle or a big furore – I knew what was to come with Amanda would take every last piece of my reserves.

'There are just no words, Alice,' Amanda said. 'I've never lived through anything as cruel as this. You are a person so warm and caring and indescribably special that I can't fathom how this could ever be okay. My faith has been tested in a way I never expected it could be shaken – if He's really there, how could He do this?' Amanda looked so truly angry, upset, and bewildered that I felt I couldn't leave her without trying to soothe the battle these emotions were fighting within her.

'I've wondered a lot of things myself, Amanda, I've been angry and sad and confused. Where I've landed after that long and turbulent rollercoaster is this: I've lived an absolutely amazing life. I've known the unconditional love of a close family, I've known what it is to find a purpose that fulfils you, I've had so much positivity that I've wanted to get out of bed every morning, I've found people to share my life with who are remarkable.' I pulled back out of the embrace we'd found our way into and looked her right in the eye as I said this. I smiled a huge smile as I continued, 'And I've known what it feels like to fall in breathtaking, perfect, life-changing, once-in-a-lifetime, soulmate love. I've had it all, Amanda, I've had every single good thing that this magical life has to offer. So, don't cry for me, cry for every person out there who lives a long, long life who never gets those bits of magic.'

Amanda nodded, but the tears ran down her face in the kind of race that young boys run – messy, disorganised, exuberant, and determined. I pulled her into a fierce, tight hug, and spoke some final words. 'Thank you for everything, Amanda, be happy, be healthy, and live an amazing life. Goodbye.'

I knew she'd never let go first, so I gently stepped out of her arms, turned, and walked through the door. The bell tinkled its final goodbye, far too cheerily, or maybe just cheerily enough.

With another highly emotional day behind me, I had to retreat to the place of serenity that recharges me in a way little else does – Dad's garden. Dad loves his garden, with the same passion and tenderness he used to pour into his trains. In the same way he seemed to know the engines he steered so they performed better for him than for the other drivers – smoother, faster, bolder – his garden seemed to respond to him too – growing, strengthening, and thriving under his soil-stained hands. He tended it with care and understanding – it was an honour just to work beside him as he hoed, dug, planted, and cultivated, and the garden seemed to reward his attention with an abundance of gifts.

He was, with his garden, as he was with his life – practical rather than aesthetic. He patched up rips in his trousers, even if they looked unsightly.

'Plenty of wear left in these yet, love, no use in throwing away a perfectly useful pair of trousers because of a line of thread where it shouldn't be – nothing wrong with that.' He would say, even as thirteen-year-old-me was going bright red in front of my giggly school friends. He wasn't much of a colour-palette appreciator either – he'd quite happily pair his mulberry trousers with his emerald green jumper (often worn over a tartan shirt!) As such, it was, perhaps, for the best that he didn't try to create visual masterpieces from the little piece of earth he was responsible for. He opted for use over beauty and our table was the grateful beneficiary of Dad's gifts. His runner beans were the only ones I've ever eaten that actually had taste and were string-less; his tomatoes were sweet and so juicy the liquid trailed down your chin; his cucumbers rivalled baseball bats for size; and his pumpkins were so bright and round that they were the envy of the street as their faces illuminated the dark on those scary Hallowe'en nights. Everything he touched in that garden of his became the best it could possibly be for my dad, much as I did.

When I asked him about his love for vegetable growing he'd explained in a way that stuck with me thereafter. He had said, in his quiet and matter of fact manner, 'Well, love, I've spent my whole life working all day to feed my family. When I retired I just had to find another way to do that, didn't I? That's what life's all about.'

For someone so straightforward my dad was the wisest person I knew.

I loved helping him out when I could spare a bit of time. I got some wonderful life lessons from Dad's garden. He had a quiet way of working his advice into our labours so that he never faced my problems head on. He knew the value of planting a seed. When I'd been going through those treacherous teenage girl years, fake friends stabbing me in the front, back, and sides, he'd calmly mentioned, 'We must clear the old to make way for the new. It can be sad, and feel difficult, but it must be done, otherwise there's no room for new, fresh growth, and without that there's no life.' I'd nodded, thinking he was referring to the dead runner beans we were clearing away, yet days later I was quietly cutting loose those toxic friends to my utmost relief. It was a system that I loved, and my dad was the definition of companionship and complete faithfulness – he never took from me, or drained me, and we could share a silence with total comfort.

As such, I sought him out for an afternoon of relief, peace, and normality, and found myself helping him with his most favourite of gardening activities – bonfires. My dad found any possible excuse for a bonfire. Before the days of recycling he even went around all our neighbours to offer to collect their old cardboard boxes to use as flame fodder. As I said, any excuse.

He had amassed quite the collection for this bonfire – we'd recently cut back the trees in the garden, so there were plenty of branches, plus three big sacks of raked-up leaves, and some other odds and ends. Dad's face was a picture of excitement as we piled up the items to create our biggest bonfire to date, looming up as if it was Ben Nevis' younger brother. I popped inside for a glass of water once we'd assembled it, and my long-suffering Mum just shook her head at me.

'You take care of him, Allie-pops, you know what he can get like.'

'Of course, I will, Mum, don't worry, he's an old bonfire hand now, but I'll keep an extra close eye on him.'

I went back outside to find Dad fussing at the bottom of the bonfire, where one of the larger branches was protruding a bit too much. Dad was heaving away at it, but it was proving very stubborn. I walked to his side, to offer my help, but he indicated with a jerk of his head for me to step back. He had stopped letting me do the heavy jobs – his way of protecting me.

As he pulled and pulled at the branch, the exertion starting to show on his face, I called out, 'Why don't you just leave it now, Dad, I'm sure it'll be fine.'

'Nearly there, love, best to get it right, hey,' he shouted back.

A moment later, the branch came loose, and with it, Dad, who fell straight onto his back, in slow motion in the manner of a cartoon – entirely straight, as if he was the second hand of a clock falling from the twelve to the nine. I rushed to him and grasped his elbow to help him to his feet.

'Are you okay, Dad, does anywhere hurt?' I exclaimed.

'Oh no, I'm right as rain, love,' Dad said, smiling, while brushing the leaves and dirt off the backs of his legs. I set about brushing down his back as he continued, 'See, I got that bastard in the end,' he said grinning. My eyes just widened, met his, and we fell about laughing together in that hysterical way that relief brings. I'd never seen Dad laugh so hard and he reached inside his baggy coat to pull out his handkerchief to dab at his eyes. Once he'd recovered enough to talk, he said a single sentence, while braced with his hands on his knees.

'Best not tell your mother about this, okay, love?'

'Okay, Dad, whatever you say,' I replied, before we both set off into hysterics again.

Chapter Twenty

Okay, so you should know Alex quite well by now. You're halfway through. His birthday is June twentieth, not that he'll have told you of course. Alex is one of those unhelpful, no fuss birthday people whereas I'm all for taking every moment of celebration and joy. He humours me on all the other celebratory days – he'll throw himself into Christmas, flip pancakes beside me on Pancake Day, drown me in chocolate at Easter, but he says since his birthday is entirely about him he gets to sit that one out. So, no banner and balloons brigade from you! But I never let him get off that easily. You have to pick him a single, perfect present. One that doesn't seem like too much to him but that he'll love and treasure, so he knows just how much you care.

I remember his first birthday when we were together. I love birthdays and we've always done them big in my family. No huge party extravaganzas as adults, but a cake with candles, lots of presents, and a day of complete and utter spoiling. So, I wanted to show him how wonderful they could be. I managed to strike a deal with the anti-birthdayist. I convinced him to let me have this one birthday to do me-style and then I wouldn't make a fuss again.

So, no, I didn't do banners, or streamers, or balloons. That could never be him. He had always been loved, in the kind of way that's there, but confined. He had always had a birthday cake, actually he had three – one carrot, one red velvet, and one Victoria sponge – because he liked all three. See, he was loved. Those fancy cakes, they were the most delicious cakes you could find. But they were not baked by the hand of a loved one, so I could only assume they lacked that little extra sweetness. And those three, perfect cakes, they never glowed with the flickering of candles. There was no raucous and terribly out of tune song, and no cheers. Everybody loves differently, I suppose. My love will never be perfect – my cakes were often lopsided, asymmetric, and sometimes even a little singed … but those cakes were bursting with care and time. And those candles were bright and beautiful, even if they dripped wax onto the cake. And that singing hurt his ears, but it sounded like love. And maybe love is better with a bit of character.

So, he needs candles. Not just those big number candles either. It has to be the exact number of individual candles for every year he's lived. You have to get them all lit at the same time. And you have to bake the cake yourself. And to be completely honest, if you're a Mary Berry baking whizz, it'd be best if you toned it down and made a mistake or two. It'll be more authentic that way. It was never about the taste.

The lights have to be turned off for the cake to be brought in and the song to be sung and it has to be loud and off-key and awfully brilliant. It was never about the tunefulness.

Alex will object to the whole thing, I guarantee it. He'll probably even bluster at first and look very angry, and he's very convincing when he's angry. But push through, you have a strong heart now, so I know you can. You're going to have to get used to doing that although I know how hard it'll be. When he starts his objections, take Alex's strong, wonderful hand, and hold it up to me, so he can feel the beating. And just say to him, 'This is for Alice.' He'll be like putty in your hands.

That first birthday I made him a 'Box of Alex'. I wrote in his card that the reason we take birthdays so seriously in my family is because they are a celebration of the fact the person arrived in this world, and in our world. I told him he had to know he was the single best thing in my world. The Box of Alex was a celebration of him. I didn't want to go overkill – we'd not cemented things too much at that point in our relationship – but I wanted to show him what he meant to me. So, I bought him a novelty gift for each part of him. Now, I know what you're thinking – how can you quantify the parts of someone else – but I gave it my best shot. At least for the obvious things. They all had a tag explaining.

So, he was given an engraved compass – 'for the traveller in you'; a football signed by his favourite player – 'for the athlete in you'; a fridge magnet saying, "I can multitask, honest!" – 'for the multitasker in you' (you'll have discovered by now – not Alex's strength); a notepad and pencils engraved with funny writer quotes on – 'for the journalist in you'. The list goes on, and I'm sure you get the idea by now! It was how I introduced the candles – twenty-four, tied up in a ribbon with a tag saying, 'for the twenty-four years in you.' He may not be a birthday man, but I think he liked it! He grabbed my hand, pulled me in for a hug, and wouldn't let go.

Best birthday moment ever.

Chapter Twenty-One

Getting progressively worse was hard, I won't lie to you. I'm a 'when you can't find the sunshine, be the sunshine' kind of girl, but all I could see were rainclouds. I had good days and I had bad days and I could handle that, but it was the fact that the bad days were slowly beating the crap out of the good ones, numbers wise, which was wearing me down. Words can't express my gratitude to my family for how they managed to cope. I couldn't cope.

My mind was frequently abducted by an unfamiliar philosopher. A reel was played, with the image of the cruel war between mortality and life; or were those dips and swings the moves of an age-old dance rather than the throes of battle? Perhaps so. How complicated the steps of the dazzling waltz that the paradoxical figures danced; there was something very *Beauty and the Beast* about the picture they made together moving across the dancefloor of my mind – the strength, brutality, and ugliness of mortality cradling the fragility, radiance, and purity of life in his beastly arms. But my God, how beautiful the dance.

I choose to believe that everything happens for a reason. I find this to be a happier thought process – that even the bad stuff has a purpose and is necessary. I believe that being happy is a choice we make every day not something that lands upon us by magic. So, I'm consoling myself that maybe the loss of me is going to happen because whoever gets my heart has bigger things to do than I ever would. Maybe she'll save the world one day or change a handful of people's worlds. Maybe she'll do a degree of good that I never could have. That will be a fair price to pay, a worthwhile trade off. I'll make sure she knows – that she must make it worth it.

I don't pretend to be a paragon of virtue though. I'm not perfect. I lose control sometimes too, just the same as everyone else. I submit to the pain of life, I give in to the sadness, sometimes. Even the strongest souls have their scars and flaws. And I'm not even claiming to be one of the strong ones.

What they don't tell you when you get a diagnosis like mine, is that they are taking away your identity. You are no longer simply you. You are you, plus a monster, plus a deadline, plus a mess, plus a glaring imperfection. Or, you are you, minus a lifetime, minus health, minus a whole. Either way, you just aren't you anymore. People treat you differently, however hard they try not to let it affect them, however normal they try to keep things. Things are never the same again. How could they be, I suppose? But it's a cruelty, being treated differently, though it only stems from good intentions. It seems that Ryan is the only one who understands that and that my sense of humour is the same, that I still love rubbish reality TV and that I still want to dance in my underwear singing into a hairbrush. So, Ryan still jokes about death, still snuggles up for *Made in Chelsea* marathons, and still does bedroom karaoke with me. He still lets me be me. And still lets me be me, not alone.

It's not that I'm ungrateful either. I appreciate people's care and their sympathy. I'm flattered by their fuss. It's just that I don't want my final days marred by their pity, I want them enhanced by their love.

So, it was a rainy day with about three weeks to go. I'd been over to Mum and Dad's for the morning and Mum had been hosting book club with a group of women rather keener on Mum's carrot cake than Moby Dick. I'd just dealt with a whole morning of tissues and tears and being called 'dear' by ladies who had won the grand prize of a full life. They were being kindly, but they were being maudlin. Treating me as if I was dead already and it was my funeral they were attending. Ryan was away. I think, deep down, I knew he was getting his space, building strength, and reinforcing his defences in readiness for the final run. So, I knew it was beginning, that the end was nigh. It had been a week without his jokes that only I got, and I hadn't watched any TV marathons (which Alex stuck his nose up at but secretly watched from the bedroom) and it had been too many days since I'd stripped my trousers off and jiggled around to crazy songs with Ryan by my side. And I cracked.

All I saw when I drove home from Mum's were children skipping along the side of the road on their way home from school. Their mothers shepherding them along, some swollen with new life inside them. I saw old couples hand in hand walking back from their daily trip to Tesco to buy their tea. I saw business men in suits blowing kisses into their phones. I saw life. I saw the essence of life all around me. For the first time, I saw myself as a deadline. A black hole.

I saw the children I would never have, I saw the grey hair I would never exclaim over, I saw the kisses Alex would never blow through the phone to me. I saw myself as a minus. Minus a future. And I saw everybody I loved minus their futures too.

Alex would never kiss my tummy when I showed him the positive pregnancy test, or spend hours poring over every pram option. He would never hold our baby for the first time, tears in his eyes. He would never teach our child to ride a bike or learn to drive. Never give our daughter away on her wedding day or make a speech for our son on his. Alex would never kiss me goodnight on the cheek when we were wrinkly, grey, and gummy, his teeth in a glass on the bedside table.

My mum and dad would never hold their grandchild for the first time or get to buy them sweets to give them in secret. My mum would never do gluing and sticking or make fairy cakes with them the way she did with me, and my dad would never sit them on his shoulders at football games. My parents would never celebrate with me when I started my own business or help us move when we bought our first house instead of renting.

Ryan would never be a godfather and teach his godchildren all about fashion and design. I would never be beside him when he married the man of his dreams or go on another best friends' holiday. He would have to do underwear karaoke alone and he'd never drink cocktails with me again while he ranted about his boss.

I saw the lifetime of moments none of us would ever live. And I broke. There was only one place that I could go to recover enough to function as myself for the next few weeks, so I got in the car and drove all the way to the beach. It was a couple of hours away and I didn't make it there nearly as often as I should have. It was the home of hundreds of happy memories – from sticky ice cream dripping down our chins, the smell of freshly made donuts caked in sugar, to sandcastle boats I sailed round the world in and jumping over waves as they splashed round our knees.

When I got to this happiest of places, I screamed. I stood at the top of that empty beach with the wind swirling round me and I screamed myself hoarse. Then I crumpled down to the cold, wet sand, and I cried. I sobbed great, wracking sobs that contorted my whole face into agonising shapes. I lay on the sand and I thumped it over and over again. I rolled around on that beach as if I was possessed. I suppose in a way I was. There's no shame in that.

Eventually, I'd cried myself out and I sort of drifted off, I think. I have a vague memory of being scooped up by strong arms, with tears plopping down onto me from above. I remember blankets and hot chocolate and my warm bed. I remember the voice of my hero telling me it would all be okay. I remember thinking, no, it won't.

Chapter Twenty-Two

There are two types of occasion I think Alex should have somebody with him for in this first year. Woohoo, you guessed it, I'd like that person to be you! Alex will be able to, or at least will have to, get through most normal days creating a new version of life, but these two occasions – weddings and funerals – are the places you feel your shadows and your empty spaces the most keenly. So, be the sun that outshines his shadow, and be the heart to fill the empty spaces in his.

I've always got the impression that people either are or aren't wedding people – the required attendance is either a blessing or a curse. I've seen the types that love the legitimate chance to get drunk as skunks, and those who have their tissues ready to dab at their carefully made-up eyes at 'you may kiss the bride.' I'm curious as to whether you're a watch-glancer, an urgent-phone-caller, a tissue-dabber, or a drink-the-night-awayer, but I suppose it doesn't matter too much as long as you show up, stay, and carry your hand around open so that Alex can hold onto his lifeline if he needs to.

Our wedding was exactly as you'd expect it to be having read some of our story – it was fun, and romantic, and unique. Now, please don't laugh, or roll your gorgeous eyes but I had a wedding full of puns. Genius, hey, and totally me. We left a little box of mints on every guest's seat at the ceremony that had 'Alex and Alice … Mint To Be' on the label; we had a huge message board with a giant sharpie pen tied to it that had a 'Our Futures Look Sharp With Each Other In Them' label attached; we had pizza on the buffet table with a sign that read 'You Stole A Pizza My Heart' – the list goes on, but I expect that's enough of that punny picture. That was my hand in the wedding plans which Alex fully supported but he had his ideas too. It was exactly right – we had so much fun planning the day together, it was truly a representation of us – both as individuals and together as a whole. Alex chose the entire playlist for the reception, half of the food, helped with the colour scheme, and his biggest request was an outdoor ceremony, overlooking the sea. I wasn't hard to convince. Neither of us are hardcore religious, but both of us believe in something more, and never is that more certain for me than when I'm staring out across an ocean. Alex and I trekked round the potential venues, eating lots of seaside fish and chips and ice creams along the way, and we found the perfect place. It was a spot that felt like safety and freedom; like home and adventure; like love and protection – and that's exactly what we wanted our lives together to be. We wanted to start as we meant to go on.

Try to contain your shock for this next revelation, hard as that may be. Ryan chose my dress. I gave him the list of must-haves and must-not-haves and he took it from there. He stole many wedding shop assistants' hearts with his intricate knowledge of all things style and class and his squeals of delight as I emerged in their creations. A lot of prosecco was drunk in those wedding dress shops and Mum came along too. Us three amigos were a force to be reckoned with, and we had so much fun. We settled on a classy, lovely, and simple number that would cope well with a breezy cliff-top affair but still look elegant and stunning and everything a wonderful white dress should be. There were to be no fluffy, puffy, billowy dresses for our trio. I mean, I totally get it, who wouldn't want to look like a princess on the most special day of their lives? And to those who can pull it off, I salute you, you have some real skills. I tried one on, just for the fun of it, after all, I would never get the chance again, and it was like I was being slowly murdered. It's just that I've always fancied being able to move on my wedding day, and to be able to breathe. I could never get comfortable either with the thought that I would need my poor bridesmaids to hold my dress up while I used the facilities – Ryan might have signed up for the gorgeous suit, and a spot in the limelight, but he most definitely did not sign up for that! Anyway, sorry for my digression, the point is, I had a simple, but let me reassure you, incredibly beautiful, dress. It was white – of course – and figure skimming, with beads on the most divine silk bodice. When I had that dress on, and I was standing at the foot of the aisle, for the very first time in my life, I felt gorgeous.

I was carrying a posy of red roses – for eternal love. I will use any of my final wishes to hope that eternal love proves true.

The clouds had been rolling in over our heads all morning. Every person present had cramped fingers from how tightly they'd been crossing their fingers for those clouds to keep hold of their rain until after the ceremony. Those clouds did not hear our prayers, for they opened right up and down the drops came. Some of the guests got flustered, but I just joined eyes with my future husband and smiled my highest kilowatt smile. He looked at me, wide-eyed, for a moment before grinning right back. Never mind all the pomp and ceremony, I couldn't make it down that aisle quick enough then, not because of the rain, but because I couldn't bind my life to Alex's life fast enough. There was not a single moment more that I could bear to not be his and him not be mine.

We went to a few weddings together after that, and we always had an amazing time, for we relived the best day of our lives every time. I think we might have got ourselves put on some wedding blacklists within our friends' and families' circles because we were so affectionate we might have won the romance contest, which could have angered the bride and groom. Anyway, I always wore my blue and white dress, so make sure you don't wear blue if you wouldn't mind. I imagine you as a red dress kind of woman, but no pressure, whatever floats your boat. Ideally red will float your boat though! And take some chocolate too please – Alex and I always snuck away for a chocolate fest if the reception became lengthy – I'm no dancer remember! After all that, just have fun! Or, as much fun as anyone can have being the wedding date of a man who has just buried his young wife. Now that I think about it, I'll keep my angelic fingers crossed that there's a free bar!

When it comes to funerals, I dearly hope that you won't be called to 'companion action' this year. However, if you are, you can rest assured there won't be any reminders of mine for Alex. If Ryan followed my wishes there will have been glorious colour, romantic and vibrant tunes (ending on the joyous melodies of the one and only Abba), and cupcakes. My funeral should have been a party not a gloom-fest. Regardless of the differences to mine, Alex will be forced to stare death and loss right in the eye again at the next funeral. It is said that hell is something you carry around with you, not somewhere you go. I believe that's true – we all have our burdens to carry. To attend a funeral though, Alex will be forced to enter a hell that he manages to contain inside in other circumstances – so he will be entirely consumed by the soul-crushing concept. I'll be fighting with everything I have to help him through from wherever I am, but please be the hand that reaches through the darkness to him and pull him out; be the light at the end of that devastating tunnel for him; save him from the hell.

Chapter Twenty-Three

My love of flowers started with my nan. Every Saturday morning for most of my childhood Mum dropped me off at my nan's bungalow and collected me just before lunch. I looked forwards to those Saturday mornings all week. Nan was the best baker in the whole of England, and she loved teaching me her masterful ways. I may be a culinary nightmare, but my nan made me a baking legend.

From an early age, I was her little helper. She'd wrap me up in an apron, the strings passing three times round my waist and the bottom flapping around my ankles. She'd pull an old wooden chair up to the work top and she'd hoist me up there, and tuck me in by her side, one warm hand round my middle keeping me steady. The skin was a little loose and wrinkles lined its surface, but it was a hand of safety. We made butterfly cakes oozing with buttercream, wings standing proud, in crinkly cases. We made wobbly layered trifles with fruits from the little garden. We made jam tarts with the jam thick and bubbling as they were pulled out of the oven. At Christmas we made mince pies under the lights strung up round the tree in her kitchen. I loved how she'd sing Christmas carols to me as we dusted the warm tops with sugar. It was a relationship filled with the smells of burnt sugar, cinnamon, and vanilla, but the smell I remember the most is the smell of my nan as she pulled me in next to her or reached across to hold my tiny hand steady as I spooned out mixture. My nan always smelled of flowers – of lavender, rose, or lilacs in the spring – and I think that's how my love was born – so many of my favourite moments, they smelled like flowers.

My love for flowers intensified the week I lost my nan. I was eighteen years old then and had been travelling since leaving secondary school, bouncing between basic jobs, saving a little here and there so I could head off again, trying desperately to find my path. I'd pulled pints, cleared tables, assembled car parts, stacked shelves, and answered phones. Nothing quite fit.

My nan passed away while I was coming to the end of a stay working on a dude ranch in Australia. I missed saying goodbye, arriving home too late, in time only to help my parents with the funeral arrangements. I was heartbroken. If I'd felt lost as I bumped my way through those years, it was nothing compared to how anchorless I felt without Nan waiting in her bungalow for me.

When Mum, Dad, and I went to discuss the forthcoming funeral in the church with the Vicar, I experienced a huge sense of loss. It was a cavernous and booming place. Every tiny movement echoed around me. For so much space it felt very crushing. Light streamed through the bright and beautiful stained-glass panels, making the divine images in them stand out against the dark grey walls as if projections, floating in the air. The holiness felt oppressing initially, but by the time I left it had become inspiring. The Vicar was deep in conversation with my mum and dad, but I remember feeling so detached, as if I were in a cloud high above them, the Vicar's white dog collar shining like a halo in the gloom.

A woman emerged then, from the choir vestry.

'My wife,' The Vicar said to my parents as the woman slowly made her way over to us. Slightly stooped and dressed mutely in worn, comfortable tweeds, she beckoned me over. Her hair was greying, her figure plump, and her face bare but generous.

'I knew your nan,' she said softly. 'She was very special.' It was all I could do to give her a tight smile and a single nod by way of reply. 'She loved flowers, didn't she?' I gave her another single nod. 'I don't know if you love flowers too, but there's a kind of secret I know about them. Well, it's not really a secret, it's just something not many people know, which is a shame because it's very wonderful.' She paused and examined my face. She must have found a hint of encouragement there for she continued, 'Every single flower has a meaning, they can send a message. These meanings can represent something, or even encourage feelings. It's hard to explain, but I thought if you were interested I could lend you a book about it, so that you could make a special bouquet for your nan for Friday. You meant everything to her.'

Tears pooled in my eyes. This lady had an air about her – a comfort, a peace. It helped. She began to shuffle slowly towards a pew, and she brought a small, green book back with her which she pressed into my hands.

'Thank you,' I said simply, in barely more than a whisper.

She reached for me, and I surprised myself by stepping into her embrace. I'd had my fill of well-meaning hugs by now, but this lady had a kind look in her pale blue eyes. She was warm and soft and held me gently. As she drew me to her, I smelled flowers.

I went home that day, carrying the book as carefully as I would a long-lost treasure. I slid into my bed and I caressed its textured surface. It was an old-fashioned fabric cover; stories and lives caught among the threads to travel on with it. I opened it, and it smelled like time – so many scents wrapped up together, bound to each other inseparably. The pages were worn – fingerprints, smudges, and coffee stains on some; all of them soft from years of thumbs flipping through them. When I opened that book, I felt like I was forging a last connection to my nan.

I read that book studiously, until I knew the name of every flower pictured within it, and all its messages. Each double page spread featured a beautiful hand painted watercolour of the flower described on one side and a breakdown of its habitats, obtainability, and the meanings it carried with it on the other.

My nan had always loved flowers. She'd smile at me and ask, 'Could you go out and bring me in some beauty, my darling?' I would trot off and pick her the most dazzling blooms I could find in her well-stocked, immaculately tended garden. Her face would light up as she accepted them from my outstretched hands and inhaled so deeply I wondered how she didn't get pollen up her nose. I could never doubt how special flowers were to her. But this book, it opened a whole other world to me. I knew it was a world in which I belonged.

A few days later, the contents of that special book were as much a part of me as my fingerprints. Collecting lilies and peonies from Nan's garden and making them into a bouquet to dress her coffin had been a profound and enchanting process. I returned to the church, cradling the book against my chest, underneath my coat. I pushed my way through the heavy wooden door into the still, airless space. It was as if the world ended outside its walls. I spotted her – the vicar's wife – arranging flowers in vases on the pulpit. I allowed myself a few moments to adjust to the completeness of the silence, the way it permeated through me, this time making me feel that I wanted to stay forever in this serenity, before making my way over to her.

As I reached her side, she turned to me.

'Alice, I was hoping I would see you again.' She smiled that gentle smile of hers. I felt like I'd arrived home.

'This is yours,' I said in a hushed tone, holding the book out reluctantly. 'I wanted to return it. I expect you feel a bit lost without it – I know I will.'

'Oh no, my dear, it's yours now. I'm merely its guardian, trying to get it into the right hands, the right heart. It's found its home with you, hasn't it, I didn't get it wrong?'

I felt such a strong sense of relief as I tucked the book safely away inside my coat next to my heart.

'No, you got it absolutely right, I love the book very much. Thank you.' I paused, eyeing the displays she'd put together. 'In fact, I would love to learn how the flowers can go together, that sort of thing. I don't suppose you'd be willing to teach me?'

'I thought you'd never ask,' Beatrice responded, her eyes sparkling and alive. 'I'm no expert, mind you, I've just muddled along over the years. But I'll pass on everything I know, and we'll have such fun doing it.'

Over the months, as Beatrice guided and mentored me, a deep friendship was born between us. She shared wisdom and grace that allowed me to grow into the adult I wanted to be. We met for coffee and cake every month and she offered me a faithful support that nourished my soul. She reminded me so much of my nan I always felt as though Nan was sipping a mug of coffee and tucking into a slice of chocolate fudge cake right along with us.

As such, I had to make a final visit to Beatrice, to deliver the language of flowers book back to its guardian to go forwards on the next stage of its journey. Alex dropped me off at the churchyard – it felt like the right place for the hand-over, an ending where there had been that fated beginning. I find it comforting to think of cycles completing. It may have only been a twenty-minute walk from the cottage to the church but even that exhausted me these days. I walked through the churchyard, with its beautifully tended, bright green lawns, dotted with bright spots of colour where flowers had been left on the graves. It is interesting how much we have always used flowers to symbolise extremes of feelings.

I reached the end of the cobbled path and stepped into the shade of the old stone porch before pushing open the heavy wooden door and walking into the coolness of the church.

'Alice, dear.' Beatrice welcomed me. 'I wasn't expecting to see you today but what a lovely surprise.' She embraced me gently. 'To what do I owe this honour?'

I produced the book from inside my coat. My thumb danced over the surface of the cover – I dearly hoped that some of my story was now woven into its threads; perhaps a lingering scent of my perfume added to the smell of time between its soft pages.

'I came to give you this. It's time for its journey to continue, for it to help the next soul who needs it. It's got a magic here, that's for sure; it saves souls, guides them.' I narrowed my eyes a fraction and nudged her with my elbow. 'Like someone else I know.'

'I don't know about that.' Beatrice blushed. 'But you're right about the magic in here.' She took the book from my outstretched hand. 'Thank you.'

I should have known that Beatrice would make this a positive encounter rather than one filled with sorrow or awkwardness. She knew, of course, why I was returning the book.

'I'm excited to think about the things it will go on to do. This book is proof of the power of one small act, the right small gesture, to change a whole life,' I said with fervour. 'I'm delighted it found its way to me, to change mine.'

Beatrice pulled me in for a tight hug.

'I'll make sure it finds its way into the right hands, dear, the right heart, I promise.'

Everybody could see that I was fading, everybody was hurting over it. However, it was only Ryan who knew exactly how to help me, who knew the only thing that could make a difference to me at this point: hope. Not the airy-fairy, rainbows, and unicorns kind of hope that spoke of miracles and getting better, but the gritty kind of hope that was made of substance and fire.

Ryan came into the cottage one day when it was apparent my time left was in short supply. He was wearing the most perfect paisley shirt I'd ever seen, swimming with sky-blues and heather-purples. He saw me curled up on the sofa in my purple woolly blanket. Cuddled in to Alex, I gave Ryan a weak smile of greeting, and he spoke three words to me that lit that fire of hope inside me.

'I've found her.'

Ryan shot a sidelong look at Alex that spurred me into action. Obviously, I didn't have a mirror to appreciate the full hilarity of the situation, but I felt my eyes widen to Bambi level and suddenly I was scrambling about like a woman possessed. I shooed Alex out of the room, claiming top-secret mission intel, and I think Alex was so happy to see me animated that he wandered out of the room wearing a bemused smile and promising hot chocolates.

'Oh my God, Ry, seriously?'

Ryan nodded, with a big, genuine, happy smile on his face.

'You're absolutely sure? She's right?' I asked him. 'Because she has to be perfect, you know? This is Alex we're talking about. I mean I was thinking looks of Julia Roberts, spirit of Mother Theresa, sense of humour of Steve Martin, heart of, well, me.' I enthused with an amused grin. 'Tell me that's exactly who you've found?'

'I'm not sure I've delivered on quite that brief, but I'm telling you, Al, she's right. She's the One, well, let's call her the Two, since you're obviously the One.'

I scrambled into a hug with Ryan, which after a moment of resistance he mellowed into fully.

'Not a moment too soon, Ryan, I'm on my last legs, as I'm sure they've told you.'

Ryan held up a finger to me in true camp style and hollered through the closed door to the kitchen and Alex.

'I'm treating myself today, so cream and mini marshmallows if you'd be so kind, Alex?'

Ryan gave me a conspiratorial smile, and although silence was returned to us, I knew that Alex would be working away in the kitchen to whip up three of the best hot chocolates the world has ever known; he takes these things very seriously.

'So, she's—' Ryan began, but I leapt up and held my hand right up in Ryan's face which stopped his sentence in its tracks.

'Stop, Ryan, we agreed, you can't tell me anything about her.'

'Please, I know that's what we said but you won't be disappointed, she's a total dream.' Ryan saw my frown. 'What's wrong?'

'It's just, you know, it's such a nice theory, but it's different when it's real. What if he prefers her to me? I really do want Alex to be happy, but, maybe, just not quite as happy as he is with me.'

Ryan pulled me back into another hug.

'Okay, no details. Trust me, beautiful, he could never be happier than he is with you. You are doing such an amazing thing, believe me, it'll mean the world to Alex, but there is only one Alice, and there will never be anyone to compare. You are it, Alice. Once a man has loved you, love will never mean the same thing ever again. Your Two, she's nice, and she will deliver what you want. But she isn't, never will be, and never could be, a patch on the real deal.'

I smiled up at Ryan from beneath brows that were still heavy. 'There's something else.' Ryan continued. 'Something amazing, albeit a little ker-ay-zee,' Ryan said, spinning his pointed forefinger around next to his temple while rolling his head about like a lunatic. 'It's a heart transplant case I came across when I was doing my Sherlocking research. It's quite frankly impossible to comprehend, and Mr Logic in me says it must be a complete fluke, or just plain and simple make-believe. But, you will love hearing it, and it'll inspire you to stay strong and keep fighting I expect. You'll be insufferable, no doubt, claiming you were right all along.' I rolled my eyes at Ryan, desperate for him to be quiet and just tell me the story. 'Luckily it's a price I'm willing to pay to make my number-one girl smile.' Ryan continued, before pausing for dramatic effect. 'Okay, here goes … the story is about an eight-year-old girl who received the heart of a ten-year-old murder victim. Their names haven't been revealed for privacy reasons because they're kids. Anyway, the recipient began having vivid, recurring dreams about the murder – nightmares about the event itself. Her mother grew so concerned about them that she consulted a psychiatrist. After several sessions with the girl, the psychiatrist concluded that she was recalling actual physical events that had been witnessed. They decided to call the police. The details the heart recipient provided about the identity of the murderer, the murder weapon, the location of the murder, and what the murderer was wearing were used by the police to find and convict the man in question. Spooky stuff.'

There was a silence while Ryan waited for me to absorb it.

'Wow, that's incredible, Ry, seriously, how can you not believe in what I say now – that our hearts are so much more than just pumping organs – that they truly do hold some of who we are? There's no other way to explain how the little girl would've known that. It's just remarkable. Oooh, this is so exciting!' I responded gleefully.

'It is quite something, I agree, that's why I told you the story, after all. And it's hard to fathom an alternative explanation.' Ryan admitted grudgingly, shaking his head in disbelief.

'What was the source? Credible?' I asked, knowing this would make a world of difference to Ryan, who placed great emphasis on such things.

'Very. It's from the work of Paul Pearsall, a scientist who looked into this stuff. I'm going to do more research, so I'll report back any findings … but, don't get your hopes up, Al – usually one story really is just a fluke. One swallow does not a summer make,' he said, seriously and sagely.

'Okay, I know. However, all it takes is one, Ry, that's all we need. It shows us it's possible.'

'Perhaps, Als, we'll see.' Ryan paused. 'Now where's that delicious hot chocolate?' Ryan shouted through to Alex at the top of his voice.

Chapter Twenty-Four

Christmas. My favourite time of the year. Alex celebrated Christmas in much the same way that he celebrated his birthday, and all other occasions – reluctantly. He was not a scrooge, I hasten to add. No, he didn't hate Christmas, not by any means. He just didn't see what all the fuss was about. Tasty meal, family together, maybe a few gifts, and he'd have a happy day. End of. To him, all the palaver and commercialism had gone too far. So it must have been a nightmare when he realised how excited I became at Christmas. I was, and always have been, Christmas crazy. I'm the girl who has a tree up and decorated the first weekend of December, complete with an ornament from every year of my childhood. I bake mince pies throughout the whole of December, just the way my nan taught me. I wear a bright, and quite frankly ridiculous, jumper with Rudolph's nose glowing off the front every time I set foot outside my front door. My biggest Christmas addiction, though, is Christmas lights. Twinkling, glowing, glorious little lights strung everywhere. I've never been able to do this outside on my mum and dad's house, but I loved going for drives around the neighbourhood looking for the most inventive and extreme decorators.

You can have Christmas Day all to yourself, don't worry. Alex and I always spent the day apart, returning to each other in the evening, tired and celebrated-out. We each loved the other's family so there was no issue that led to this way of spending the day; our families were just so different, and we decided that we had each other every single day so our families deserved us every Christmas, without having to share. It worked great for us all. Even if that hadn't been the case, I would never ask you to be apart from your loved ones on such an important day for families, though, confession time, I hope Alex might be on that loved ones list by now anyway. So, Christmas Day is all yours! And so is the present you get Alex – you'll know him well enough by now to get him a wonderful gift. He's easy to please. He's marvelled over T-shirts a size too small, exclaimed over CDs for bands he hates, and he's loved homemade fudge that was congealed and disgusting, so you can't sink to a lower gift-giving level than that. Alex loves the thoughts.

Your task to bring me to him for Christmas will take place well before Christmas Day itself. You'll need to start preparations the last week of November and dedicate the entire first two days of December to it. You know how it works by now – I'll tell you the story first, then what your version of it should be. Okay, here goes.

The first year we were together we'd grown very close by Christmas time, and very serious. We had agreed to spend the day itself apart, with our own families, but we were a loved-up couple, who enjoyed walking hand in hand through the streets under the glow of the Christmas lights of an evening. One day in early December, I'd driven home from work a slightly different way, in order to check out the displays of Christmas lights on the houses in the streets surrounding ours. There were some crackers, let me tell you. See what I did there? Christmas pun alert!

Sorry, anyway, Alex noticed me pulling up from the wrong side and as I walked through the door he asked if I was okay. I said 'yes' and explained my Christmas lights addiction. He has this funny little 'pfft' noise he makes when he thinks I'm making too much of something – you will know the one I mean, you must have earned it yourself a few times by now. So, I did the only thing anyone could do in such circumstances, I got his thickest coat off the peg and helped him into it. I grabbed some thick mittens from the box and pulled them onto his hands. I put his wellies in front of him and signalled that he should step into them. He gave a humongous sigh and asked if he had any choice at all? I, of course, said he had none whatsoever. I clasped his mitten covered hand in mine and led him out the door. I knew just the house to take him to. We didn't know the people personally – they were a few streets away. But believe me, these were people as Christmas crazy as me. Theirs was a plain house, kept neatly but subtly the rest of the year round. At Christmas time, though, their house came alive, it lived and breathed Christmas. Not with the brash and gaudy Santa and elf inflatables that some houses favoured, though they have their place too, but with tasteful and classy displays. This year was a nativity scene made from chicken wire figures with soft white lights woven through. There were gentle spotlights trained on them from the grass in front. It was breathtaking. It was everything Christmas should be. I stopped Alex in front of their drive and I said, 'Give it a chance.' He looked at me for a long moment and after a short while he squeezed my hand.

'Maybe you're right,' he said quietly. 'I see it now. I see it.' He slung his arm around my shoulder and walked me home in a settled silence.

It was the weekend after that when Alex told me he couldn't make it to Sunday lunch with my parents because something had come up. He ushered me out the door earlier than we normally left and told me to stay on with them for the afternoon since he might be a while and could use the quiet. It was dusk by the time I went home. I drove right past our driveway the first time, but my eyes were glued to our garden as I rolled by, I just didn't realise it was ours. After I'd found myself totally dazed in the rabbit warren of streets surrounding our house and circled back carefully, I realised. This magical grotto of a home was mine. It was covered in white lights. Literally, covered. The lights twinkled through the trellis covering the front porch replacing the jasmine that flowered there in summer, the lights glowed from the brickwork, and shone from the old, gnarled trees in our garden. Lights lined the path from the parking space to the front door. It was a fairy land. I was crying silently. It was indescribably beautiful, and it was for me. I stood outside the car, taking it all in.

Alex opened the front door and called out to me, 'Allie, come on, you'll get too cold.' He was grinning from ear to ear. It was only as I set foot over the threshold, wiping my wet boots on the doormat that I noticed Alex's attire was a little different from normal. Right there, all round his neck, and along his sleeves, were knitted snowflakes, brilliant white against the grey backdrop. It may have been subtle, but there was no mistaking it, this was a man wearing a Christmas jumper. This was my Alex of all people, wearing a Christmas jumper. Fresh tears sprang in my eyes.

Alex pulled me roughly into him and exclaimed, 'What are you crying for? I can take them all down if you want?'

I just shook my head and mumbled into his woolly chest, 'You're amazing. Do I tell you that enough?'

'Not nearly enough, but you're worth everything, Allie.' He went to brew me up his signature hot chocolate and a tradition was born.

In the years since then we've done the lights together. Each year we try to do something different. Now, I have to warn you, you know how people can be? Well, we have lovely neighbours, but boy do they enjoy a bit of friendly competition. So friendly in fact it seems to have hit a 'the rules are, there are no rules' situation the last year or two. Our street is infamous for its Christmas lights displays. We tend not to get sucked into all the craziness, but it has a habit of sneaking up on you so watch out!

I've come up with a final design for this year, but this time it's just for Alex, so I hope you have your DIY belt handy. I want you and Alex to build a huge frame out of chicken wire, in the shape of an angel. Thread as many white lights as you possibly can through it, so she is stunning and glorious and sensational. She needs to be nestled in an otherwise plain tree, I was thinking the huge old oak right in the middle of the back garden. Your task, and you need to do this part in private, is to build an appropriately sized heart for her. Just before Alex unfolds the ladder to lift your gorgeous angel into that old oak, fix that heart into her chest. Look Alex dead in the eye and tell him 'she's here, Alex'. I will be, I promise. I'll be floating around somewhere next to that oak tree too, remembering those glowing lights that first year. Remembering how our love was enough to light up that cottage, how our love twinkled in every bulb. Keep the lights shining for me, won't you, lovely!

Chapter Twenty-Five

As I've mentioned before, Ryan believes most strongly in things he can prove. I expect that when he first saw a sign on a wall saying wet paint he walked away with coloured fingers from where he'd touched it to be sure. He respects what is known, known for definite. So, I'd been a little surprised by his lack of scoffing at my idea of the manual. I'd expected a barrage of preaching about how crazy I was, how silly it was to believe that my Two would get my love – but I knew full well those thoughts were flying around in that wonderful head of Ryan's. Alas, that was revealed to be the truth when he came whizzing into the cottage all in a flap one day. Alex had popped out to the supermarket – yet another thing that frustratingly proved too much for me these days – so it was perfect timing.

Ryan is synonymous with energy. Good, fun, bubbly energy, and that was such a wholesome thing to be surrounded by when I so sorely lacked it. I felt lifted up inside just to have Ryan with me, and with so much passion spilling from him, I was infected before I even knew what he was here for.

'Hiya, Al. My God you're looking rough,' he said, with an inflection that made it an amusing start rather than an insulting one.

'Mmmm-hmmmm, don't I know it,' I replied, trying to inject the sass I knew Ryan was searching for – as evidence I was still all right. I must have been more convincing than I felt for he continued full steam ahead. I never knew how he managed to talk for so long without taking a breath, I just mused that he'd missed a stellar career as an underwater Houdini. Think how much he'd have loved the show and performance!

'So, you know what I'm like about my facts and evidence, Al, and you know I love you more than life itself? But I was worried about your sanity when you started up with this whole "I'll still love him because my heart will and it will still beat" bunkum.'

I raised my eyebrows at him and he flapped his hand at me to dismiss my admonishment.

'It turns out maybe you're onto something. That story I read out to you the other day … wait for it … it wasn't a fluke! Now I've found your Two, I thought I'd better look into how seriously I need to take this stuff, and it turns out there are more fascinating cases out there – stories from transplant recipients you just would not believe. I certainly didn't believe them at first, even when I'd read the very words in black and white on the page. So, I managed to do some digging and got some phone numbers and I spoke to a couple of them. You just couldn't make this stuff up, Al, I'm telling you. Even a hard-hearted cynic like me is converted to your airy-fairy malarkey after this.'

I admit to being intrigued and excited by the stories, but even more so by how delighted Ryan sounded and with the knowledge that with this new attitude he'd do the most incredible job of delivering the manual and the set-ups just right.

'Did you bring any of them with you? Tell me, tell me!' I demanded.

Ryan had been pacing the lounge floor in front of the rustic coffee table up to this point – he liked to be moving – but at this he produced a folder from his shoulder bag with a flourish and settled down next to me on the sofa, all scrunched up with me so that I could read as he did. The drama queen in him didn't leave it there, he wanted to read all the stories out to me. I have to confess the theatrics did add to the occasion. These stories deserved a bit of occasion.

'Okay, so these cases are all taken from the work of Paul Pearsall, same as that first one. I've looked into him more and he was a neuropsychologist and a man of international renown and acclaim in his field.

'Okay, so the first story we have is Sara and Susie's. I'll just read them as they came off the website, so they haven't been altered by my theatrics one bit.

'Sara was a nineteen-year-old woman killed in an automobile accident. The recipient was Susie – a twenty-nine-year-old woman diagnosed with cardiomyopathy secondary to endocarditis. The donor's mother reported,

"My Sara was the most loving girl. She owned and operated her own health food restaurant and scolded me constantly about not being a vegetarian. She was a great kid — wild, but great. She was into the free-love thing and had a different man in her life every few months. She was man-crazy when she was a little girl and it never stopped. She was able to write some notes to me when she was dying. She was so out of it, but she kept saying how she could feel the impact of the car hitting them. She said she could feel it going through her body."

'The recipient reported, "You can tell people about this if you want to, but it will make you sound crazy. When I got my new heart, two things happened to me. First, almost every night, and still sometimes now, I actually feel the accident my donor had. I can feel the impact in my chest. It slams into me, but my doctor said everything looks fine. Also, I hate meat now. I can't stand it. I was McDonald's biggest money-maker, and now meat makes me throw up. Actually, whenever I smell it, my heart starts to race. But that's not the big deal. My doctor said that's just due to my medicines. I couldn't tell him, but what really bothers me is that I'm engaged to be married now. He's a great guy and we love each other. The sex is terrific. The problem is, I'm gay. At least, I thought I was. After my transplant, I'm not … I don't think, anyway … I'm sort of semi- or confused-gay. Women still seem attractive to me, but my boyfriend turns me on; women don't. I've absolutely no desire to be with a woman. I think I got a gender transplant."

'The recipient's brother reported, "Susie's straight now. I mean it seriously. She was gay and now her new heart made her straight. She threw out all her books and stuff about gay politics and never talks about it anymore. She was really militant about it before. She holds hands and cuddles with Steven just like my girlfriend does with me. She talks girl-talk with my girlfriend, where before she'd be lecturing about the evils of sexist men. And my sister, the queen of the Big Mac, hates meat. She won't even have it in the house."'

Ryan wiggled his eyebrows at me like they were a pair of deranged caterpillars. 'What do you think?' he asked.

'I think it's amazing. Next one, next one!'

Ryan grinned at me before replying, 'Your wish is my command! How does the whole world not know these stories?' I shrugged. Ryan continued. 'Okay, which one next? Ah, that's right, we'll go with this fellow. Ready?'

I nodded eagerly. This was exactly what I'd hoped for.

'The donor was a thirty-four-year-old police officer shot attempting to arrest a drug dealer. The recipient was a fifty-six--year-old college professor diagnosed with atherosclerosis and ischaemic heart disease.

'The donor's wife reported, "When I met Ben [the recipient] and Casey [Ben's wife], I almost collapsed. First, it was a remarkable feeling seeing the man with my husband's heart in his chest. I think I could almost see Carl [the donor] in Ben's eyes. When I asked how Ben felt, I think I was really trying to ask Carl how he was. I wouldn't say that to them, but I wish I could have touched Ben's chest and talked to my husband's heart. What really bothers me, though, is when Casey said offhandedly the only real side effect of Ben's surgery was flashes of light in his face. That's exactly how Carl died. The bastard shot him right in the face. The last thing he must have seen is a terrible flash. They never caught the guy, but they think they know who it is. I've seen the drawing of his face. The guy has long hair, deep eyes, a beard, and this real calm look. He looks sort of like some of the pictures of Jesus."

'The recipient reported, "If you promise you won't tell anyone my name, I'll tell you what I've not told any of my doctors. Only my wife knows. I only knew that my donor was a thirty-four-year-old very healthy guy. A few weeks after I got my heart, I began to have dreams. I would see a flash of light right in my face and my face gets real, real hot. It actually burns. Just before that time, I would get a glimpse of Jesus. I've had these dreams and now daydreams ever since: Jesus and then a flash. That's the only thing I can say is something different, other than feeling really good for the first time in my life."

'The recipient's wife reported, "I'm very, very glad you asked him about his transplant. He is more bothered than he'll tell you about these flashes. He says he sees Jesus and then a blind flash. He told the doctors about the flashes but not Jesus. They said it's probably a side effect of the medications, but God we wish they would stop."'

Neither Ryan nor I had heard Alex return, so caught up in the story were we, but we certainly heard his thumping about as the lounge door crashed shut and he thudded through to the kitchen. My eyes met Ryan's and widened with alarm – I knew Alex would have hated to hear any talk of the after stage. I jumped up from the sofa, albeit like an old granny such was my deteriorating agility and rushed through to the kitchen to join Alex. He was pushing food into the fridge with such ferocity I worried we'd have an omelette where we should've had a carton of eggs.

'I'm sorry you had to hear that, Alex, really I am – we didn't hear you come in.' I paused to let that work. 'But there are some incredible stories in there, that are so moving, if you wanted to give them a chance I think it could help.'

'No thanks, Alice, you know how I feel, I won't give those thoughts a moment of this time – I'll be living with them for eternity and that will be more than I can bear.'

I thought about it for a second. I understood – I think I would have felt the same if the positions had been reversed. However, I knew these stories could bring him a tiny piece of comfort when the time came and might also help him believe when my Two began her magic. So, I left him with his egg-crushing after a final question:

'Okay, I understand, really I do. Maybe I could ask Ryan to leave them though, safe in the drawer in the coffee table – so you have them, just in case you ever want to take a look. Would that be okay?' I went to him and wrapped my arms round him from behind. I felt some of the tension drain away from him.

'Yes, that would be okay, Allie,' he said softly.

I went back into the lounge where Ryan was sitting still on the sofa, looking contrite.

'Sorry, Al, I didn't know he was there, is he okay? Shall I go?'

'You have nothing to be sorry for, Ryan, we're not doing anything wrong. And, no, stay right there, mister, I need another story. We have time for one more while Alex puts the food away. Please tell me you've saved the best until last?'

'As a matter of fact, missy, I think I have!' Ryan said with a smile. 'The donor was a sixteen-month-old boy who drowned in a bathtub. The recipient was a seven-month-old boy diagnosed with tetralogy of Fallot (a hole in the ventricular septum with displacement of the aorta, pulmonary stenosis, and thickening of the right ventricle). The donor's mother, a physician, noted, "The first thing is that I could more than hear Jerry's [donor's] heart. I could feel it in me. When Carter [the recipient] first saw me, he ran to me, and pushed his nose against me and rubbed and rubbed it. It was just exactly what we did with Jerry. Jerry and Carter's heart is five years old now, but Carter's eyes were Jerry's eyes. When he hugged me, I could feel my son. I mean I could feel him, not just symbolically. He was there. I felt his energy. I'm a doctor. I'm trained to be a keen observer and have always been a natural-born sceptic. But this was real. I know people will say that I need to believe my son's spirit is alive, and perhaps I do. But I felt it. My husband and my father felt it. And I swear to you, and you can ask my mother, Carter said the same baby talk words that Jerry said. Carter is six, but he was talking Jerry's baby talk and playing with my nose just like Jerry did.

'"We stayed with the ... [recipient family] that night. In the middle of the night, Carter came in, and asked to sleep with my husband and me. He cuddled up between us exactly like Jerry did, and we began to cry. Carter told us not to cry because Jerry said everything was okay. My husband and I, our parents, and those who really knew Jerry have no doubt. Our son's heart contains much of our son and beats in Carter's chest. On some level, our son is still alive."

'The recipient's mother reported, "I saw Carter go to her [donor's mother]. He never does that. He is very, very shy, but he went to her just like he used to run to me when he was a baby. When he whispered, 'It's okay, mama,' I broke down. He called her 'Mother', or maybe it was Jerry's heart talking. And one more thing that got to us. We found out talking to Jerry's mom that Jerry had mild cerebral palsy mostly on his left side. Carter has stiffness and some shaking on that same side. He never did as a baby and it only showed up after the transplant. The doctors say it's probably something to do with his medical condition, but I really think there's more to it.

'"One more thing I'd like to know about. When we went to church together, Carter had never met Jerry's father. We came late, and Jerry's dad was sitting with a group of people in the middle of the congregation. Carter let go of my hand and ran right to that man. He climbed on his lap, hugged him, and said, 'Daddy'. We were flabbergasted. How could he have known him? Why did he call him dad? He never did things like that. He would never let go of my hand in church and never run to a stranger. When I asked him why he did it, he said he didn't. He said Jerry did and he went with him.'"

Chapter Twenty-Six

I never wanted this to be some kind of manual for life from beyond the grave. Being handed a death sentence doesn't make me any more qualified to advise others on their mistakes and regrets, believe me, I know that. But, if you'd be so kind as to overlook this one little exception, I would love to share my one regret so there's a chance our heart doesn't have to hold that hollowed-out feeling twice over. I'm sure you'll have heard it before, after all it's in every quote book, it finds its way into films, and it's spouted by so many people: tell the people you love that you love them. At every opportunity, and with complete conviction. Also, tell the people who brighten up your day that they made the sun shine. Smile at someone and remember that the people who can't smile back are the ones who need it the most; hold the door open for someone; help someone with their shopping; really look someone in the eyes, see them, see what they need right now in this moment, and do it for them – strangers, friends, loved ones. Don't let the opportunity to be something good in that person's day pass you by. Tell everyone who ever brought goodness or brightness into your life that they made the world a little bit lovelier just by being in it. That's the stuff which can change someone's whole day. That's the stuff which can change someone's whole life. And we all need every little piece of goodness we can get. Don't underestimate its impact or power.

Say the things that deserve to be said; don't let the words die in your heart.

Chapter Twenty-Seven

It's no secret my mum and I are rather huge fans of the classic afternoon tea. Scones piled high with sweet strawberry jam and thick clotted cream; tiny little crustless triangular sandwiches; dainty tarts and cakes; and the wonderful company of my mum – those were some fantastic afternoons. We had ventured to lots of different venues over the years, our favourites being stately homes. Being in Oxfordshire, we were fortunate to have plenty of country houses nearby and believe me, we'd done the rounds. We went back to our absolute favourite – Hartwell House – every year. We always threw ourselves into it and felt so (unusually!) ladylike – we waltzed up the sweeping drive, white pebbles crunching underfoot, arms linked, an extra spring in our steps, our heads held a fraction higher than usual, giggles escaping from both of us every so often. The grand door would be opened for us by a doorman dressed traditionally, and it was like stepping back in time. The rooms were so elegant and refined, the service impeccable – it was truly like we were two ladies of the manor, and we loved this massive treat so much. I always felt like an imposter though, dressed in my modern-gal attire of dark jeans and a blouse. I've never felt any inclination for dresses so puffy they look like they should be *on* the afternoon tea as a pastry, yet in those moments of grandeur I felt like I would be open to giving one a go – anything else seems so common, ordinary, and boring. Anyway, Mum and I love feeling like we're on the set of a period drama, and I had a plan to spoil Mum with a trip to the mother of all afternoon teas – at The Ritz in London. It had the reputation of being the fanciest, grandest, most impressive of all afternoon tea options, and no one could have deserved an experience like that more than my mum. It meant a trip into London, which Mum didn't like to do very often due to the frantic busyness of the capital, but I knew it would be worth it and I'd planned it for a Sunday to avoid the worst of the bustle.

I upscaled everything to give us a girls' day to top them all, starting with first class tickets on the train. This meant enough leg room to Morris dance in our seats had we so wished (we didn't), and a regular procession of smiling servers offering us tea, coffee, bacon rolls, panettone, fruit, and all manner of refreshments. It was lovely, and we took advantage of it all, it momentarily slipping our minds that we had to work our way through a feast in a few short hours. This wasn't my first afternoon tea rodeo though. I knew I would be consuming nearly my entire bodyweight in cakes over the course of the afternoon – so I'd worn a loose dress with plenty of room for, well, expansion. Mum, however, seemed to have forgotten life's lessons from years of second scones, since she was wearing a rather snugger ensemble which she looked beautiful in, but didn't leave much room for a food baby – oh well, she could always fall back on the 'open button of the trousers' play if the need arose.

We arrived in London, and I ushered Mum into a black cab to whisk us there in style (at least, style on my budget). We chatted amiably to the taxi driver who informed us that he had indeed heard that The Ritz offered the finest afternoon tea of them all which amped our anticipation up even further. It made me happy to see that Mum seemed so delighted. Never usually one to show much excitement, she seemed close to spinning her scarf around her head, whooping, and running through those revolving doors into The Ritz.

The taxi driver pulled up right outside the majestic hotel, and having been infected by our enthusiasm, even got out to open the taxi door for us with a flourish and a bow.

I settled up with our sweetheart of a driver, and we stood before The Ritz. Mum linked arms with me immediately, giving mine a squeeze, as we took a breath to absorb the moment.

The building itself was a beautiful, old, sandstone structure. It was impressive and imposing. The whole frontage oozed quality and luxury. There were striking navy awnings covering the doors and windows, edged, of course, in gold trim. There was a doorman, standing straight-backed wearing a dapper uniform of tails, and he opened the door for us as we approached. Stepping through that door was like stepping into another world. The whole interior was magnificent – a level of luxury I'd only seen in photographs and films. We were shown to the restaurant by a very smart lady, with hair so immaculate I wondered if she had a layer of invisible cling film secretly laid over the top (my locks went rogue moments after I'd tried to tame them, and even the tame version looked positively childish next to this chignon of excellence).

It was like a scene from *The Great Gatsby* in the restaurant, at least to Mum and me. The diners wore clothes that looked more expensive than our cottage and held themselves as though they'd spent a lifetime being berated by a posture coach. The afternoon tea stands were towering up out of the tables, piled high with items that looked like they belonged in an art gallery, not my tummy. Oh, dear, was all I was thinking, The Ritz didn't know what it had let itself in for! Mum and I have good table manners I assure you – it's not as if we'd be holding a chimps' tea party in there – but we'd be devouring those scones where the other ladies were picking at them; and we'd be giggling together where there were barely broken silences at some of the other tables. We were here for a culinary journey of delight – we were planning to enjoy every second and each mouthful.

Once we got settled and had ordered our teas from the dazzling array, our towering stand of delights was brought out to us quickly.

'Mum, just when we thought it couldn't get any better than tiny triangles – they've managed to go one step further – these pinwheels are so adorably dainty!'

'I know, I feel like a queen!' Mum was beaming. 'It just looks too good to eat.'

'Too good not to eat, I say! But we can enjoy the view for a minute longer. Oooh, I know!' I exclaimed, before making eye contact with a waiter who appeared magically at our sides in an instant.

'Would you mind taking a photo for us, please?' I asked.

'Of course, madam,' the waiter replied with a smile. 'Special day is it?'

'Very,' I said. 'We're celebrating each other.' The waiter looked a little surprised but responded smoothly.

'Well, I can't imagine anything better to celebrate,' he said softly and kindly. I passed him my phone, camera loaded.

'It's just the big button at the bottom.'

After a few clicks, he showed us the screen, which showed two happy, lovely ladies grinning from ear to ear with the most heavenly (and huge) cake stand between them. It was perfect.

'Thank you,' I said from the heart. He floated off, and we tucked in.

We started with the petite pinwheel sandwiches, which were so perfectly sized it looked as though the chef had used a protractor. The cream cheese and cucumber ones were weightless, the roast beef and horseradish were rich and zingy. We moved onto the scones, which melted right onto our tongues, the jam sticky and sweet, the clotted cream full and satisfying. We finished with the cake selection. The pastries were fluffy, flaky, and light, the cheesecake like silk, the macaroon bright and cloud-like. It was lucky the cakes were so delicate, otherwise I don't know how we'd have found room, and as much as Mum is a pro at the wrap-up-in-a-napkin-into-the-handbag slide, I think even she realised that wasn't the 'done thing' here.

'Do you think anyone would notice if I opened my top button?' Mum asked, eyes darting about.

'I think if you're sneaky you'll get away with it,' I whispered back.

We stayed for another cup of the very special tea (with actual leaves, that we had to smell and approve before they poured it!) and then headed for home. We got taken care of in first class again as though we were royalty, although I was worried that I would have to roll Mum up her path after she'd been unable to refuse even more refreshments, some of which went the way of her handbag.

'You can't say no, Allie-pops,' she'd hissed, 'they're free.'

I dropped Mum off at home, popping in for a quick hug from Dad, before pulling up at the cottage rather late, and completely exhausted. I wouldn't have swapped that day for the world though. Alex was waiting up for me and having taken one look at my weary face and sunken eyes he bundled me into the shower, before polar-bearing me with the fluffy white towels and carrying me into bed, where he tucked the duvet in tightly around me and sent me off to sleep by drawing on my back, repeating over and over again with his finger 'always'.

♥

I must have overdone it with Mum in London because the next day was one of my bad days. It was also the beginning of the end, though of course I didn't know that at the time. I opened my eyes with a splitting headache, the kind that feels like the world's strongest man is in there somewhere, repeatedly swinging an axe against the sides. I must have groaned as I woke up because Alex, still very groggy himself, reached for me.

Alex is a slow waker. The kind of man who sets thirteen alarms and hits snooze on the first twelve of them. Yes, he plans that, he plans twelve snoozes. Men are from Mars, hey. Even on that last shrill ringing he emerges from the safety of sleep like an angry sloth who has been ripped away from his lads' night. If sloths have lads' nights that is, which, of course, they can't do, I suppose. I'm the opposite end of the waking-up spectrum to Alex – I'm that annoyingly perky, bright eyed, and bushy tailed person who everybody detests at eight o'clock in the morning on the family holidays – awake early, humming away, irritatingly cheerful, and ushering everybody along to the day's activity. So, I'm a morning person, and I'm damn proud that I am!

Anyway, Alex slung an arm my way, and pulled me to him, nuzzling my neck as he did so. I feel bad about what happened next, I really do – I shrugged him off. I know, I know, we had so few mornings left together, and I did that. I felt like a pantomime villain, believe me, all purple velvet suit, long gnarly fingernails, and an evil cackle. My only defence is that words can't describe the level of pain that was trying to rip my head off my body, so I just had to get up to find something to do to distract myself from the pain as well as getting to the painkillers in the kitchen straight away. Alex would normally fall straight back to sleep. So, I lifted his arm up, and wriggled out. I looked back, when I was in the doorway, and his eyes were closed, his thick, dark lashes resting still. I was in the shower a few minutes later, pain killers taken, when he came thundering in, shouting.

'Alice, are you here, Alice?!'

I popped my head around the steamed-up shower screen and replied, 'I'm here, it's okay, and could you not shout please, I have a terrible headache.'

Alex was all in a rage.

'What happened, Alice, I've told you before to wake me up and let me help. I could've got you the painkillers. Besides, how do you think I felt when I woke up and you were just gone?'

'Well, first, I'm always up before you, so why would you think anything at all? Second, you know I don't want you to remember me this way – needy, pain riddled, and dominated by the monster.'

'Alice, don't you get it? I want to help. I need to help. I signed up for this remember, in sickness and in health. So, stop taking these things away from me, please. I want to be involved, we're supposed to be partners, it's not fair for you to choose when to rely on me and when to go it alone.' Alex's voice was rising again, he was getting increasingly agitated. 'And, obviously I worry now that something could happen to you and I sleep through it.'

'Alex, please be quieter. We can't live like this. We can't let it win. I'm not willing to give it any of our moments together. It will poison these remaining days if we submit to it.'

Suddenly, it turned. Clearly months of emotion had built up and, like the walls of a damn bursting, waves were coming at me like a tsunami now.

'Fuck you, Alice. Stop fucking preaching to me, acting like some heaven-sent angel of wonder with all the fucking answers.'

'I'm not saying I do have any answers, Alex, I'm just trying to make it easier.'

Alex dropped his head into his hands and slid down the bathroom door until he was like a puddle on the floor, broken.

'Well, just stop, please. It's not going to be okay at all. You're the lucky one. You have it easy. You get to go. You get to leave all this fucking hurt and pain and mess behind. You get to leave and be free, as you say frolicking around in heaven. And I'll be here, all alone. You'll be gone, and I'll have to live every fucking day for the rest of my life without you. I have to live in agony forever. Don't pretend that's okay.'

A violent silence stretched between us, separating us more effectively than any chasm could.

Then I felt it. The monster attacked me so quickly I stumbled out of the shower, water flying everywhere, and just made it to the toilet in time. Monsters like mine are crueller than anyone imagines. They take everything. It is so undignified, sitting naked on your wet bathroom floor with your head leant over a toilet, retching up bile. I didn't want Alex to see me like this, so I tried to usher him away. I'm lucky that he's such a hero because he let the tension flow out of his body and he came and knelt behind me, and he held my hair out of the way while he rubbed my back. When it was over, he wrapped me up in a towel and held me close to him.

'I'm sorry, Alice, I just don't know how I'll do this without you.'

'Do what?'

'Live. Breathe. Exist.'

Chapter Twenty-Eight

For this next instruction, you're going to have to be spontaneous – grab life by the snowflakes and go wild. I'm sorry but I can't help to organise any of it for you and neither can Ryan this time since you might be waiting years for your chance to help this memory along, or it might fall into place this first year around. Sorry, sorry, I know, again with the puns – fall into place – because snow falls! I just can't help myself, but don't worry you've not got to put up with my punny-ness for much longer – this is one of the last instalments.

So, this one is a chance to have some seriously good fun. And to make some wonderfully entertaining memories. If you find a blanket of pure, beautiful, crisp snow has fallen then drop everything, pick up the phone, call Alex, and arrange to meet him on the hill. He'll know where it is – it's on a map in the folder attached to this so that you can find it too. Don't worry, it's not far away from our cottage.

You'll need to gather the following things together before heading straight to the hill, and to Alex: carrots, pebbles, a hat, scarf, and gloves, three lumps of coal, an old wooden toboggan, and a flask of hot chocolate. If you haven't got a toboggan, text Alex to bring ours. It goes without saying that you should wrap up warm. You can't don a hat too woolly or a scarf too snug for what lies ahead. I won't try to micromanage you – at least, not beyond the excessive level that this whole manual already does – but if I can offer a tiny, friendly tip it would be to have most of the list ready and assembled if snow is forecast so that you get minimum worry about remembering everything and maximum enjoyment when the time comes.

Now, I appreciate that you don't have be Sherlock Holmes to guess what you have in store, but you definitely won't understand the magic and fun until you live through it yourself.

Alex was originally, just like with all occasions, not against snow per se, he just didn't understand the point of spending time in it. According to Alex, snow was for the young. He believed you had to leave the gleeful abandon of snowball fights and the unadulterated joy of lying on the soft, cushion of snow, and becoming a snow angel, behind you as fond memories of childhood times. I say believed because just like Pancake Day, and his birthday, and Christmas, Alex indulged me and my snowy flights of fancy, and even though he'll most likely not admit it, he's now the one who throws the first snowball, instantly flings himself down, and flaps his arms to create angels in the snow and who drags us out the door, cumbersome toboggan lodged underneath his arm, when the world goes white.

The very first snow we shared together was during our second Christmas in the cottage – the year after the Christmas lights tradition began. It had snowed for the first time that year and it was a great fall, inches thick, absolutely pristine, and perfectly powdery. I think Alex jumped out of his skin when I ran into the bedroom first thing in the morning screeching, 'Get your things, this is so exciting!' I was literally bouncing up and down in front of him, while he tried to get enough sense out of me to figure out what his reaction was expected to be. When he understood that I was this excited about the snow he launched into a long diatribe about not seeing the point. Don't fall into the trap of engaging with that if he springs it on you too, just remind him of how I'll be feeling if I'm there with you both, hearing his lack of snow-born happiness. That should jolly him along a bit I hope.

Not to be dissuaded, I ran to the woollies box and gently but enthusiastically smushed a bobble hat onto his head, pushed his arms into his thickest coat and coaxed mittens onto his hands. I grabbed our supplies and just said to him 'let me show you?' to which he nodded and off we set, hand in hand.

Now, I don't know if you're a city girl or a country girl, so I don't want to presume that you have or haven't been in fields of undisturbed snow before. I'll tell you all about it in case you haven't experienced it but please forgive my ramblings if you have. That day the snow was perfect, and I was so familiar with the area around our cottage that I knew just the peaceful wilderness to take Alex to. We got to the first stile into the fields nearby and as Alex hopped down to the ground on the far side of it he gasped. Until you've seen snow like that you can't imagine the brightness. Your eyes squint up to offset it but they desperately want to open so wide to take it all in. The other thing you can't imagine is the silence. There is no other silence quite as strong, or complete, as a snow silence in nature. It feels like time has been paused. There is a stillness surrounding you that makes you feel as though everything has just stopped, everything except for you, and in this case, the man you love.

Alex and I were so in tune with each other, always, not just that day, that I could feel that it was at that moment that he let go. He let go of all his adult expectations, responsibilities, reluctance, and disappointments, and he threw himself into this escape from time and from reality, with wild abandon. I was half over the stile and he scooped me up underneath the knees and around my back, full romance style, and he twirled me round and round. 'You're completely and utterly magical,' he said to me. 'I simply can't believe someone as totally spectacular as you, actually exists! And I'm the one holding you in my arms.' Alex bent his head to mine and he kissed me deep, long, and hard. Then, he let us both fall to the ground and he rolled us around before grabbing a fistful of snow and shoving it underneath my scarf. I shrieked, and somehow it echoed around that open space like a booming gong of release. Alex's face was hilarious – he looked like a cheeky, impish, little boy on Christmas morning. I was so happy. This man who had been raised within boundaries, and taught to be contained, had been let out, and he was loving it. Perhaps loving it a little too much if the frozen, wet, ice, and water against my neck was the overwhelming evidence.

I shouted like a war cry, 'Oh it's on, you have no idea what you've started!' I grabbed fistfuls of snow and tried to find my way to some skin to rub them into. Alex was far stronger than me and he gripped my wrists with a delighted grin on his face and kissed me again. I enjoyed a few minutes of that – who wouldn't – but he'd started something, and boy was I going to finish it. So, I wriggled out of his grip and scrambled away. Now, this is where you have the chance to gain the upper hand, just like I did. What I lacked in strength I made up for in snowball crafting skills. I was almost an artisan snowballer. Alex had a childhood lacking in snowball fights and had gained no match practice since, so whereas his efforts slid off his hand or arced a few feet before crumbling apart mid-flight, my snowballs were torpedo-like balls of weaponry. Luckily, I also had a stonking arm, if I do say so myself, so those little balls of cold greatness hit their target every time; and with a thud. Breaking apart on impact, they did their job. Alex soon gave up on his own snowball forming and simply dedicated himself to, quite literally, taking down the enemy. He chased me round that field like Tom chases Jerry. I was agile, and let's not forget, I was armed and firing, and only a marine would be able to continue on despite my frozen hits square in the face. Alex may have been a hero, but he wasn't marine level, so the chase went on.

He will protest until he's hoarse that he beat me fair and square, but, truthfully, I let him catch me. He wrestled me to the ground and we lay side by side, hand in hand, for a few minutes while we caught our breaths. Never mind marathon-running there is no harder cardio workout than an adult-only snowball fight, let me assure you. He then rolled on top of me before kissing me again and whispering into my ear, 'You're the most beautiful thing I've ever known.'

So, take out the hand-holding and the kissing, and start this snow-fest. Get Alex to climb the stile first, and then jump onto his back, with a snowball in your hand ready to push down the back of his neck as you leap on, ninja style. Jolly him along if you have to, but snowballs must be thrown, chasing must occur, and no end of fun must be had. If you're an experienced snowballer then so much the better, but if you're a snowy novice then don't worry, you can switch roles and be the Jerry to Alex's Tom – he's had a lot of practice since that day, and Alex is great at everything he puts his mind to. Suffice it to say, I don't have to let him win anymore.

Once you've had your fill of the fighting fun, lead him onto the next phase, the hill. If you thought that those fields were an oasis, then you're about to enter a wonderland. Wind your way along the footpath in the next field (you'll need the signs to guide you) and you will see a copse of trees climbing a hillside. There's a path through these trees from the bottom of that hill to the top. It is narrow and it's steep but if you're lucky the sun will be shining like it often does after a snowfall and those sun beams will find their way between the tree branches to light up the path. As they stream through, making the enchanted snowy forest even brighter, you will wonder how you ever thought you'd seen beauty before, until today, until you're standing in that snowy tree-lined tunnel, looking at Alex.

When you see the hill, don't be afraid. Yes, the narrow path is lined by spiky hazards, and, yes, some serious speed and momentum is gathered, but, since you're alive anyway, why not live a little!

You will find it a tight squeeze on the toboggan with Alex, but I suggest you ride with him the first time or two, since he knows how to steer it, and how to stop it, and if all else fails he'll cushion your landing. He's very gallant like that. Besides, like with most things in life, this is far more fun when shared. The only way to squeeze you both on will be for Alex to climb on cross-legged and for you to squash on, flush against his chest, sat on top of his crossed legs, with your legs tucked right under your chin and your feet resting on the ropes on the front that Alex will be holding. He'll keep you safe, honestly. He's got the mad hero skills remember. Then, you need to dig through all the parts of yourself until you find the piece that spent a former life in the belly of a bobsled – Cool Runnings style – and bring that piece right out to play. Alex will push you both off the brow of the hill and you will fly. The air will be too still to whoosh past your ears, and even if it could, the bobble hat will block it out, but you will feel like you're slicing through space. You'll gather momentum quickly and the trees will pass by you in a blur so close you could reach out and feel them brush your mitten-clad palm. Alex's arms will be pressed tightly to your sides and you'll move with him as he sways to steer the toboggan out of the trees' path. I used to feel totally surrounded by him, his breath on my cheek, his chin resting on my shoulder. We were so connected it felt like we were the same person, that there was no end to me and beginning of him.

We flew so fast down that hill that the air dragged tears from our eyes and whoops from our lungs. I felt more than I'd ever felt before. There was no easy, gentle stop at the bottom, though. Alex had to roll the toboggan, so I found myself lying on the soft snow, arms tangled up with Alex's arms, legs tangled up with Alex's legs and there had never been a more beautiful mess.

Erghh, I'm so jealous of you right now, but that's exactly how it should be, because that will mean Alex has let go, has let himself have fun again, has let himself find his way back to the man I love with all my heart and soul. So, don't let even an ounce of guilt creep into that day. I'll be smiling right beside you if you've managed to get him on that toboggan. And if you can get him shouting with wild abandon on his way down, know that you've hit the mother lode, and that never mind me being an angel, the real angel will be the girl on the toboggan shouting along with him.

You will want to keep going on that toboggan until you physically can't climb back to the top again. You will, of course, have both forgotten about the long walk home. That flask of hot chocolate will be just what you need to fuel you up for the way. You will have to drag yourselves, and each other at times, back across those scenic fields to the cottage. When you finally make it there you will collapse in a heap on the sofa, and, I expect not move for a good while.

That first snow day it was me who roused us eventually with a sudden, and probably startling, exclamation of, 'Okay, snowman time!'

Alex let out a long and melodramatic moan before replying with, 'Come on, Alice, surely not, I can't move.' I somehow found the energy to bounce up, grab his hands, and start trying to pull him up.

'Please, please, please. The snow could start melting any moment.' I could feel Alex's weary gaze stare deep into my eyes,

which must have been bright and sparkling with excitement, before he let me drag him up.

'Fine, a snowman you say? Your wish is my command.' He paused, and then a eureka look exploded in his eyes. 'First, a full-works hot chocolate! The snow can wait five minutes, and this is a hot chocolate day if ever there was one. It'll fuel us through this crazy snowman idea of yours.'

I nodded with a big grin and followed Alex through to the little kitchen. He never let me help, the hot chocolate recipe was his best kept secret, so I just fidgeted and chattered to him while he whisked and warmed and then squirted the cream on top. I tucked in so fiendishly that I got that cream all over my upper lip.

Alex laughed when he saw me and said, 'Ha, my very own Santa!' Before promptly coming over and kissing it all off. That kiss got longer and deeper and Alex made a very persuasive argument for there being far more exciting things to do than build snowmen, which was tempting I assure you, but I reminded him that our bed would be there all night and the snow wouldn't. Sorry – a case of too much information!? Mental pictures that can't be unseen and all that? Well, I'll move my ramblings along then. Alex was so amazing, he dutifully pulled his hat back on, and his mittens, and without any suggestion from me he burrowed around in the fridge for a carrot which he brandished with glee.

You need to include the hot chocolate, if for no other reason than to regain strength between such strenuous activities. Besides, as you surely know by now you've not experienced culinary mastery until you've had Alex's hot chocolate swirling round your mouth. So, ask him to brew up two mugs, insist on whipped cream, though hopefully you can be a more elegant drinker than me and avoid the moustache mistake.

The front garden of our cottage, as you know, has a patch of lawn next to the parking space in front of it. It seemed the right thing to do to give our snowman the companionship of other fellow frozen friends that had taken up residence in the front gardens of some of the neighbours. There was plenty of undisturbed snow on our patch, and it was the ideal snowman type – crunchy and with enough air in it to compact solidly and with stability. I could tell early on that this would be a mighty man. It was a lovely place to do it, with the giggles of neighbouring children music to our ears and our little rustic picket fence, complete with picture perfect robin perched on top making it feel one hundred per cent like home.

For someone so averse to the concept, and so inexperienced in the ways of forming small men from snow, Alex took charge both very rapidly and very capably. He set me off rolling the snow around to form the bottom body-ball while he went off to gather the coal, sticks, hat, scarf, gloves, and pebbles. He hunted, and scavenged, and entertained the children with his questions to them about their magnificent snowmen. He built everyone up that day, like he always did, not just the snow.

I patted, and I compacted, and I sculpted, and I shaped until I'd built a snowman with a rocking bod. He was everything a snowman should be – portly, and round, and three tiered. Alex gave him a wolf-whistle when he appeared round the side of the cottage armed with sticks with mittens on the ends. He proffered them to me, but I insisted he do the honours. Alex placed the sticks into the snowman's upper body with painstaking precision. He set the bobble hat upon his head with care and he pushed the carrot and the pebbles into his face with tenderness. He made our snowman dapper with his coal buttons and he stood back proudly to survey our masterpiece. He collared one of the children to take a photo of us with Jack – Jack Frost of course. We crouched down beside Jack, put our arms around him and smiled the most authentic and genuine smiles there are. Redder-nosed than Rudolph, Alex was breathtakingly handsome that day. I'm sure you've lost your breath yourself when you've seen the photo – it's the one that sits proud as punch in the centre of the mantelpiece.

You need to make Jack his Jill. So, pink hat, and scarf – tell Alex that he needs to make sure of that, since you will no doubt be tasked with Jill's actual creation. You can't pat too hard, or roll too smoothly, trust me. Make sure you get your own photo, and as a last gesture to me, maybe you could make Jill a tiny bit less magnificent than Jack? I know it doesn't make sense, but somehow it makes me feel better to think of it – of Jack keeping his top spot as number-one snowman to rule the cottage's lawn.

Only one thing left to do, I promise. Either side of Jill, lie down in the snow and spread your wings. Make some beautiful angels. Never will soggy pants have been so worth it. But, thinking about it, do add a spare pair of knickers to that list of things to prepare. It'll be worth the sogginess, but why suffer all the way home, hey?

Make another snow angel for me and ask Alex to lie hand in hand with her for a while, with a mug of his finest hot chocolate beside that snow angel-me.

Your day will be complete at this point, but if you're anything like me you'll have felt when the vibes have seemed off. Please know, if anything, this means you've delivered a stellar performance. Alex and I had such painfully happy memories of snow, but it will be bittersweet for him this time, perhaps, for this upcoming memory will remind him so acutely of what he has lost. This is as personal as it gets so it's a between you and me one – but you deserve to know in the spirit of full disclosure, and so that you can be there for Alex to lean on if he needs it. That first snow day, the one I've told you all about, finished in bed that night with more hot chocolate (and more moustache kisses, and the rest, of course!). We were cuddled into each other, cosy and warm under a duvet so plush and fluffy I regularly got lost in it. It was winter-dark, the lights were off, and I was drifting off into sleep when Alex asked me, 'Allie?'

I mumbled, 'mmm-hmmm,' in reply.

'How would you feel about adding to our snowman dream team ready for the next year we have snow?'

'What do you mean?' I was still groggy and sleepy, and very slow on the uptake.

'I mean, half-you, half-me sounds indescribably perfect. If they're a boy, he'd have to be called Jack, now, but if they're a girl, I'm open to suggestions.' I looked up into Alex's eyes to see a hopeful smile on his face. 'What do you think?' I sat up slowly and pulled out of his arms to sit cross-legged, facing him.

This was huge. And unexpected. But completely marvellous.

'The half-you, half-me part sounds appealing. There's just one problem.'

Alex's face dropped, he looked forlorn, so I let him know my intentions with a soft smile.

'Three is just a bad number, you know. If we want to be serious snowman-ers we'll need to go big. We'd need four of us, maybe even six, to do it right. How do you feel about big teams?'

Alex was fidgeting in the bed with excitement now, his face decked out with a lunatic of a smile.

'I feel great about big teams, they're my absolute favourite kind.'

Chapter Twenty-Nine

Having struggled so much at the end of the afternoon tea at The Ritz day with Mum, and then the horrifying physical aftermath the following day, it became apparent that I was deteriorating, and rapidly.

The only way the airline would allow me to fly was if I required no medical assistance, so we knew I had to get over to America with a few days spare, so that I could fly while I was still fit to travel. The clock on that had just started ticking.

Alex had struggled at first to understand why it was so important to me. I didn't want to tell him about the manual, and my plans for the recipient, since I wanted that to come as a surprise after he'd had time to grieve. I know that grief can be a pain that never goes away, but I didn't want the manual events to interfere with the initial grieving process. I'd explained to Alex that I believed my heart carried almost all of who I was. So, it mattered that my heart would continue its life with someone I could trust with … the essence of me. I must have managed to convey how much it meant to me, because Alex agreed to support the trip. I managed to entice journalist-Alex out, who was so intrigued by the system surrounding British organ donation rules that he delved into research on that for a while, after which he became a champion of choice, and, with that, fully on board with the America planning.

It felt right, therefore, that it was Alex who booked me in for an urgent appointment with Dr Hunter the day after the headache incident, and who whisked me back to those lumpy felt chairs that chafed.

After the initial pleasantries, I got stuck in.

'I'm getting worse, Dr Hunter, and fast,' I said.

'What sort of timeline are we talking about?' Dr Hunter questioned.

'Well, my symptoms hadn't progressed much beyond the ones I had when I first came to you, that is until a couple of weeks ago when I had a terrible day of vomiting. Since then I've felt a steady decline, but no symptoms I haven't been able to cope with – no pain or loss of function. Two days ago, I went to London with my mum for the day. We had a lot of fun.' I smiled. 'But I was really poorly by the time I got home – more exhausted than ever before and I had a headache creeping in. Yesterday I had a debilitating headache, and a lot of vomiting which I thought would never end. No vomiting this morning, and the headache has eased enough for me to function, but the tiredness … it's like they say – in my bones. Plus, sometimes there are black spots in my vision.'

I could feel Alex's angry stare boring into me – I hadn't told him about those yet. They had only started last night, and there had been no need to worry him until we heard what it meant from the expert now sitting before us.

Dr Hunter pinched his lips together so that they shrunk into a very thin line. His eyes sunk a little, and although I'd come into this room knowing it was bad news, my heart still dropped when Alex grasped my hand so tightly the bones crunched together – he knew how to read a situation. He had read this one and found it wanting.

Dr Hunter rested his fingers together to form a steeple, which he looked at for a few moments before talking.

'I think, based on that timeline, and on your specific form of cancer, that things will happen very quickly now, Alice.' Dr Hunter looked at me with sympathy. 'I will prescribe you different medication to take to help with the headaches, ease any pain.' He paused, as he put the green slip of paper into the printer to provide my prescription. He looked me levelly in the eye before continuing. 'Is your plan still to fly to America for the final stage?'

'Yes, it is,' I replied.

'Then my recommendation is that you fly immediately, Alice. In another few days you won't be well enough to manage a long-haul flight.'

'Does that mean …?' I asked, my voice trembling slightly.

'It means, my best estimate would be less than a week.'

Alex let out a quiet moan of despair and was rocking back and forth on his chair. Dr Hunter looked over at Alex, and there was pain in his eyes too. How did Dr Hunter manage it, I wondered, to live among this sorrow, day in day out? We do not understand how many heroes walk among us, dressed in suits, or white coats, or overalls.

Alex composed himself, and the conversation turned to the details of the plan – Dr Hunter wanted to understand the provisions and arrangements; and he was going to liaise with the whole team in New York to ensure things went as well as they possibly could. Dr Hunter pulled me in for an unconventional hug in parting, a whole world of warmth and caring in his grey eyes. Alex and I walked away side by side, hand in hand.

We got home, and Alex insisted on packing for both of us. He hauled suitcases about and thrashed his way around the cottage in a frenzy. It was a new form of his physical working out of things, I just feared this was something that couldn't ever be worked out. At the very least, it let Alex feel in control of something, and that will have been the most helpful thing to him at that moment.

Ryan had made the provisional travel arrangements for all the family, plus my mysterious recipient, though with her being so unwell I knew the flight situation was more complicated. Somehow, though, with his amazing magic touch, Ryan had sorted this too. I wanted to help but he insisted on keeping me out of it – a heaviness I didn't need, he said.

I called Ryan.

'It's time, Ry, book the flights,' I whispered.

Ryan had charmed his way onto a priority waitlist for every flight from London airports to New York there was, meaning that as soon as he gave the go-ahead he'd be given five tickets on the next flight out. He booked our five seats, and we flew, all of us together.

My recipient flew ahead, with special medical support. Ryan had managed to wangle this as part of the pro bono package from the hospital in New York.

Ryan had secured us a comfortable people carrier as a taxi to the airport and I'd made sure his bottom landed on the seat next to mine.

I muttered to him, 'Ryan, please let me pay you back for the flights, I'm sure I could manage it. It feels like too much.' I'd been badgering Ryan since he mentioned the flight cost and that he'd cover them, but he remained obstinate.

'As I've said, what must be, fifty times already, Als,' Ryan hissed back exasperated, before softening his tone to finish the sentence, 'this is what's happening. You're my light. I'll do anything I can to keep you shining on.' Before I had a chance to respond, Ryan chimed out loudly to the back of the taxi, where Mum and Dad were sitting on the back bench, and Alex was on his own in the middle row making a phone call, 'Anyone for a bottle of water? I've got still or sparkling. Got to keep hydrated for the flight – your complexions will thank you later!'

'Still, if you don't mind, son.' Dad was first in. 'Very kind of you, thank you.'

'Oooh, Ryan dear, sparkling sounds wonderful,' Mum responded.

'Still, thanks,' Alex mouthed, between words in his conversation.

Ryan handed the bottles round, including a fizzy one for me. Then he settled back, a satisfied look on his face – he was so thoughtful and caring, and he loved to be able to be so.

We arrived at the airport and there was immediately a flurry of activity around us. Ryan continued to take charge and organise us all. I asked Alex to keep Mum and Dad close, as people were marching about so fast I was worried it was just a matter of time before one of them got sucked into another queue and their luggage checked onto a flight to Timbuktu. Ryan looped his arm through mine as he pushed the trolley with everyone's luggage on it.

Ryan shepherded us all to check-in where the queue was thankfully short and the process smooth. This was harder than I'd naively expected. One foot in front of the other, keep moving, Alice, I told myself. We made it through security without any beeps or pat-downs, which we all know constitutes a minor victory, and before we knew it we were standing in the middle of the departure lounge.

'Do you fancy something to eat, Anne, John?' Alex asked. 'We have,' he checked his watch, 'two hours before we're due to board.'

'Oh, sure then, son, but we're easy, whatever's going will suit us fine,' Dad replied.

'Well, you can have almost anything you could possibly imagine, John,' Alex said with a smile, gesturing to the array of options around us.

'Why don't we find our way to the airline lounge, and see if that's a bit quieter?' Ryan suggested.

'What do you mean?' Alex asked.

'It's all a bit hectic out here, it'll be more restful in there, away from the hullabaloo, and they do food and drinks in there too,' Ryan said with a casual shrug.

'No, I mean, there is no airline lounge, Ryan, for economy travellers,' Alex said, painedly.

'There must be, where else would you go for a comfortable, composed sit down, and a head and shoulders massage before the flight?'

Alex gestured around at the seats laid out in their severe uniform rows, bolted to the floor in the main concourse area.

'Take your pick,' he said, amused.

'Oh dear, no, there must be some mistake.' Ryan looked alarmed. 'It's so noisy here.' I knew how much fun Alex would have with this, and how wound up Ryan would get, so I quickly grabbed Ryan's elbow and steered him to the Starbucks, knowing that the offerings of that green and white siren would mollify him a bit.

'Look, Ryan,' I said, turning him to face it. 'Why don't we get a lemon and poppy seed muffin for the flight and one of your fancy coffees to get us started.'

'Oooh, yes, good thinking, Als.' Ryan replied, brightening.

I shot Alex a stern look and said to him, 'While we go and get coffees for everyone, why don't you find us some seats and work out where Mum and Dad would like to eat?'

'Of course, Allie,' Alex said with a rueful grin.

An hour and a half later we had full tummies from the meal we'd just devoured and were boarded and settled in our seats. Ryan had booked us seats all together and Alex was in the window seat in our row, with me in the middle and Ryan in the aisle seat. Mum and Dad were behind, in the middle, and aisle seats. A young man dressed from head to toe in black, and with headphones appearing to be surgically attached to his head, slouched in the window seat next to Dad. It was a lovely arrangement, and we could all chatter freely.

Ryan was the last to sit down, having stowed everyone's bags in the overhead lockers for us in the jigsaw puzzle that it always turned into. As soon as his sculpted behind touched down on his seat he exclaimed, 'Oh my!' Ryan pressed down on the call button on his armrest and almost immediately an air hostess appeared by his side. She was dressed in a red, below-the-knee skirt, a white blouse, her blonde hair was in a perfect bun, and she wore lipstick the same shade as her skirt, which struck me as a huge achievement.

'Good afternoon, sir. How can I help you?' she asked Ryan with a professional warmth.

'Well,' Ryan began, glancing at her name badge, 'Claire, it seems that there has been a mistake, we've been allocated the wrong seats.' Ryan told the air hostess, gesturing to our row, and flashing Claire an apologetic smile. 'So, I wondered if we could be moved to the correct seats please?'

Claire took a dismissive look at the seats, complete with all of us and the confused expressions on our faces.

'I'm sorry, sir, I'll look into it, but I'm afraid this flight is full. So, there are no unallocated seats. What seems to be the problem with these seats?' Claire's smile didn't move a millimetre – I was very impressed that she managed to keep it and talk through it.

'The issue is the restricted leg room – they must be children's seats, aren't they? You see, my legs are all crammed in, they don't fit right.'

'That is the standard economy leg room, sir, exactly the same as everybody else's. Why don't we look at your boarding card to make sure you're in the right place?'

'But there must be some mistake.' Ryan implored as he handed her his boarding card. 'I always have plenty of legroom and space to make myself comfortable.' He pointed at his knees, which the seat in front was skimming. 'This seat is quite literally crushing my knees, they'll bruise. It can't be right,' he exclaimed flamboyantly with his eyebrows raised so high they'd all but melded into his hairline.

'Unfortunately, sir, these are your allocated seats so there is nothing I can do,' Claire continued, clearly annoyed.

Ryan took the briefest second to assess the situation, and clearly realising any further efforts would be futile, he let his shoulders drop, his indignation fell away, and he replied, 'Well, I suppose it isn't your fault is it, Claire, my dear? You hardly bolted these chairs down yourself. You must get no end of grief from passengers all because of the greed of those big boys in the boardroom. I'll just have to live with these purple knee caps, at least purple is my colour, hey.' Which earned him an eye-roll and the flicker of a smile from controlled Claire before she walked away. There were no limits to his skills.

'I think there must be forms of torture more comfortable than this,' he huffed.

I could hear Mum give a gentle chuckle from the seat behind mine. Ryan had that effect on people – his grumblings were never outraged, or carried the energy of someone angry, they were genuine amazement at incompetence or misfortune, and they tended to gain support from those around, as happened next when the passenger across the aisle from Ryan leant over and said to him, 'First time flying economy, mate?' This burly bloke asked him. 'They call it cattle class for good reason – pile 'em in and squash 'em up.'

'Not my first time in economy, but my first time since I was a child. It's nearly inhumane in here!' Ryan exclaimed.

'Too right, man, too right.' The passenger sighed, before flicking open his newspaper.

'Cabin crew, seats for take-off.' Was announced over the tannoy and a few moments later we were airborne. Mum and Dad coped admirably with the ascent, given they'd not flown much. I'm sure Mum gripped Dad's hand tightly but Dad will have been steady as a rock for her.

Ryan had taken every care to make sure I was comfortable, having brought a little cushion along which he'd tucked in beside me. Alex fussed with a blanket until I felt like a swaddled baby and had to thrash around just to break free of the blanket's claustrophobic grip.

Alex seemed in a bit of a daze, and I recognised this distance as a sign he was struggling to cope with the situation. I leant my head on his shoulder for a few minutes, and he cuddled me into him. I ignored the armrest cutting into my ribcage to let Alex have this time – he was hugging me so hard I was worried the armrest would snap right off. Dad must have seen us from between the seats, and in his customary way knew exactly how to help ease the pain. His face appeared right up against the space between the seats and he exclaimed through the gap, 'Hey, Alex, son, have you seen these films?' Dad was waving the entertainment guide about. I squeezed Alex's leg as he let go of me to twist round to speak to Dad.

'I haven't looked yet – is it a good selection?' Alex replied with a tired smile.

'Amazing. I'm going to be glued to the screen the whole way. I'm hoping I can squeeze three of these good 'uns in. That's if I can figure out how to work this thingy-majiggy.'

'Once the seatbelt signs are switched off I'll get you all set up. It's easy to work once you know how,' Alex said generously.

'They've even got that one we were going to see on the big screen together, before … all this,' Dad chatted jollily, tailing off at the end.

'Oh, you mean, *Dunkirk*, fantastic, John, maybe we could both watch it as our first one, so we're watching it together?' Alex asked Dad.

'That'd be marvellous, son, just marvellous,' Dad responded, grinning happily.

Alex had just made his day. It's the small things sometimes.

The plane levelled off soon after that, and the ping of the seatbelt sign turning off brought a flurry of activity in the cabin. Alex stood up and spoke to Mum.

'Would you mind swapping seats for the first bit, Anne, so that John and I can watch *Dunkirk* together?' Alex asked my mum.

'Not at all, Alex, that sounds like a lovely idea. John was so excited about seeing that with you,' Mum replied with a warm smile before easing herself up and out of her seat. It was a bit of a palaver getting everybody swapped around but well worth it to see Dad's delighted face as the opening scene played out, and for the nudge Mum gave me as she said, 'Well, this is nice, hey, Allie-pops, lucky me.' She had a twinkle in her eye as she beamed at me.

Ryan had got himself all set up with his flying gear out – he had a soft cashmere scarf wound around his neck so the absolute minimum of skin was exposed to the recycled air; he'd taken out his silk eye cover and that was strapped over his head like a headband, even though this was a day flight. He had a litre of water stashed in his seat pocket which he took a sip from every few minutes, passing it to me to do the same.

'Dehydration, darling,' he said, knowingly, every time.

As soon as we were all settled in and sorted, Ryan pressed the call button on his armrest … again. A few minutes later the flustered-looking air hostess returned.

'How can I help you this time, sir?' she asked, in a friendly way, as if expecting to be amused, but with the fixed customer-service smile plastered tightly onto her heavily made-up face. It made me think how lucky I was to have found Alex when I did for with all the 'contouring' (what on earth does that even mean?) and drawn-on eyebrows women seemed to favour nowadays, it seemed that every woman was a Pablo Picasso level artist, and I simply wouldn't have kept up.

'Well, I just wanted to let your team know that since I like to wear this during the flight while listening to my zen rhythm playlist,' Ryan pointed to his eye mask, 'it might seem like I'm asleep, but I don't want to miss the first round of prosecco. Always helps tickle me along on the journey of relaxation.' Ryan gave a little giggle of endearment. 'So, if you don't mind leaving mine with gorgeous Als here,' Ryan gestured to me, 'I'd be very grateful?' Ryan gave the air hostess a disarming smile, and a knowing look, yet this was the first I'd ever heard of zen rhythm playlists, so I'm not sure Claire would "know" as familiarly as Ryan thought.

'Well, sir, I'm not sure what you're referring to by the prosecco round?'

'The introductory drink to get the flight started, usually you lovely ladies, or sometimes it's a dashing gentleman, of course, bring a tray round as soon as we're settled on our way.'

'Perhaps you're used to flying business class, sir?' she replied, with a cheeky edge to her voice. 'For there is no such service here in economy. The drinks service will be round in an hour or so, but there is certainly no prosecco.' She paused. 'Now have a …' she paused, and the corners of her mouth teased up, her eyebrows raised a fraction, '… comfortable flight.'

'Fancy that, Als,' Ryan said to me when she'd walked away. 'How disappointing. I was looking forwards to you getting the luxury treatment.'

'You're the only luxury treatment I need, Ry, don't worry. I think you've just spent too long living the high life – your feet have well and truly left the ground.' I said with a smile.

'This will bring me back down to earth with a bump at least.' Ryan held a hand up against his mouth, aghast. 'Did I just say that? While we're hurtling through the air at hundreds of miles an hour in a metal tube? Oh, my dear Lord, please let that idiocy be forgotten.' Ryan looked heavenward, theatrically. Once again, I didn't think he was joking.

'I'm not becoming one of those poncey types, am I, Al? You'd tell me, right?' Ryan looked concerned. I gave a little giggle.

'No, Ry, but you edge a little closer with all your talk of zen rhythm soundtracks, prosecco service, and economy lounges.' I pointed out gently.

'Oh, good heavens, you're right. You must correct this at once, Als! Chain these Italian leather clad feet to the ground from now on.' Ryan instructed. 'Well, actually, let's leave it until after our New York shopping spree. Prada needs me.'

'I'll do no such thing, Ryan, you're spectacular just the way you are. Don't go changing on me, okay. You promise?' Ryan nodded. 'Now, since there's no prosecco heading to us, let's treat ourselves to those lemon and poppy seed muffins, shall we?' I suggested playfully.

'I like the way you think, Alice Richards,' he responded with a grin, fishing the delights out of his bag.

The flight proceeded peacefully, with Dad and Alex enjoying their shared *Dunkirk* viewing experience, Ryan and I chattering away, with Mum joining in on the girl-talk in between ploughing her way through her latest book club read, which was thicker than my thigh – no mean feat!

However, as, 'cabin crew, seats for landing' was announced over the tannoy, New York laid out below, we all shared looks between us. The fear and pain in everyone's eyes spoke of the same thought – the elephant in the room we'd all done such a good job of ignoring so far: we were flying out as five; they would be flying back as four.

Chapter Thirty

Your next task is one which involves a bright red hat, trimmed with the most unconvincing white faux fur, and topped with a white pompom – a veritable polyester paradise. It also involves the choosing and manhandling of a six-foot, spiky tree that works very hard to prick you and get needles caught in the most uncompromising of places as you drag it into position. Don't worry, I promise it'll be worth it!

Decorating the Christmas tree was always the most special of traditions for Alex and me. It always took place on the first Sunday of December, so you'll have to keep that free please and it has to be done on that exact date. I'm worried that Alex won't get a tree if you don't help him along with it – it will be a terribly difficult thing for him to do alone now. Alex has lost so much that he can't lose the essence of his home too, and our cottage just couldn't be his home without that piney scent flying up his nostrils for the whole month of December, coloured lights twinkling from the branches, and little decorations nestled between the tree's green arms, making their homes among the needles.

The whole of that first Sunday of December was always dedicated to the tree – we'd drive out to get the Christmas tree in the morning. Alex's family never liked the mess of a real tree so this was a new experience for him but there could never be a worthier mess so don't let him slip back into old habits. Early afternoon would be decorating time (my favourite part), closely followed by the wrapping of the presents we'd already got by then, accompanied by unlimited hot chocolates of the most extravagant variety. The presents would be put under the tree to complete the process and we'd finish the day by snuggling up on the squishy sofa in the lounge to watch a Christmas film in the evening, with the door open so the tree glowed through to join us.

We always made the half hour drive to Santa's Christmas Tree Land to choose our tree. This was a plot which – you guessed it! – became a Christmas tree paradise for the month of December. They wove lights through all the paths between the trees, blasted out cheesy Christmas songs over the field and I don't think they granted anyone entry without at least a Santa hat or Christmas jumper, so the place was made from Christmas cheer. My mum and dad had always scraped the funds together for a real tree, and I've kept that tradition alive with Alex.

Alex and I went to Santa's Christmas Tree Land every year on a mission – we wouldn't just bring any old tree home, it had to be The One. Much like us ladies, those trees come in all shapes and sizes – it seems like there are pear-shaped, apple-shaped, hourglass, top-heavy, triangular, and any other shape you can dream up, every year in that field, and as everyone has different Christmas tree tastes, they all find a home. For

Alex and me, when it came to our Christmas tree, perfect was not perfect. We needed a tree with character, one that felt right for us. We went for tall (six-foot was ideal), not too bushy, not too skinny, no bare patches – we didn't mind the odd bulge or crooked branch. After all, I have a bulge or two that I would rather be without! The whole point of it was to have a real, natural, actual tree after all. So, no tape measuring for the perfect shape cone was allowed! The most important thing of all was to make sure there was enough space between the branches for the decorations – they are the jewel in the Christmas tree's crown. Once we'd picked the tree, we asked for Bill – he knows us well – I don't think many of his other customers lingered so long between the rows of trees, chattering about which one belongs with them. We knew we'd found The One because we couldn't leave without it – it always felt like it was meant to be ours. Alex always acted long-suffering as we traipsed about for hours, examining every tree carefully, but no one defended their tree-choice once they'd made it more passionately than Alex did. He would huff and puff when we got back to the car because we'd been there so long the windscreen had iced over; but he merrily mulled the wine for us as soon as we were home, whistling 'O Christmas Tree' as he added the oranges.

You'll be on your own at Santa's Christmas Tree Land though this first Christmas, I'm sorry. I think the best plan is for you to choose Alex's piney pal yourself and then arrive with it at the cottage door – Alex won't be able to turn it away then.

So, choice made, ask Bill to load your precious cargo up onto the roof of your car and then whizz over to the cottage. Put that Santa hat back on (that's a requirement for Christmas

Tree Day, not a suggestion) and ring that doorbell. Have a spare Santa hat with you to gently tug onto Alex's head and lead him to the car to unload the tree and get it safely into its spot in the cottage. Watch out for those pine needles – as I said, you just won't believe where they end up, and they deliver quite the prickle!

We have an unusual bay window in the hallway – between the lounge and the kitchen, at the bottom of the stairs, where the Christmas tree always goes. It welcomes us home from there, and the smell permeates all through the cottage. It's the sight that greets us when we go downstairs in the morning, so we start and finish our day with Christmas spirit, and top up lots of times in between. Alex will have to get the stand for it out of the garage and ask him to make hot chocolates while you put a Christmas playlist on. It must feature 'Do They Know It's Christmas?', 'All I Want for Christmas Is You' and 'Santa Claus is Coming to Town' to get you both in the mood. Can you hold back a smile when you hear Slade blasting out 'Meeerrrrry Christmas Everybody'? – I think not! So, get it blasting!

Now comes the important part – the decorations. We keep the tree very simple – just lights, the few decorations we've collected and an angel on the top. The ornaments themselves will be the hard part, but you have to persuade Alex to push through the pain because I wouldn't want our endeavours over the years to have been for nothing – for the stories of each ornament to stay tucked up on a shelf somewhere in the dark, getting dusty. Those decorations carry memories that need their moments in the light – those multicoloured Christmas lights to be exact. I will leave it up to you to decide how to bring up the decorations and to convince Alex to go and find them – you'll have known him for almost a year now and have shared so many amazing moments together that if you can't manage it then he's throwing you a stubborn curveball that even I can't straighten out.

First things first – the Christmas lights. Due to the tree being simple, and the decorations so special, the lights have to be plentiful – it's their job to light up the magic memories; and they have to be coloured – for the warmth and cheer. It's always my job to untangle them, and yes, I always put them back into their box in a perfect roll, and they emerge in a massive knot – I'm convinced fairies must go in and tangle them all up just so that Alex can have a good giggle as my frustration mounts. Once I've battled my way through the untangling process, I feed them to Alex as he places them on the tree. He shimmies around it, and dives beneath it to get them just right. He makes a real meal of it, and I always have to kiss his tummy better that night as he shows me his war wounds from the spiky tree.

Once the lights are all in place, and tested, it's angel time. I made the angel when I was in nursery so please handle her with care – she is now rather fragile, her wings are wobbly, and her once brilliant white, felt dress is now a rather dull shade of grey – but she always does her job perfectly, protecting Alex and I over the festive period.

Last, the ornaments. So, the story here is that every single ornament is different, and each one has a memory attached. Our tradition is that we each buy a new decoration every year, with a special meaning or history behind it. Ask Alex to tell you the stories of each one as he finds the perfect spot for each to dangle among those bright green arms.

He'll tell you about the snowman I bought for him last year (a bauble snowman head, complete with carrot nose and frosty hair) which Alex scoffed at and said was hideous, until I told him it was Jack Frost, for our snowman, and our snowman team building plans at which point he scooped me up in his arms, kissed me breathless, and Christmas tree decorating had to be put on hold while we had yet another practice run for that matter immediately.

That same year he gave me a hand-made clay Christmas bell that was far too heavy for the branch so sagged down pitifully, but which Alex made with his own hands the morning he looked after his young cousins. A practice-run, he called it when he came home and gave me the bell.

You'll hear about the old-fashioned fabric Santa Claus we bought from the Christmas market we went to in Oxford the year we moved into the cottage. The traditional beauty of the city added to the authenticity of the market to create a fabulous vibe. The stalls were all decorated beautifully, with gorgeous wares, and smiling vendors. The smells were mouth-watering, with roasted chestnuts, warm mince pies, and mulled wine around every corner. Alex will tell you that we tried churros for the first time that evening (one of mankind's finest creations!), and he had to kiss the chocolate sauce off my chin because I made such a mess. As he did, a kindly choir decided to assemble around us (the ladies dressed in long, billowy, heavy red and green dresses and bonnets; the men dressed in white stockings below puffy green three-quarter length trousers and matching tunics). They formed a circle, all joined hands and began regaling us with 'All I Want for Christmas Is You' while a lanky teenage choir member stood on his tiptoes to hold a bunch of mistletoe over us. I went as red as my gaudy Christmas scarf, but Alex pulled me into him for a slow dance, kissed my forehead and whispered, 'How magical is this?' With sparkles dancing in his eyes.

He lowered me into a dip and grinned at me before leaning down for a deep kiss. The choir loved it, the volume increasing enough to attract rather more attention than I'd have liked, until the circle the choir had formed had parted to allow a keen elderly man to lead his white-haired wife into the centre to join in with the dance. They looked over at us and smiled before gazing deep into each other's eyes and shuffling the steps of a dance together. Before we knew it a mini-party had started, the choir getting far more than they bargained for, and having to improvise with a rather more modern repertoire than they'd perhaps been imagining, to satisfy the crowd of dancing duos which had formed before them. It was Christmas magic and Alex and I threw ourselves into it with gleeful abandon.

There are plenty more ornaments, and some very special stories, every single one overflowing with love, but I won't spoil any more of them for you, I want you to lose yourself in the moment, standing before that twinkling majestic beauty of a Christmas tree. Just please make sure our stories get their chance to be dusted down, brought out, and remembered. There is one more thing. I need you to buy a Christmas ornament yourself to add to the collection for this year, so that Alex knows I'm still with him in heart. It needs to be simple, but beautiful.

It can be red or gold, it's up to you; sparkly or glass, whatever you decide, but it needs to be a heart. A strong and glowing heart, just like ours. Save it for the end, hang it on once all the other decorations are in place. Put all that love back up on that spectacular tree, right where it belongs.

Chapter Thirty-One

Ryan had booked us all into one of New York's most impressive and luxurious hotels for the first two nights. It was a wonderful treat for everyone and lovely for me to stay out of the hospital for as long as possible.

After we'd all checked in, Mum and Dad went for an early night in their room and Ryan knocked on the door to mine and Alex's room. Alex greeted him warmly and Ryan marched in and made himself right at home laid out on the sofa next to the king size bed.

'I just wanted to make a plan, if that's okay?' Ryan asked us.

'Of course,' I answered with a wry smile of amusement – I must have heard Ryan utter those same words thousands upon thousands of times before.

'I'm sure you won't be surprised to hear I've had some ideas for how to spend the day tomorrow,' Ryan began enthusiastically. 'We just can't have made it to New York, Als, and not soaked up the wonder of Times Square. Plus, we've spent years dreaming of a shopping spree in New

York, so how about some retail therapy? I could really do with a sharper suit for my afternoon of publicity meetings tomorrow.' He hesitated before continuing, 'With Ben. I mean, Dr Casey.'

'Times Square sounds great and you've spent years dreaming of a New York shopping spree, Ry, so that has to be top of our to-do list. You'll need your trusted companion, and advisor, obviously.'

'Obviously, because I always look so hideous when left to my own fashion devices.' Ryan teased me, and we shared huge grins with each other. Alex rolled his eyes affectionately as he flipped another page of the New York Times over.

'So, shall we try it tomorrow morning, if you're feeling up to it? I'll knock for you at eight o'clock sharp, we'll grab breakfast and a coffee at one of these chic New York coffee houses, we'll have the full experience. Alex, do you fancy it too?'

'Sounds like a plan, I'll be ready,' I replied.

'It does sound tempting,' Alex said generously, 'but since I don't know my Prada from my Gucci I'll leave it to the experts. I'll join in the chic breakfast though, if you don't mind – I've never been labelled as chic before, but if I'm somewhere like that in the company of the world's most stylish man, maybe I finally stand a chance – I don't want to pass that opportunity up. I have to see Alice's face when she sees Times Square too, so I'll tag along for that please and then peel off right before the torrent of Calvin Klein and friends.' Alex winked at me, and Ryan smiled.

'Perfect. Eight o'clock then. I will see both of you lovelies then.' Ryan nodded excitedly, jumped up, and gave me a long, tight hug goodnight.

Ryan knocked on our bedroom door at exactly eight o'clock the next morning. I knew to expect him, since he was always punctual, but I also knew that at times of stress he became even more organised than usual. Where he may give himself a minute's leeway normally he'd allow himself no such liberties over the next few days. We had breakfast and coffee at an espresso bar selected by Ryan which was the fanciest coffee shop I'd ever set foot in. Decked out from top to bottom in pale rustic wood, with beautiful glass domes lined up along the sleek counter top, housing exquisite looking pastries, and offering coffee options that even I, a coffee addict, had never heard of, it was a fabulous experience. Alex and I whispered our orders to Ryan since we were a bit overwhelmed by these fast, professional New Yorkers speaking the foreign coffee language, and Ryan delivered our simpler request like the suave and stylish modern man that he was. He had the barista giggling in seconds and she plucked the three biggest pastries for us, so Ryan's charms had worked once again. Once we were zinging from the strong coffee and satisfied by the delicious flaky pastries we hailed a yellow taxi to take us to the one and only Times Square.

As we whizzed around New York in our nifty taxi to the music of blaring horns, we all took the city in. The streets in the posher parts were wide, with beautiful broad trees thriving amid the pavements. There were older buildings, called brown stones by the New Yorkers, which were grand and traditional. Then there was the slick, glass, and chrome more business and banking district that looked to me like it arrived from the future. There were small coffee carts, wafting wonderful, strong aromas through the air to offset the smog. Ryan asked the taxi driver to pull over next to a hot dog trolley, and even though it was still only mid-morning we all shared one, complete with mustard and ketchup squirted in a squiggle out of two of the brightest bottles I'd ever seen.

'It's my mission to tick as many Yankee experiences off our lists as we can,' Ryan said, earning him a glare from our taxi driver. Ryan wiped a speck of ketchup from the side of his mouth. 'I have to confess that wasn't my favourite experience– I'm more of a Michelin star man myself, I realise.' Alex rolled his eyes at me. 'Let's hope Times Square is more delightful.'

It's safe to say it was. The taxi driver dropped us off a 'block' away, telling us we had to walk in to achieve the full affect. We made our way slowly up the road, Alex holding my arm on one side, Ryan on the other. I was the type of person to be more blown away by stunning beaches and diamond skies than by city scapes, so I didn't think Times Square was ever going to feel the most special for me. As a wilderness and wilds girl, city scenes feel too humanised, and great as us humans can be, we have a knack for ruining things – it horrifies me to think that something as spectacular as Javan

Tigers are extinct because of us. However, Times Square did have a certain kind of magic. It was full of colour from all the animated advertising billboards, and it was bustling with hordes of people bringing along a bold energy. It was a sight that filled your eyes, and even more excitingly there were all sorts of fun shops lining the street.

'Oooh, look, can we pop in there?' I squealed excitedly, pointing to the giant red, orange, blue, green, and yellow M&Ms that made up the signage of an M&M shop. Ryan rolled his eyes and shook his head.

'Als, the New York shopping spree that my dreams are made of was more Gucci and Prada than M&Ms,' Ryan said, his nose scrunching and his lip curling in mock disgust. 'But, I suppose we can never have too much chocolate.'

We wandered around a few shops, having a jolly time, until I was hit by a wave of nausea.

'We need to find a toilet,' I said, agitatedly.

'What, why?' Ryan asked.

'Allie's going to be sick,' Alex fired back, already steering me to the back of the shop we were in. He rushed me into the disabled cubicle, locked the door behind us, and swept my long, loose hair back into his grip just as the first round of vomiting hit. Alex rubbed my back and spoke soothingly to me as waves two, three, and four followed a few minutes apart.

'Okay, I think we'll be all right now,' I said quietly to Alex when it was all over. 'Thank you.'

'Always.'

Alex kissed my forehead tenderly and wrapped me up in his arms for a few moments.

As we emerged from the cubicle, a very distressed Ryan greeted us. Complete with a knot in his brow he'd clearly nearly worn the soles of his finest Italian leather shoes out from all the pacing he'd been doing.

'Is that a common thing, now, Als?' he asked, upset.

I just nodded.

'We need to get Allie back. You seem to have the best luck with the taxis – could you try to flag one down for us?' Alex asked Ryan.

'Err, no. I need to go on the shopping spree with Ryan,' I protested firmly.

'Allie, you need to rest. You look as white as a sheet,' Alex responded, concerned.

'Make that green tinged just like a Trebor Extra Strong Mints wrapper, Als, my gorgeous girl. We don't need to do the shopping spree, I wouldn't dream of it if you're feeling grotty.' Ryan proclaimed.

'But you said you needed a new suit for your afternoon with the gorgeous Dr Casey,' I said with a cheeky smile. 'Besides, after all you've done for me, Ry, I wanted to do this for you – the pair of us on a New York shopping spree like we've talked about for years.'

'Ben will just have to make do with last year's Armani. He wears scrubs all day, so I doubt he'll even notice the difference. It'll be far nicer to snuggle up with a film and try to make some headway through this mountain of M&Ms we seem to have acquired.' Ryan insisted.

'Ryan, you still have to go!' I said aghast. 'I'll only agree to go back to the hotel if you promise to take the New York Gucci and Prada shops by storm. I'd hate it if this wretched thing had cost us another dream,' I said passionately.

'Okay.' Ryan gave in, not that I gave him much choice.

'I'll meet you back at our room at five o'clock, and I'll be requiring a full fashion show.' I instructed Ryan with a grin. 'Complete with your absolutely fabulous strut, twirl, and a lot of, "darlings". Deal?'

'Deal,' Ryan said with a small smile.

'See you later then. I'll save us some fashion show M&Ms.' I promised.

The following morning was typical of New York in late May – a chill biting around our exposed pieces of skin, but dry, still, and bright. Ryan had a busy day ahead with meetings at the hospital, most of which were with Ben. The fashion show had been a roaring success, Ryan was going to look sensational, and we'd both been in stitches by the end of the night. It seemed that the story was gathering momentum, not least because of the camp, gorgeous man with the delightful English accent who was spearheading it. If Ryan had been flush with admirers before (which trust me he was) he now had a whole new fan club this side of the Atlantic. I had a suspicion that Dr Casey might have been the fan club's founder – fingers crossed for my best friend!

So, it was Mum, Dad, Alex, and I together for the day, with Ryan joining us for dinner later. I feared it would have to be room service on our laps again, since I was finding it too exhausting sitting up in restaurants for hours later in the days, but that was okay because it was much cosier for everyone that way – more like our old tradition of fish and chips out of newspaper on Friday nights. It was more comforting to sit with the familiar.

Mum and Dad knocked on mine and Alex's hotel room door at nine-thirty. I'd needed Alex to help me get dressed that morning which had been a new low and having been sick the previous evening, I was hungry and depleted. There was only one thing for it.

'Mum, Dad, I have a special request to make. I need comfort food of the most supreme variety. There is only one place to go, don't freak out, Mum, but I just need it this morning, so please say yes. Can we get breakfast at McDonald's?'

Alex was fighting hard to keep spirits and energy up, so he punched the air as he shouted, 'Yes!' I shook my head in amusement and smiled at him. Dad grinned at him when Mum wasn't looking but remained silent.

'Well, if that's what you want, Alice, of course we can,' Mum answered, surprising everyone with her immediate willingness.

There was a McDonald's right around the corner (I think there must have been golden arches around every corner in New York), so we were there within minutes, peering up at the big, illuminated menu board. Alex and Mum had stepped ahead and were talking between themselves. It gave Dad and me a chance to enjoy our final McDonald's moment together.

'Oh, good heavens, look at all these extra options. What on earth are they? "McGriddle?", "biscuit?" – it's a whole amazing other world. What shall we do? They look so tempting – that griddle thing looks almost like pancakes,' Dad exclaimed, his mouth nearly watering.

'There's only one thing for it, Dad – we have to get one of everything. We can't miss out and never taste the wonders of breakfast biscuits and McGriddles. We can share them between us. How about it?'

Dad looked delighted and excited, as he nodded eagerly. Alex turned around to talk to us.

'I think we're decided, how about you two?' Alex asked.

'Yep, we're ready. If you're ordering, could Dad and I have one double sausage and egg McMuffin.' I smiled at Dad – a smile full of memories, 'one double sausage and egg McGriddle and one double sausage and egg biscuit, please?'

Alex's eyes widened but he grinned.

'Aha, you've gone for the try everything plan. I fully support it. Can I get in on that action?'

'Of course!' I laughed – this was already a lot of fun. 'Have you managed to find something you'll be happy with, Mum?' I asked, hesitantly. Alex was making a face that suggested he was struggling to stay upright and not roll around on the floor with uncontrollable laughter. My eyes widened.

'Oooh, yes, I'm going to try the pancake stack, with extra syrup, and a caramel frappe,' Mum said.

There was silence among the group, all except for Alex, who let a chuckle slip out, which he quickly masked with a throat clear. This, from Mum, was not only hilarious but also astounding – I don't think she'd ever let a single drop of syrup enter her cupboards before, never mind requesting extra of it to grace her plate.

Alex placed the order and carried the mountainous tray over to a booth in the window when everything was ready. We had no booth neighbours, which was nice and private. We unwrapped the options, Dad looking gleeful as we did so, and Alex cut ours all into thirds, so we could each try the American McDonald's' breakfast trifecta. Mum was making great headway into her pancakes, letting out little sounds of satisfaction I didn't think she was aware of. Alex and I exchanged looks of entertainment – Alex had been involved in the convincing of Mum that proper fish and chips on a Friday night wouldn't do any of us any harm (he'd used his persuasive journalistic methods to remind her how important eating fish was for health), and it was Alex who was tasked with getting Mum extra mushy peas to keep her vegetable consumption high enough.

Dad had started with his old favourite, and he was clearly on a mission to maintain our cover.

'Who knew these were so absolutely extraordinary?' Dad mentioned very convincingly. 'Not that your cooking isn't heavenly, of course, Anne, but as a treat, you know, these are quite something.' Dad was wolfing down the McMuffin.

Mum was quiet for a long minute, looking Dad squarely in the eyes.

'Oh, give over, John,' she said, fondly. 'Do you really think I don't know about your breakfast habits? No man needs that much compost, you old doofus.'

'What?! Why have you never said anything?' Dad asked, shocked.

'Didn't want to spoil your fun, did I? It was such a lovely, simple treat for you and Alice to share, there was nothing to gain from me letting on – it would've just ruined it for you. The secrecy was half the fun, I think,' Mum said affectionately.

We munched on quietly for a few minutes – all enjoying the comfort of our filling breakfasts. Dad and I shared a few nudges and surreptitious grins, revelling in our breakfast extravaganza. Even with our cover blown and not a bag of compost in sight, it tasted as fantastic as ever.

'There's nothing like it, hey, Dad?' I asked, rubbing my belly.

'Nothing like it, love,' Dad replied, rubbing his, with a look that rewound time.

Alex finished first, and as Mum was having a good slurp of her decadent caramel frappe, Alex said to her,

'I have a weakness for those myself, Anne. It's a slippery slope though, trust me, once you start the caramel frappe habit, you'll never stop.'

'I know, Alex, dear, you're exactly right. I was so relieved when they started doing them all year round, instead of just in summer. Wiped my brow I did,' Mum replied vehemently.

Always on the lookout for a story, Alex immediately clocked what Mum had just unwittingly revealed. This beautiful lady, who had forced nearly inhumane quantities of vegetables on me for my entire childhood, had been frequenting McDonald's for what must have been years, in secret, to enjoy these cream-covered, sickly-sweet beverages. Within our family, this was a Pulitzer-Prize-worthy discovery.

Bless him, Alex exchanged a sidelong look with Mum, keeping his realisation to himself, but after a few moments I clocked on too.

'Hang on, Mum!' I exclaimed. 'You mean you're a regular caramel frappe consumer?' I was trying for the outraged look, but I couldn't help a smile from slipping out. Mum looked at Alex for a second, but must have realised the jig was up, because she nodded silently. 'When do you sneak those in?' I asked.

'On the way home from my maths after school club on a Wednesday – trust me, if you had to deal with that group, the only thing that would revive you would be one of these darlings,' Mum said defensively, while looking lovingly at the remainder of her frappe.

Dad burst out laughing then, and Alex looked relieved to finally be able to release his mirth, joining in instantly with a hand slapping his thigh for good measure.

'What a palaver, Anne, love. What are we like, hey?' Dad said, between chortling fits. Once Mum realised it was all in good fun, she joined in too, and we laughed until our tummies hurt.

'Alex, you make sure you take this pair of funny old sticks to get their fixes under the golden arches back home at least once a month, okay? Fancy all this! I would never have guessed.' I instructed him in mock consternation before giggling again. Mum, Dad, and Alex all froze comically for a moment, the reality hitting them right between the eyes for a second. My continued giggling broke through it though, for a moment later we were all falling about laughing uncontrollably once more.

Chapter Thirty-Two

This may be hard for you to believe after reading about so many of our romantic moments already but I'm about to tell you about the most romantic moment of my entire life. It makes The Notebook look naff, Romeo and Juliet stupid and Bella and Edward plain second rate. At least, that's what I like to think, but I do accept that my glasses are as rose-tinted as they come where Alex is concerned. The point is, this is romance at its absolute, mushiest, finest. But also, at its simplest, most real. So, in readiness for the next instalment, may I suggest you dash off to fetch either a box of tissues, or a sick bucket, depending on your feelings towards big romantic gestures.

It will be your biggest challenge to date, getting all the cogs turning in sync for this one but my hope is that it may turn into a real occasion; that the love experienced will be shared and spread around. You will have to enlist Ryan's help fully – he will be invaluable in getting this done just right, and he's primed, ready to go, and very excited. He knows this story off by heart, down to the tiniest detail. I phoned him up straight after it happened for a full BFF debrief. He squealed with glee and raced right over to mine with champagne, magazines, and chocolate. He even got Alex talking about stationary and shades of lavender that evening which was a sound I never expected to hear, even if I'd lived for a century! It is quite possible that Ryan was more excited that day than I was, which was nigh on impossible. I've set things up pretty thoroughly for this one myself though, too, since it matters so very much. All the right people will be expecting your call, all the ducks are in a row. So, there's no need for stress! Let the pressure turn you into a diamond. You've got this! And anything you drop, your new GBF will catch. This is your big one, a moment of monumental importance. I know you can do it, and I hope you enjoy yourself along the way. Let the magic sweep you up! I know it swept me up beyond my wildest dreams.

Although it didn't happen on the date I died I would like you to action it for the anniversary of my death. It feels right, somehow. To celebrate the best moment of my life on the day it ended – like a highlight montage. Also, it fits a lot more snugly in your timeline with Alex – it would have come far too early in both Alex's grief, and in the strength of your relationship with him, if we'd done it accurately in the calendar year. He'll need to be open to it, and he'll need to trust you. The final important piece of context for you is that this is a one-off. You'll be doing pancakes, the bat house, Christmas lights, birthday celebrations, and all the other bits every year if I have my way. But this one is a one-time-only scenario. So, make it spectacular!

It was a totally normal day it happened on. I suppose that's always the way. One moment is all it takes to change your life, and so very often you don't see that moment coming until its hit you square between the eyes. Alex had been away for a week researching a big story for work. I'd missed him so much. Each minute we should've been together felt like a day, each day like a month. I was lost without him, which I know sounds pathetic for only a week apart, but the heart is a law unto itself, it wants what it wants. As I write this, I feel so hurt thinking of the pain Alex will go through feeling that way forever. I had the consolation that he was coming back, that he loved me. All he'll know is that I don't even exist anymore. At least with you doing this he will know he's still loved by me, however impossible it seems. We have to make this amazing.

Anyway, back to the story. I was hopelessly in love. We'd been together for somewhere around eighteen months. We'd been living together for six. We were happy. On the day, I met Alex off the train at the station. There's something wonderful about train stations, don't you think? The lovely old ones anyway. They just sort of welcome you. All the history, and the stories they have to tell, the trains whizzing through so fast they push you backwards, then the stillness that follows. All those lives moving around. I love train stations, anyway. And ours had an extra story to add to its history books by the time Alex and I walked out of its doors that day.

Alex had asked me to meet him on the platform, which was unusual – I usually met him at the entrance – but I didn't think anything of it beforehand – I know, I know, bright spark I am! When I arrived, there was Alex standing outside the train. He was dressed to impress in my favourite of his suits – a gorgeous dark grey – with a pale blue shirt underneath, open at the neck. He looked nervous, and he looked spectacular. I was worried initially – Alex isn't an anxious person, ever, apart from where bats are concerned of course, hehe! I rushed over to him and wrapped him up in a big hug. I whispered into his ear, 'Are you okay?'

'I will be, I hope.' He replied as he gently grasped my shoulders and pushed me back. He looked flustered, shifting his hands around in his over-the-shoulder-bag. I was totally puzzled at this point. I was just supposed to be casually meeting Alex at the station, this all seemed peculiar.

'What's going on, Alex?' I asked him. 'You're being a little odd.'

He smiled a wry and worried smile and said, 'You'll see.' He clearly found what he'd been rooting around in his bag for and produced two sets of headphones – the chunky, bulky, make you look your ugliest possible self, type. He gently placed one set over my ears and the other set over his and he led me back from the tracks a bit. He positioned me so that we were standing squarely opposite each other, a foot or so apart. Nope, I still had no clue what was happening. He then plugged the headphone cords into a splitter already in his phone and pressed play.

Quiet chords started thrumming in my ears. They were slow and melodic. Alex spoke to me, the headphones blocked out his speech, but I could make out the words 'humour me' formed by his lips. So, I did.

Other passengers were paying attention by now, some giving us sidelong glances as they made their way around us, others stopping to look. We were two people facing each other, headphones on, man looking worried, a little red, and clearly orchestrating a planned debacle. Let's just say there were some brighter sparks than me on that platform. Those bright sparks were looking excited, elbowing each other in anticipation. I was still confused. I think it made it all the sweeter in the end – the total and complete surprise.

The soft strumming continued, and Alex leant forwards in a deep bow, proffering one hand to me. 'May I have this dance?' he mouthed. I nodded and stepped towards him. I was never one to let other people stop me having my magic moments, and this was quite clearly turning into one, even if I didn't yet realise just how magical, so I threw myself into the magic moment with complete abandon. The world around me disappeared, time slowed down. There was nothing but me, and Alex, and this beautiful music.

Now, I know you'll be getting impatient, but please bear with me, and please just take the time to do this next bit right as you read it – it'll be worth it, I promise. The song that was winding its way through those headphone cords and into my ears was a song I'm sure you will know, but the cover that Alex played changed it completely. It is sensational, and haunting, and beautiful, and wonderfully romantic. I want you to have the full effect, so please find it on YouTube, or Spotify, or wherever you can, and play it out loud as you read on. I want you to know exactly how it felt, I want you to feel the magic, so that you know exactly what it is you have to replicate.

Okay, so here we go, get ready to type:

Sleeping at Last, '500 miles'.

When you're up and running, when it's playing, and when you've heard those mesmerising first few chords, imagine yourself cradled in the arms of spectacular Alex, him staring deep into your eyes, moving you back and forth in a perfect, slow rhythm. Imagine him mouthing the words to you as they play.

When the last word rang out, Alex gently removed my headphones, and reached up to stroke my cheek softly. Then he lowered himself onto one bended knee, with tears glistening like diamonds in his eyes. He fumbled in his grey suit pocket and pulled out a navy velvet box. It snapped open and he asked his strong, clear, simple question.

'Alice Hadley, will you marry me?'

I was shocked, and delighted, and entirely overwhelmed. I looked deep into his chestnut brown eyes and I knew with every fibre of my being what the only possible answer could be. The answer shaped in my mouth and poured out tasting sweeter than sugar.

'Yes.'

I felt the wetness of tears soaking my cheeks, and then the tight grip of Alex's arms hugging me and spinning me round and round. Then, I heard the claps and the cheers. Looking up I saw the circle of people around me, holding up their phones, videoing, some crying right along with us. Imagine all that magic.

Now, I expect you're thinking that it's going to be a hard thing to re-create, just please promise me that you and Ryan will try? If Alex hasn't let his drawbridge down so far, this might be a memory so big, emotional, and totally 'us' that he manages to let it down and feels me for just a second; and that would be enough. I've contacted the train station, and some of the people who videoed it on their phones. In the pack attached to the manual is a CD with a video reel I've made of clips put together to show the full story. The same CD also has the song on it.

What I want you to do is to ask Alex to meet you at the station. Stand on the platform where he was standing – you should be able to tell the exact spot from the video. Then, nod to the stationmaster who has agreed to help – he remembers me well. Even the most unlikely types seem to love a successful proposal and this stationmaster was as proud as punch that his territory had been the home of a happy-ever-after moment. I could hear him sniffle through the phone line when I told him the ending had turned out not to be quite as happy after all. When he sees your nod, he will then play the song out through the overhead tannoy system so that it booms through the whole station with its beauty. Every single person in there will be a part of the magic. The video will then start playing on all the monitors, so Alex will see every magical second of it surrounding him. Then, step forwards and dance with him. If you're nervous of dancing, or have stage fright, please don't worry – Alex and I never did anything more elaborate than a slow shuffle back and forth. Unless you have a club foot, or no legs at all, you'll be able to do it wonderfully. Place his hand on our heart and let him feel me. Ryan will be nearby, and will no doubt be getting his boogie on. I've asked him to get some of the other passengers dancing along too. This was the happiest of all days, I want to give a little of that to anyone who wants to share it. Ryan has an incredible knack of turning ordinary, subdued people into dramatic celebrators so don't be surprised if you look up and see a flash mob situation. Ryan can create a spectacle anywhere.

When the song finishes, Ryan will step in with a bunch of my favourite flowers for Alex to lay on that spot. Place them in Alex's hands and then walk softly away. Give him his time and space. He will never have needed them more.

There is something else you should know. The significance doesn't end there. Alex's memories won't end there on the platform. That song played out through the speakers of the marquee the night I wore my once-in-a-lifetime white dress. I was standing cradled in Alex's arms again, this time with a little band of gold on the ring finger of my right hand. Our first steps together as husband and wife were to those same strumming chords, and that same haunting voice. Just like the first time, the world melted away and time slowed down so all that there was in the world was me, and Alex, and the music. Just like the first time, magic danced around us like fireflies on a dark night.

I'm sorry for putting such a heavy weight on your shoulders, but I hope you can understand that this represents everything to me. This represents a love of a lifetime. This represents the entire contents of my heart, of our heart.

How does it sound? I hope it sounds great, because this is the big one. This is the magic, and the heart, and the forever.

Chapter Thirty-Three

I woke up the next morning with the worst headache yet, the blackness creeping ever more over my vision and it being so hard to move I felt like my body had been strapped to the bed. I knew it was time to get moved to the hospital and settled in there.

Alex helped me to get dressed, sadness crawling over his face. He packed up our few things and he half carried, half dragged me down to the taxi waiting for us outside. Mum, Dad, and Ryan were waiting inside the cab for me, their faces peering out silently and white as Alex folded me carefully inside.

The journey was quiet. It was such a short distance there wasn't time for much chatter. Mum was the only one inclined to fill silences with small talk and since she wasn't getting much engagement even she fell into silence, fiddling constantly with the strap of her handbag.

The taxi driver pulled up outside the impressive entrance. The hospitals in America try so much harder than their NHS counterparts to balance functionality with aesthetics

– here there were bright spots of vibrant flowers dotted about, fresh signage, and privet trees in tubs. Alex ran off to find a wheelchair while we waited for him, Ryan paying the taxi driver while clinging tightly to my hand. Everyone was leaking in their own ways – Ryan's constant need for contact; Mum's fiddling; Dad's glassy and sunken eyes.

I was going to be spending my time in the Oncology Department Ryan told us all, but we were heading to Cardiology first, to meet the team there and for a work-up, since they were the ones responsible for me being here. Apparently, the Chief of Cardiology, Dr Casey, had tirelessly and passionately campaigned for my case to be taken on pro bono by the hospital board. Ryan had talked to him extensively to discuss the situation and to make arrangements. From the language Ryan used he held this doctor in high regard, a status few people achieved.

As we all exited the lift at the Cardiology floor there was a flurry of movement. The nurse at the main desk took one look at us all and immediately asked, 'Are you Alice Richards by any chance?'

'Yes, that's me,' I said with a smile.

'Oooh, it's great to finally meet you, we've all heard so much about you. Could you just hold on a minute while I get Dr Casey – he'll want to see you straight away.'

The nurse dashed off, and I looked round at Alex who was pushing me – his face was shuttered. I glanced at Ryan whose hand was resting on my shoulder. He gave me a strong smile.

'Nice team, hey, Als?' he said.

I nodded, and he gave my shoulder a squeeze.

A moment later the lyrical sound of laughter filtered through from a side room as the door opened and a tall man came out. The nurse who had greeted us was behind him. This man was arresting. He had sandy blonde hair that was cut short, but long enough to be tousled, his skin glowed, his eyes sparkled, and he was built like Michelangelo's David. It was his easy smile that drew you in though, and the way his startlingly blue, twinkling eyes danced. He had a presence surrounding him, but not in a big way, rather that somehow, he exuded warmth.

I felt Ryan's hand tighten on my shoulder a fraction.

'Hi, guys, I'm Dr Casey,' he said warmly.

Ryan stepped forwards and made the introductions.

'It's absolutely fabulous to see you again.' He started with, shaking Dr Casey's hand for a few moments longer than any of us were expecting. Eventually Ryan took his hand back and used it to gesture to us all in turn. 'This is, of course, the very special Alice; her husband, Alex; and her marvellous parents, Anne and John.'

Dr Casey stepped forwards to shake everyone's hands. His hands were cool and his shake solid and strong yet gentle. I'd known this man a few moments, but I felt a great trust in him already. He could secure this for me; for Alex.

'If it's okay with you, we'll do a full work-up of you now, Alice. I want to make sure we know every millimetre of that important heart of yours, and exactly what it needs and wants. It's far too important for us not to find out everything we possibly can about how to best look after it.

By the time we're done I'll be able to tell you it's favourite colour.' Ben spoke warmly and with a subtle humour. 'There's a cafeteria a few floors up that does a mean slice of pie (not that I'm supposed to promote pie, of course, forget I said that!) You could wait up there if you like, it's very comfortable – they obviously got first dibs on the best chairs.' Ben joked. He had a magic touch of putting us all at ease. I hoped that magic touch extended through his surgical gloves – it was just what I needed, and he was more than I'd dared to hope for.

'That sounds great, Dr Casey, thank you,' Mum responded. Dad was looking vacant.

'Yes, you Americans and your penchant for pie – it's around every corner it seems. I have a soft spot for cherry myself, so I hope that's the cafeteria's speciality,' Ryan replied.

'You three head on. I'll unpack Alice's things in her room so it's homely and comfortable for when she's finished here,' Alex said, sombrely. 'Then I'll survive Cardiology's chairs and wait for her.'

'Okay, I'll see you all soon, then,' Dr Casey finished before wheeling me away.

An hour or so later all the imaging was finished, the electrodes were peeled off and Alex was indeed waiting for me on those uncomfortable Cardiology chairs. He had his head in his hands as the nurse wheeled me to him and his shoulders sagged with defeat. When we approached, and he looked up his eyes were black, and his face was far too pale. This was really taking its toll on us all.

Alex smiled a bright smile when he saw me though.

'Everything go okay?' Alex asked, far more cheerfully than he looked. He had always liked to light the way for me. I nodded.

'I can't wait to get snuggled up in my room now, though, I'm ready for a bit of quiet us-time.' I told him. 'Did you find the way?'

'Umm-hmm,' Alex said. 'I'll wheel us up there as fast as I can. Some us-time sounds the best thing in the world right now.'

'Will Ryan, Dad, and Mum know where to find us?' I asked, realising they must still be off having a coffee.

'Yes, I popped up to see them on my way back down from sorting your room out. They were quite settled in there. That Dr Casey was right – it's a very comfy café, all plush armchairs and cushions.'

'I'm glad. Mum and Dad especially will need somewhere to go and rest, where they can just switch off from all this for a few minutes.'

Alex didn't say anything. There was a pause before he continued.

'I told them I'd give them a call when you were all finished, and we were back up there. They'll join us as soon as they get the green light.'

'Can we leave it a few minutes? Do you think they'll mind? I could do with a few superhero minutes.' I turned around to smile at Alex who smiled right back – eyes to eyes, heart to heart.

'Absolutely. Superhero ready and waiting, at your service,' he replied, chuckling softly.

The Oncology Department was two floors up from Cardiology and had a very different feel when the lift doors pinged and parted. It was so still, and silent. The nurses glided in a way that looked as though they didn't even want to disturb the air. There was almost no movement, and certainly no joy. I supposed that was to be expected. I felt like I didn't belong here. My bright smile felt out of place, my positivity felt like an insult to these hallowed halls. It worried me instantly – I wanted to be able to spend my final days as one hundred per cent me.

I shouldn't have been concerned though, because as we neared the end of the corridor, having passed lots of other rooms, curtains drawn across each, there was a brightness coming from an open door at the end. The hallway was dull, lights deliberately dimmed, but illuminations were spilling out of this spot at the end. As we reached those sliding doors, I could hear music playing gently, and I recognised the unmistakeable lyrics of Kodaline's 'The One' playing out. It finished as we wheeled in, and the melody of Abba's 'Super Trouper' started up. It was 'The Story of Us' CD playing out. Alex had brought it; and it was the perfect welcome. He was my superhero indeed.

The sight before me shocked me delightfully. This was my room. Alex had worked his magnificent magic once again to make this room a home for me. There were extra chairs pulled up on both sides of the bed – four in total so that we could all sit together. Brightly coloured throws were covering them – orange, yellow, blue, and pink – so they didn't look like hospital chairs at all and they livened the room up with their vibrancy. There were fairy lights woven through the arm rails and top of the bed so if I squinted enough I could convince myself it wasn't a hospital gurney. There was a sideboard with a kettle sitting on it alongside a portable hot plate, pan, and the jars of Alex's top-secret hot chocolate ingredients. Our two favourite hot chocolate mugs had pride of place in front. The final perfect piece of this beautiful puzzle was laying spread out over the bed. It was purple. It was woolly. It was home. It was me and Alex.

Alex gently scooped me up out of the wheelchair and tucked me into the bed. He pushed the wheelchair outside the doors and drew the curtains. For these few superhero minutes we didn't have to be in a hospital at all.

'The works, Allie?' Alex asked with a smile as he stood before his hot chocolate creation station.

'Of course!' I exclaimed.

'Your wish is my command. Coming right up.' He said as he started pouring and whisking. We chattered away like always until the song changed to '500 miles'.

Alex stopped whisking and braced his hands on the sideboard, head bent over, motionless. More than anything I wanted to leap out of bed to wrap my arms around him tightly, but I couldn't move.

Alex slowly turned around, and his shoulders started shaking with sobs. His face was soaked with tears, his cheeks glistening, and my heart cracked.

He walked over to the side of my bed and reached for me as the chorus played through. He put his arms around my shoulders and eased me forwards until I was standing up. I was thinner now, and frail, so it was no effort for Alex to lift me up a few inches and put me down gently on top of his feet so that his feet would carry us both. He pulled my body in tightly to his, holding me up in his strong arms. He nestled his face into my neck and he danced us ever so slowly and ever so gently around as the song meandered along. When it spoke of being the man who's lonely without you and growing old together, we both broke. I heard a moan come from deep within me and Alex's body shook harder with his sobs. We couldn't hear the music over the sound of those two hearts splintering into fragments, but our cries had quieted enough for those final verses.

We clung to each other for a long time after the last note faded, and then Alex tucked me back in, steeled himself, and manoeuvred his face into the semblance of a smile.

'I will love you forever, Allie.'

'I will love you forever, too.' My voice was trembling. 'An Alex Richards signature the works hot chocolate would be out of this world fantastic right now,' I said, knowing there was nothing else to do but make the most of these precious minutes.

Alex set-to, and when he'd placed these towering marvels down beside the bed, he clambered on, drew me in close, and pulled that purple woolly old friend right up to our chins.

It was later that same day. We'd spent some time together getting settled into the room and making arrangements for the coming days. Alex was going to stay with me at the hospital full-time, while Ryan, Mum, and Dad would return to the hotel overnight to get some proper sleep.

'Can I take Alice on a little trip, just around the ward, maybe while you three get a cup of coffee?' Ryan asked Mum, Dad, and Alex. I had no idea what he wanted to do, unless it was another wheel to the Starbucks, where he'd snuck me off to once already and which I'd really enjoyed.

'Okay. We'll be back in twenty minutes,' Alex said. He eased me out of bed and into the wheelchair before giving the handles over to Ryan with a look passing between them. It was a look that held the conversation "take care of her", "I will".

Mum, Dad, and Alex all filed out of the room. They were looking crumpled, worn. A coffee would help. After they'd left, Ryan wheeled me back down to Cardiology. Dr Casey was waiting for us outside the lift. He took great care of me, but his eyes followed every move Ryan made. Ryan changed a little around Dr Casey, as though he thought about everything he did a fraction more. I smiled to myself.

'So, Als, Ben, I mean, Dr Casey, has said there is someone he'd like us to meet. He's ready and waiting for you, just around the corner, a few rooms down. How does that sound?'

'It sounds great, if you both think it'd be helpful. I'm feeling drained though, so I'll do my best.'

'Of course, Alice,' Dr Casey said with a smile. 'The gentleman I would like to introduce you to is called Mr Moorcroft. He's a patient here in Cardiology. He's a heart transplant recipient.'

I exchanged a look with Ryan, who smiled enthusiastically at me.

'And you're in on this, Ry?'

'Not fully. Obviously, I've chatted away to Ben all about you, what you're doing, and why. All I know is Ben thinks it would be good for us to meet with this Mr Moorcroft – he thinks it will help, somehow.'

Dr Casey gave us a big smile.

'Okay, then, let's go,' I said good-naturedly.

Ryan pushed me along and into the corridor. The hospital was immaculately clean and modern. The nurses seemed to have taken a shine to me for they all greeted us warmly as we wheeled along. Maybe it was my big smile – there aren't too many of those around here.

We stopped outside some sliding doors, the curtains drawn over them so that we couldn't see inside until the doors opened.

'Mr Moorcroft had his transplant three days ago, so he might tire quite quickly. Having said that, he's been wowing the nurses with his new lease of life,' Dr Casey said with an amused smile.

I just nodded up at him and Dr Casey gave my shoulder a gentle squeeze as Ryan began to wheel me into the room.

As soon as the doors slid open and we entered the room I was stunned. The clinical, neutral feeling of the hospital had been obliterated by a riot of colour all around us. Sellotaped onto every piece of equipment and blue tacked to all the walls were pictures from an artist's workbook. The pages were filled with phenomenal sketches – there were waterfalls; interesting faces; flowers; angels; a jaguar; and all manner of wonders. The one that mesmerised me the most, though, was a toucan sitting on a tree in the rainforest. It was like another world in that room; a far nicer one. It was magnificent, spectacular, and glorious.

'Quite something, hey?' Dr Casey whispered, nudging Ryan, who he was standing beside. 'Good afternoon, Mr Moorcroft, how are you feeling?' Dr Casey asked the gentleman. He looked to be in his fifties with greying hair but a ready smile. His hospital gown covered a sturdy torso and his brown eyes that were the colour of coffee held a bright twinkle.

'On top of the world, Dr Casey.'

'These are the visitors I was telling you about. Are you happy to see them now?' Dr Casey asked.

'Oh, yes, most definitely,' Mr Moorcroft said with a smile. 'Come in, come in.' We had been hovering just inside the doors and Mr Moorcroft beckoned us in. Ryan scooted me forwards to be close to the bedside and pulled the high-backed visitors chair over to sit next to me. Dr Casey left us to it.

'I'm Alice, and this is my best friend, Ryan.' I made the introductions.

'I'm Wes, it's a real pleasure and an honour to meet you,' Mr Moorcroft replied. 'The whole of Cardiology is abuzz with your story, Alice.' I smiled humbly in response.

I turned towards the nearest sketch – a towering mountain range – precise and powerful

'Your drawings are quite spectacular, Wes.' I admired. 'Have you done all these since you were here?'

'No, I only started once I came around from the op, once I had my new heart.'

'It must be comforting to have your work to do while you recover?'

'I think that's why you're in here with me, little miss,' Wes replied. 'You see, this is not my work.' He gestured around the room. 'It's his.' He said simply, patting the left side of his chest, over his new heart.

Ryan leant forwards in his chair, as he asked, 'What do you mean?'

'Well, before I went into that operating theatre, I couldn't draw so much as a stick man. When I came to, the first thing I asked is, could you pass me my pencils? Since then I've hardly been able to stop my hands. My new heart tells them and then they do it, they just know how to move, it's not me, they just … draw.' Wes explained in amazement.

'It's more than that, though, it's a need, a deep, burning need. When I'm drawing, I feel at peace, calm, and happy. When I stop, I get agitated.' He paused. 'I've never even seen one of those fancy birds before.' Wes said, pointing at the drawing of the toucan. 'Or whatever that thing is.' He gestured to a sketch of the Taj Mahal. 'So, the good Lord knows it couldn't be coming from just me.'

I was excited now.

'How do you feel about it?'

'I think it's great. Who wouldn't? I go in as a lifetime loser at Pictionary and come out as the next Rembrandt. And the drawing itself, it makes me feel so good. I truly … love it.' Wes answered, with a big smile.

'Do you really think it's your new heart that's done it?' Ryan asked.

'I don't think it is, Ryan, I know it is. There is no other possible explanation. It would take skill, years of training, expertise, and inordinate talent to draw these pictures. How would I have developed them in the exact same instant my new heart went in unless it was the heart itself that gave me them? I'm telling you, it's not even me doing it. It's coming from here.' Wes pointed again to his heart.

There was a pause while Ryan and I absorbed everything Wes had said. Then Wes continued.

'So, little miss, it'll work you know, what you're trying to do. Take it from someone who knows. My guy, he loved to draw, more than anything, I can feel that. So, if you love your man enough to do what you're doing, your recipient will remember, will feel. Look around you.' Wes gestured to the oasis of colour and images covering the room. 'This is the power of a heart that loves.'

Ryan was gazing around the room in awe, and tears were falling silently down my cheeks.

'Thank you,' I whispered.

'You are most welcome. You're an awesome gal.' He turned to face Ryan. 'Could you tell her I'd love to meet her, if she'd like to?' We all knew he meant my Two. 'You have one hell of a heart.' He nodded at me. 'I want to know it again.'

Ryan just nodded, tears trekking paths down his cheeks now too. He wheeled me slowly out of the sliding doors.

Dr Casey was waiting for us at the main Cardiology reception desk. He took one look at both of our wet faces and said, 'It's truly remarkable, isn't it? It gives you hope, though, hope, and faith. We need them.'

'Do you know?' I had to ask. 'Can you tell us, please? The donor – were they an artist?'

Dr Casey looked at me levelly, giving nothing away in his expression.

'We're not supposed to say, but given the circumstances, it's worth it.' He took in a big breath and sighed it out. Then, he smiled, with eyes wide with awe.

'Yes, he was an artist. He was hit by a car right outside his first big exhibition at New York's most prestigious art gallery. He was really something special. Just the same they are, too. I had to see for myself. The headline piece at the exhibition, it's a toucan. The one Wes has drawn, it could be a print copy.'

♥

The next morning, I felt diabolical. Exhaustion pinned my limbs to the bed, and a blackness swam around my eyes. I still wanted to get out of that room though and have a wheel around the hospital. Ryan insisted he'd take care of me for half an hour while Alex went to the hotel to shower.

'Trust me, Alex darling, everyone will thank you for it.' Were Ryan's words of persuasion, and they worked a treat.

'I'll be back the second I can, Allie,' Alex said, his eyes haunted.

The hospital had a large main cafeteria serving all manner of hot food, but whose coffees were, according to Ryan, distinctly under par. Suffice it to say, they did not serve double shot, soy, mocha lattes. So, it was with delight that we'd discovered the Starbucks stand tucked away in a corner of the hospital near the Oncology Department. It was obviously the place to be though, for there was always a long line of scrub-clad people waiting for their paper cup of stimulation.

There were tables and chairs around it too, so it had a café feel, and Ryan wheeled me to a table in the corner before striding over to the counter to order our drinks. I thought the sandy blonde hair of the person in front of Ryan in the queue looked familiar, and as he turned to pick a lemon and poppy seed muffin out of the cabinet I recognised him – it was Dr Casey. I craned my neck and half leant out of my chair, so I could get a better view of the encounter. I was close enough to hear everything, and I sensed this was not a moment I wanted to miss. The connection between the two of them was undeniable, though, of course, Ryan denied it. That was to be expected – you needed a huge battering ram to break down Ryan's walls. Fortunately, I suspected Dr Casey may have such a thing lying around.

Dr Casey seemed not to have noticed Ryan standing behind him, and Ryan was looking uncertain, working out whether or not to say something. The cheerful barista handed Dr Casey his coffee and the paper bag with his lemon and poppy seed muffin in it at just the moment his pager went off. I could see Dr Casey scrambling, trying to hold the coffee and bag with one hand while fumbling to see the screen with the other. He had turned and paused in the main thoroughfare and was too engrossed in the pager's message to notice another doctor in scrubs hurrying behind him. This man tried to skirt past him, but jolted Dr Casey at the last moment. As if in slow motion Dr Casey tipped forwards, landing square in Ryan's chest, sending Ryan's coffee clattering to the ground. Ryan staggered for a stride, and then took a firm grip of Dr Casey's broad shoulders and helped steady him. Dr Casey looked up and seemed to double take when he saw who had broken his fall.

'I'm so sorry, Ryan. Are you okay?' Dr Casey asked Ryan concernedly.

'I'm fine, more worried about you getting knocked about,' Ryan replied.

'Oh, I'm tough.' Dr Casey told Ryan with a cheeky smile. 'But I'm so sorry about your coffee.' Dr Casey paused. 'I have an emergency surgery, so I have to fly, but can I buy you a replacement, sometime tomorrow?'

'You don't have to do that, really,' Ryan answered, shaking his head.

Their eyes met, and there was a millisecond of a pause, while they both absorbed the moment.

'Perhaps. But I want to,' Dr Casey said earnestly, taking hold of Ryan's hand for a moment and squeezing it, before running off through the swinging doors.

I don't think I've ever seen a blushing Ryan, but right there and then he was a few shades pinker than ever before. He looked all a flutter, flailing around over there. I didn't want to say anything to him yet – this was his moment.

Nothing could have made me happier – we all know where a simple cup of coffee can take you. It looked like Ryan might have found himself a superhero; and there was no one who deserved it more.

The following day was my last one. It was sunny and bright. My room at the hospital had a window, which was such a blessing – I love to see the sunshine. It was a good start, it gave that sombre day a shred of hope. Ryan had been true to my wishes and I didn't know anything about my recipient, other than that she was perfect; and that she was called Helen. I like the name Helen, it's good, pure, and strong. I hoped she'd live up to those things. Rather, I knew she would – Ryan had picked her, after all. She didn't know Ryan yet, or anything about me, and she was already here in America being prepared. Ryan had excelled with his sleuthing in ways even I'd not dreamed possible.

All she knew was that a heart was due to become available in America and that she was a match. She didn't know it was my heart.

Somehow, I knew today would be the day. I felt a weakness, an exhaustion, that ran deeper than ever before. For the first time, there was no break in the metaphorical clouds for a sliver of sunshine to filter through. It was all storm clouds. It's lucky I love storms.

We were all sitting in the hospital room together later – Mum, Dad, Alex, Ryan, and me. They were all so different, but united. The surroundings were bare and clinical despite Alex's amazing efforts. Cool greys and stark whites. There was new equipment all around, skulking in corners as well as brashly standing tall in plain sight. It gave the room an ominous feeling. It represented the bitter truth that no one would address but filled everybody's minds – in a few hours, there would be a team of medical elite around me, slicing through my skin, and taking pieces of me away. I would be gone, and I would never be coming back.

Everyone was trying so hard to hold it together and make these precious last few minutes positive. But the cracks were snapping loudly in the composed exteriors, and slowly those cracks were being prised apart. Dad grew quieter, his words lower and rare. Mum grew tearful, and weepy, and I was quite positive I would have fingers stained with purple bruising from where she was squeezing them so tightly. Alex was heroic Alex, save for a few minutes where he left the room and then came back, ashen and with a strong smell of spearmint on his breath, a faint odour of vomit lying underneath. Ryan was the biggest surprise, this strong, confident, and bouncy man became small, hunched, and seemed completely lost. The most striking thing about that scene was that the cold grey, the impersonality of the clinical equipment, and the monster in my head that was about to claim my life, couldn't taint or diminish the warmth of the love that was contained in those four walls. There was so much love it was surprising the room didn't break apart from the pressure of it. Whatever else life hands you, if it hands you that much love, you're one of the luckiest ones around. For that's all that matters when you feel the darkness closing in. That love lights your path home.

Alex and I had said what we wanted to say earlier – in the stillness and silence of the hospital at night. Having a private room meant we could lie side by side on the bed and create a world that stopped at the edges of our intertwined bodies. Alex stayed with me at the hospital; Mum, Dad, and Ryan having gone to stay at the hotel for a few hours' sleep. Alex and I hadn't slept at all, we'd clung onto each other all night long, and we'd said our goodbyes with the twilight as our witness – the words had been tender and painful and private. They had gone a little something like this:

'Just leave me with one promise, Alice?' Alex asked me.

'Anything.'

'Promise me you'll wait for me, wherever you get to? Promise me you'll keep safe a place by your side?'

'Always.' I reached up to stroke Alex's cheek tenderly, his tears falling over my hand, searing my skin with the pain leaking from him. I had a flow of my own tears to match his. We were always each other's moons, pulling the other's tides with us.

'Because that's all I'll be doing, every day for the rest of my life – finding my way to you again.' Alex pressed his forehead to mine for a few seconds before kissing me deeply and for an eternity that was contained within a few fleeting moments.

Back, sitting waiting for the clinical reality of the end, Alex was silent now. His knuckles were white. His face was pallid. Tears were streaming down his face, more joining them every second. He was sobbing inconsolably but without sound, his body wracked with heaves of pain. My heart was shattered.

Mum sent me home, really. It could never have been anyone else. She'd delivered me into this world, protected me all my life, held me up when I fell down, dried my tears, cleaned up grazed knees, kissed sore bits better, sang me to sleep every night, and was a friend every minute of every day that I'd known. She was beside herself, but she found a way to be strong enough to say some final words. I will never know where she got that strength from.

'Alice, you're the most beautiful, extraordinary person I've ever known. I'm so proud and grateful to have been your mum. My heart is breaking but I know you're going to be free. You will find yourself in a place more magical and wonderful than we can even imagine. Everything that's good will surround you for the rest of time. God wants you home, and you will be welcomed by angels with arms outstretched, singing a chorus of 'Hallelujah'. You have always been my angel, so I know you'll be among friends.' Her voice broke before the last part. 'Just, say you'll be waiting there for me. When I come home I want it to be your face I see, your arms I step into. For if it's not you I go home to, then I won't be going home at all.'

I was too far gone to reply but I squeezed her hand tightly beyond the very last moment. Mum sang as I went, she sang 'Hallelujah'. She sang it strong and clear and beautiful. I prayed that she was right, that I would be greeted by angels with warm hugs, feathery wings, and shining halos. I thought maybe that would be okay. All I heard was hallelujah. Mum sang 'Hallelujah' until the darkness fell around me. When it came for me, I was ready.

Chapter Thirty-Four

I will leave you here, on New Year's Eve, with a huge thank you for doing this for me, and some final words.

I can't imagine that anyone with my heart could stop themselves from letting that tsunami of love spill out and into their soul. It always felt like too strong a love for my heart to hold – I sometimes felt my heart would surely burst from it all. If I'm right, and you do feel that love yourself then know I'm happy, I get to keep on loving him that way. But the most important thing I want to say, as my last goodbye, is although it's my heart, and my love, it's inside you. This is your story now, your love. I hope a little bit of me will keep shining through, but I would never want to take away from your magic.

This life is cruel and nasty at times, bad things happen to good people far too often and pain can cut so deep. I have a promise for you though: you have a strength in you now that will never desert you. You're stuck with me, and I'll always be with you, fighting in your corner.

So, when you think you can't hold on; hold on.

My brain struggles to comprehend how simple twists of fate work, how single little happenings can change the course of a whole life; how tiny threads weave together, each one so fragile and inconsequential alone, to change the course of events, the people whose lives we touch, the things we encounter. Until, suddenly, one of those simple twists of fate becomes the twist of fate that changes everything. 'Aha', we think. 'So that's why!'

Most often, we never see those moments coming; and doesn't that just make them all the more interesting? There is a certain excitement to knowing that at any given second of any given day it could be moments away; our time to say, 'Right here, right now, this is it. This is the moment everything changed.'

It was the alarm clock that didn't go off that made me five minutes late leaving my mum and dad's house for work that morning. Then it was the closed road which meant I had to detour into the next town over to get my proper morning coffee. The cancelled train was the reason Alex was in such a hurry in that same coffee shop queue. And that spilt coffee was the thing that led Alex to me.

The next day there we were, sharing a coffee, infinite love ahead of us.

That was my moment when everything changed, that the threads pulled together, that my cover was whipped away, and I saw him, sitting there: Alex, my spectacular technicolour masterpiece.

However, that same alarm clock that didn't go off, that same closed road, that same cancelled train, and that same spilt coffee, they were threads in an image beyond my wildest imaginings, because they were also the simple twists of fate that led me to you. Without my meeting Alex, there would be no manual, without the manual our lives would never have touched, without my heart, you'd never have met Alex.

Aren't we all just searching for the things that soothe our souls? Alex was a lullaby to my soul. I pray that you will be a salve for the wounds in his, and that he will be the hero that protects yours.

Part Two

Chapter Thirty-Five

The first thing she saw when she opened her eyes was a beautiful man dressed supremely in a sky-blue and heather-purple paisley shirt. He was flawless with startling blue eyes, an aquiline nose, cheekbones you could cut glass on, and a chiselled jawline. This man must have seen her eyes flutter open for he jumped up out of the chair in the manner of an alarmed cat and in the next instant was towering over her. As his startling eyes met hers she felt a wave of comfort wash over her; of relief; of safety. She felt like she was home. She'd never seen this man before and yet she was sure she'd always known him. It was out of her mouth before she knew it was forming:

'Ryan.' This statement softly sounded and tender, made the man's startling eyes widen, and his mouth shaped an O as he let out a tiny gasp.

'Helen.' He reacted, shocked, as he took her hand in his. Helen nodded.

A moment later, Ryan let go of her hand to pull the high-backed chair up close to her hospital bed. Ryan then pressed a button on a control unit attached to the bed and they waited a couple of minutes, silently, for a cheerful nurse to appear through the door. There was a whole universe of unspoken words and unanswered questions hovering in the air around them.

'Well, hello, my lovely. It is great to see you. How are you feeling?' The nurse asked warmly. She was a busty and bustling woman, and she fussed around Helen's bed.

'Tired, but good,' Helen croaked.

'Can I get you anything?' the nurse asked.

'I don't think so, thank you.'

Ryan spoke up then, he oozed a magnetism that the nurse clearly fell victim to when she looked at him properly for the first time.

'Could Helen have a glass of water, please …' Ryan glanced subtly at the nurse's name tag. 'Maggie? And would you be able to help sit her up? That would be helpful so that we can talk.' Ryan smiled a winning smile that evidently clinched it for him.

'Of course, my dear,' Maggie replied, before setting to with Ryan's requests.

Once Maggie had finished and Helen was propped up on a small mountain of pillows, glass of water on her bedside table, Ryan got himself organised. Calm as he was when it came to matters of planning, he'd rehearsed this next event many times over in his mind. His palms were slightly clammy, and he fumbled with the folder in his hand. He knew Helen better than she could ever imagine, and she truly was perfect. She was quiet, but dazzling.

She was young, twenty-four, with no family to speak of – her parents had been killed in a car accident a few years previously. This had made her strong but had taken away a bit of the fizz she'd been known for before. She was highly intelligent, and beautiful, and quirky, and she'd do amazing things; Ryan was sure of it.

He looked deep into her eyes as he said, 'Helen, I have something really important to talk to you about. Are you up to that?'

Helen nodded, just a single, but sure, nod.

'Do you know who I am, Helen? It's just that you said my name earlier, and I wasn't expecting that.'

'I know that you're Ryan.' Helen gave him a weak smile. 'I know that I know you, that you're special. You make me feel … safe. But that's all.'

Ryan nodded pensively.

'That's a wonderful start. We will be great friends, I hope.' The look in his eyes reassured Helen, and she relaxed a fraction. That look was love. 'I have something to give you, and it might take a bit of time to process. The heart you have now, it used to belong to my very best friend. Her name was Alice. She was the most magical person in the whole world. She was, in her own way, my soulmate.' Tears were flowing like a waterfall from Ryan's eyes. Helen noticed the way the drops fell on his shirt, darkening it, adding to the already busy pattern. She always noticed the small, beautiful things. She was a painter.

Ryan paused and gathered himself for a moment. Helen grasped his hand and held on. 'Alice wanted you to have this.' He reached with his free hand for a folder that was tucked in the chair beside him. He passed it to Helen. Its cover said simply:

The Manual for My Heart

Helen went to open it, but Ryan stopped her with his words. 'Before you start you should know that this meant everything to Alice. I'll help you with anything you need for it. To be entirely truthful with you, I chose you personally, because I believed with all that I am that you could do this.'

Ryan took a deep breath and settled back into his chair. Helen nodded slowly, opened the folder and read:

So, hello there my special new friend! Since you're reading this you must have my heart! Can you do me a favour? Lay your hand right over it and feel it. Feel it beat underneath your hand for me. Ah, now that's something to savour! It worked!

Helen did as she was instructed, and she felt Alice fluttering. It felt glorious.

Before we go any further I want to tell you what you're going to read. This is the key to my heart. A manual if you like. You see, what you're feeling beating right now beneath your hand is the part of me that loves. You might not believe that, but I do. And since it's spent twenty-six years being mine, I think what I believe counts for something at least, don't you? Let me tell you, that heart of ours, it's so good at what it does – it loves like you've never known love, until now I suppose. Now that love is inside you, so you must be able to feel it, you must know its magnificence. If the strength of that amazing love feels overwhelming, please don't be afraid, that's what this manual is all about – showing you what to do with all that love. Let me explain …

I always told him that my heart beat for him; and I believed that with every fibre of my being. So, since it's still beating, you have to make him feel that love still. After all, what's love with nowhere to go? That heart of ours couldn't take that.

This package you've been given works in two ways. First and foremost, this is the story of my heart – I thought you'd want to hear that. Secondly, this is a request – to take action to help my love live on. I've organised things so that by the time you get this, and things have been sorted, it should be just into the New Year. I'll cover a full year for you – all the things you need to do at every special occasion, season change, anything that could crop up that would be a defining moment in my love story. These things I've planned will deliver a piece of me, and my love, back to my husband. You see, I can't let those precious memories become tainted for him – I want those beautiful moments we shared to be the thing that pulls him through the grief, not what sucks him under. I need you to help him remember in the very best way and to hold his hand through to the other side. I need him to know that those special times will never die or be gone for as long as they live in our hearts. My heart will beat on so my love will still be alive, he needs to feel that. I pray it's not too much to ask, and that it's a price you're willing to pay. These things I have planned will deliver a piece of me, and my love, back to my husband. I pray it's not too much to ask, and that it's a price you're willing to pay.

So, let's start at the very beginning. I'll start where you'll start. And you'll start with coffee. That's the very first thing to do – have a cup of coffee with him. That's how we met. It's the oldest cliché in the book – we were both in a rush at the coffee shop line. He spun round and spilled it straight down my shirt. I lived for my morning coffee so this was a crime tantamount to murder – he'd literally killed my morning zest. That was until I looked up into his huge brown eyes and that old ticker you can feel beating, it skipped a beat. Ready for cliché number two? – I honestly knew in that moment that he was my One. That I would love him for as long as I lived. I was so right. And that brings us back round to you, and now. You have that piece of me and it's living. So, the love lives on. Meet him for a coffee – he'll know to expect your call. Don't meet him in a coffee shop though, that would be too much. Besides, I want you to show him that he's still loved – by me – not to fall head over heels in love with him yourself! Believe me, you'll be tempted. Unless you're a nun, which would be disappointing – my heart wants adventure! Or unless you have a thing for the ladies, which I think would be unfair, since although I don't have an issue with it – live and let love I say – I don't think your new apparatus will help you out with the heart racing feeling for another lovely lady if you know what I mean.

Sorry, back to the coffee. So, you need to do it in the kitchen at our cottage. Intimate enough – how could it be any other way – and yet not creepy, I hope. He likes it strong – pour that instant in. And he likes it with just a dash of milk, the smallest splash.

At this point, Helen had a single thought: the milk must be skimmed – that's important.

She looked back down at the page, and had the fright of her life when she read:

And the milk must be skimmed. That's important.

Oh, and his name is Alex.

She stopped reading there, though she didn't look up, she couldn't, not yet. She felt so much, she felt more than she'd ever felt in her life. She felt like her chest would explode from all the feelings. It felt like warmth, and sunrises; it felt like Christmas lights and toboggans; it felt like flowers and lopsided birthday cakes; like chattering bats and thunder and lightning; it felt like snowmen and big teams; it felt like pancakes and puns; it felt like train station platforms and wild sea views; it felt like spilled coffee and homemade CDs; it felt like heroes and dancing in the rain; like hot chocolate and scratchy wool blankets.

It felt like everything.

It felt like forever.

After an eternity had passed, contained within a few moments, Helen looked up, deep into Ryan's eyes, and with a face soaked in tears she whispered:

'I remember. I remember everything.'

Author's Note

Cellular Memory

The heart transplant cases that Ryan shared with Alice in the story are all real cases, taken from the article published by Paul Pearsall, PhD, Gary E. Schwartz, PhD, Linda G. Russek, PhD, extracted from Nexus Magazine Volume 12, Number 3, April – May 2005 entitled 'Organ Transplants and Cellular Memories' - they have not been embellished or changed in any way. This article can be found online via: http://www.bibliotecapleyades.net/salud/esp_salud25.htm

The scene with 'Wes' is fictional but is based upon real accounts.

Reports are regularly made, by organ transplant recipients, of changes to taste, personality traits, interests etc. Doctors have, up to now, deemed these to be the result of anti-rejection medications, the psychological effects of surgery etc.

It is important to note that only anecdotal evidence for cellular memory exists, there is no empirical evidence. There are many naysayers who disregard cellular memory as nonsense. However, the individuals who most avidly believe in it and support it are the actual transplant patients; the ones who have experienced the phenomenon themselves. Therefore, it remains up to you as an individual to form your own opinion on the matter for now.

The vast majority of doctors and scientists believe that the heart is merely a pump. However, recent research shows that cells in the heart synthesise catecholamines – which were thought only to exist in the brain. Additionally, neurologist Dr Andrew Amour from Montreal, Canada has discovered a sophisticated collection of neurons in the heart organised into a small but complex nervous system, containing about 40,000 neurons called sensory neurites.

Most scientists also believe that our consciousness – our soul, if you believe in souls – lies in the brain. However, these lovers of facts and evidence have never managed to define consciousness nor prove specifically where it's held in the body. A few pioneering scientists have started to question the conventional belief that our consciousness is contained in our brain. They claim that our memories and characters are encoded not just in our brain, but throughout our entire body. They say that consciousness is created by every living cell in the body acting in tandem: a hypothesis they call 'Cellular Memory'. Under this theory our hearts, and every single organ in the body, store our memories, drive our emotions, and imbue us with our own individual characters. Therefore, if any of these organs should be transplanted into another person, parts of these memories – perhaps even elements of the soul – might also be transferred. Studies are currently being conducted into the field of cellular memory.

It is over fifty years ago that cardiac surgeon Christian Barnard completed the first successful human heart transplant in South Africa in 1967. For many of us alive today that means that when we were born human heart transplants simply did not exist. In those fifty years heart transplants have gone from medical revelation to ordinary and common place. Where will we be in another fifty years? We are still a very long way from a full understanding of the mysteries of the human body, heart and soul but it seems that perhaps science is opening the door to some fascinating concepts and discoveries.

Organ Donation

Legislation goes before the UK parliament in 2018 that may change organ donation from an opt-in decision to an opt-out process.

Donating your organs can include: your kidneys, heart, liver, lungs, pancreas, and small bowel. A single organ donor can save up to eight lives.

Donating your tissue can include: your corneas, heart valves (not possible if you've already donated your heart), skin, bone, and tendons. A single tissue donor can improve up to fifty lives.

There are ways to donate, even in life, that can do extraordinary good and save lives: donating a kidney; donating blood; donating bone marrow; and donating stem cells. More information about these can be found at:

https://www.blood.co.uk/ for blood donation. Giving blood involves registering to become a blood donor – either online, by phoning 0300 123 23 23 or by attending a donation venue. You can then make an appointment to give blood which is aimed to be completed in less than an hour.

http://www.nhsbt.nhs.uk/bonemarrow/qa/index.asp for bone marrow donation.

www.anthonynolan.org for stem cell donation (via blood or bone marrow). This organisation works to cure blood cancer and blood disorders. For people between the ages of 16 and 30 in good health a postal spit kit can be completed which puts you on a register to donate if a match is found.

You can give your consent for organ or tissue donation by:

Joining the NHS Organ Donor Register online.

Telling a relative or close friend about your decision to donate.

As touched upon in the novel, there are very tight regulations governing organ donation in the United Kingdom. For deceased donations absolutely no conditions or directions are allowed at all. There have been attempts by individuals to leave organs to family members, or to leave conditions for the organs such as, in one case, the organ only being given to a white recipient. The laws surrounding organ donation mean that these requests are disregarded, and consent for unrestricted donation is assumed. So, the requests are ignored, and the organs are still used. There are less strict regulations in place in America, where individual preferences are given more consideration. Living donors in the UK are allowed to specify the recipient in an entirely directed way. It is an interesting field.

Acknowledgements

Since I wouldn't be myself without the following people, they need a world of thanks for the existence of *I Give You My Heart*. I love you all so much!

Thank you to my mum, Belinda Ford, for everything. There are no words beautiful enough for you.

Thank you to my dad, Russell Ford, for the truly unconditional love and infinite belief in me.

Thank you to my brother, Elliott Ford, for the laughs and the memories – past, present and (God willing) future. I'm so proud of you.

Thank you to my nan, Valerie Airton, who bought me my first dictionary, who did the first proofread of this book, and who has been there for me my whole life with wisdom and strength.

Thank you to my beloved Gramps, Frank Airton, who is the purest, gentlest, loveliest soul I've ever had the tremendous honour of knowing.

Thank you to everyone else who's been a part of my twisty journey or who lent a helping hand or heart along the way.

Thank You!

I'm so happy and grateful that you've chosen to undertake the journey of reading *I Give You My Heart* – thank you ever so much!

If you're at all curious about me or would like to connect further, then the following might help:

My website – www.sarahjaneford.com – which has further information about yours truly, a mailing list sign-up as well as a contact form and social media links.

My Facebook Page – www.facebook.com/sarahjanefordauthor

My direct email – I'm on the other end of sarahjanefordauthor@outlook.com

I absolutely love hearing from my readers so please do get in touch if you'd like to!

Lightning Source UK Ltd.
Milton Keynes UK
UKHW01f1840240718
326220UK00001B/1/P